"I absolutely refuse to live in the harem."

Ali's dark heavy eyebrows met in a frown. "We shall see. We will need to confer about the conference. That would be inconvenient if you were at the hotel."

"Nevertheless, that's where I'm going to stay."

"You will be more comfortable in the harem."

"My staying in your harem with your wives and concubines is quite impossible."

"We have no concubines. The women in the harem are wives, sisters, daughters, relatives of our family and the families of the ministers. They all live very well, I assure you."

"But wives are separated from their husbands."

"Not all of the time. The wives spend time with their husbands."

"At night?" Genevieve's green eyes sent sparks of anger his way.

His lips twitched in a smile. "Of course, at night," he said. "When they are sent for."

Dear Reader,

The holidays are almost here, and with snow whipping through the air and cold winds blowing—at least in my part of the country!—I can't think of anything I'd like more than to escape to a warm climate. Let Barbara Faith help you to do just that in *Lord of the Desert*. Meet an American woman and share her adventures as she is swept into a world of robed sheikhs and sheltering desert dunes. You may not want to come home!

This month's other destinations are equally enticing. The Soviet Union is the setting of Marilyn Tracy's *Blue Ice*, and intrigue and danger are waiting there, despite the current spirit of *glasnost*. Paula Detmer Riggs returns to New Mexico's Santa Ysabel pueblo in *Forgotten Dream*, the story of a man who has forgotten much of his past and no longer has any memory of the woman he once loved—and is destined to love again. Finally, reach *Safe Haven* with Marilyn Pappano. When Tess Marlowe witnesses a murder, her only refuge is a secluded house in the Blue Ridge Mountains —and the embrace of Deputy U.S. Marshal Deke Ramsey.

In coming months, look for new books by such favorite authors as Nora Roberts, Heather Graham Pozzessere and Lee Magner, as well as a special treat in February: four brand-new authors whose debut books will leave you breathless.

Until then, happy holidays and may all your books be good ones.

Leslie J. Wainger
Senior Editor and Editorial Coordinator

BARBARA FAITH

Lord of the Desert

SILHOUETTE·INTIMATE·MOMENTS®

Published by Silhouette Books New York

America's Publisher of Contemporary Romance

SILHOUETTE BOOKS
300 East 42nd St., New York, N.Y. 10017

ISBN: 0-373-07361-5

First Silhouette Books printing December 1990

Printed in the U.S.A.

Books by Barbara Faith

Silhouette Intimate Moments

Silhouette Special Edition

Silhouette Books

BARBARA FAITH

is very happily married to an ex-matador whom she met when she lived in Mexico. After a honeymoon spent climbing pyramids in the Yucatan, they settled down in California—but they're vagabonds at heart. They travel at every opportunity, but Barbara always finds the time to write.

Me, cruel Queen! you ever captivate,
From valiant knight to puny pawn translate;
And marshal all your force and ply your arts,
To take my castles, and myself checkmate!
—Omar Khayyám

Chapter 1

She sat across from him at the conference table, poised, self-assured and verbal—all of the things Ali Ben Hari most disliked in a woman.

She was taller than he liked his women, slender and sleek from the top of her beautifully though severely coiffed blond hair, all the way down to her shapely legs. She wore an elegantly plain royal-blue dress, a strand of pearls and small pearl earrings.

When he had been introduced to her this morning, he'd naturally assumed she was a secretary. But when the meeting began, it wasn't she who took notes; it was the young man who sat so deferentially behind her. Only when the young man said, "Excuse me, Miss Jordan, would you mind repeating that?" did Ali realize that she was one of the vice presidents of the company.

A woman vice president! He certainly didn't approve of that.

Ali had contacted Cunningham, Tabler, Randall and Jordan two months ago, when the date had finally been settled for the Kashkiri conference. It had taken him a long time to convince his father, known to the Arab world as Sheik Turhan Ben Hari, that although Kashkiri was one of the richest oil-producing sheikdoms in the Middle East, it was considered a backward country by other nations.

"If the conference is to be held here," Ali had told his father, "we must have help. We know little of protocol. What will we do if the representatives from the non-Arab countries bring their wives? We should have help from someone who understands these things, someone who can handle the foreign press."

It was Rupert who had suggested the New York public relations company. "That's their business," he'd told Ali. "Cunningham, Tabler, Randall, and Jordan helped get the last president of the United States elected by changing his image. They've done the same for other top officials. Two years ago, when Lozarini Bengal declared its independence and the new government invited dignitaries from all over the globe, they stepped in and arranged everything. Made a wonderful impression, thanks to one of the company's top executives, a fellow by the name of Jordan."

Only Jordan wasn't a fellow; she was a Miss. A Miss Genevieve Jordan.

"Mr. Randall had originally been in charge of making the arrangements for your country's conference, Mr. Ben Hari," she said now. "He's had to take a leave of absence, but he's given me all of the information he'd garnered. There are, however, a few questions I'd like to ask." She looked at one of the papers in front of her. "In addition to the Arab leaders, will any other countries be involved?"

Ali barely glanced at her before he turned and spoke directly to C.J. Cunningham. "Representatives will come from the United States, England, Germany and Japan."

Cunningham steepled his fingers and looked at Genevieve, who said, "I presume the men from the non-Arab countries will bring their wives."

Ali frowned. "I presume so."

"Then of course you'll want the wives of your father's chief advisers, as well as his wife, to take part in the social activities."

"My father has three wives, none of whom will have anything to do with the conference, Miss Jordan. Nor will any of the wives of his advisers."

"May I ask why, Mr. Ben Hari?"

"It is our belief that women have no place in the business of men."

"I see." Then, with a kindly chuckle she said, "My goodness, Mr. Ben Hari, I can certainly understand why you need help."

His eyes darkened with anger, and for the slightest fraction of an instant Genevieve felt a chill of fear, and of something like the anticipation that comes with an interesting challenge, run down her spine.

Ali Ben Hari was an impressive man. Genevieve judged him to be well over six feet, probably close to six-three, and he must have tipped the scales at two hundred muscled pounds. His neatly trimmed hair was thick and black. His brows, over Omar Shariff eyes, were deep and dark. He had a straight jutting nose and a sensuously angry mouth. His hands, resting on the mahogany table in front of him, were strong and tanned.

At thirty-six he was the prince of Kashkiri, an oil-rich country roughly the size of Cuba, and heir to the sheikdom. Though he had been educated at Cambridge and had lived for a year in Paris, she did not think he was too acquainted with Western ways.

Perhaps that was why the Englishman was with him. Blond, blue-eyed and ruddy-cheeked Rupert Matthews appeared to be a few years older than Ali Ben Hari. He had, Genevieve learned, been Ali's tutor at Cambridge, and after Cambridge he had gone back to Kashkiri to become Ali's right-hand man, as well as his confidant and adviser.

Matthews sat next to Ali, papers spread in front of him, and when Genevieve had suggested the lack of women in Kashkiri's government might be what was wrong with that country, he had barely been able to suppress a smile.

But if Rupert Matthews felt like smiling, Genevieve did not. She had never shied away from taking on a difficult assignment, but she knew it would be almost impossible to work with a man like Ali Ben Hari. If his father, the sheik, was anything like Ali, and apparently he was, no wonder there were problems in Kashkiri.

The next two months would be a challenge.

Sometimes it seemed to her that, in one way or another, she'd been doing battle with men since the day she'd been born. The youngest in a family and the only girl, she'd grown up having five brothers to contend with. She'd learned early on that if she wasn't going to be shoved in the corner, she would have to speak up, to defend herself, to prove herself.

When she'd applied for a job at Cunningham, Tabler, Randall and Dillon ten years ago, the first question she'd been asked was, "Can you type?" It had taken her three years to rise from junior secretary to executive secretary, to Chad Cunningham's assistant, and finally to account executive. A year later she'd landed the multimillion-dollar Quality Tire account, and she'd been named a vice president of the company.

She'd worked hard to be where she was today, and she still worked hard. She was at her desk at seven-thirty every morning, and she stayed long after the other executives left at night. She survived business lunches by sticking to club soda with a twist of lime, and she had never dated a client or a business associate.

And now, though she enjoyed a challenge, she found herself regretting that John Randall had turned the Kashkiri account over to her.

"You're the logical one to take my place," he'd said. "You've lived in Morocco and Tunisia. You know and understand the Arab world better than any of us."

And while it was true that she had lived in those countries, there was much she didn't understand about the Arab world.

During the next two hours Ali Ben Hari continued to direct his questions to the men, but invariably it was Genevieve who answered, Genevieve who had all of the facts and figures concerning Kashkiri in front of her. And it was Genevieve who asked most of the questions.

"Kashkiri has a new hotel," she said. "Will it accommodate all of the delegates and their wives?"

"The Hotel Kashkiri has three hundred and fifty rooms and one hundred suites. It's lavishly furnished, and its employees are well trained," Ali said.

Genevieve nodded approvingly. "Then we won't have to worry about that, other than arranging for fruit and flowers to be sent to the rooms." She glanced down at the papers in front of her. "Something will have to be scheduled for the women who will be accompanying their husbands, of course. They'll want to visit your hospitals and schools." She hesitated. "Are your schools coeducational, Mr. Ben Hari?"

Ali shook his head. "Boys go to a boys school, girls to a girls school."

"Does that also apply to high school and universities?" Joseph Tabler asked.

"Of course not. Girls in Kashkiri go to school only until they're thirteen."

Genevieve raised an eyebrow. "I see."

With a deepening scowl, large hands flat on the table, his dark eyes boring into hers, Ali said, "In Kashkiri we don't think that it's necessary for a female to have a more formal education. A woman's job is to attend to the needs of her husband and take care of her children."

Genevieve tapped long, polished fingernails on the table-top. "What about museums and libraries, Mr. Ben Hari?"

"The library in Kashkiri City has one of the finest selections of books in the Middle East. Our national museum concentrates more on the history of Kashkiri and of the Arab world and artists than it does on Western artists. Our pride is in our own culture, not the culture of foreign nations." He turned to Cunningham. "When the representative from your company comes to Kashkiri, he will see for himself the richness of our culture, Mr. Cunningham."

"Yes, I'm sure he... uh... he will, Mr. Ben Hari." Cunningham cleared his throat. "Mr. Randall had planned on going, but since he's unavailable, Miss Jordan will go in his place."

Ali's nostrils flared, but before he could say anything, Cunningham said, "Miss Jordan's father was with the State Department in both Morocco and Tunisia, and she spent a great deal of time in those countries. She understands the customs far better than I or any member of our staff. She lived in Washington when her father transferred there after Genevieve's mother died, and while still in her teens she acted as her father's hostess. Not only is she well versed in

Middle Eastern culture, she's also knowledgeable when it comes to protocol.''

He smiled at Genevieve, who frowned back at him. Ignoring the frown, he said, ''In my opinion she's the perfect person to help you prepare for the conference.''

''She's a woman.''

The words were an accusation rather than a statement. Genevieve glared at Ali Ben Hari, and he glared back at her.

A woman! Ali thought. Preposterous! It wasn't as though he didn't like women. Of course he did. They were delightful creatures, wonderful ornaments on a man's arm, a necessity if a man wanted children and absolutely irreplaceable in bed. But as far as he was concerned, that's where it ended. A good woman was a silent woman.

He opened his mouth, but before he could speak, Cunningham pushed his chair back and said, ''I think we've talked enough for today. We can take up where we left off in the morning. Mrs. Cunningham and I are attending a reception for the Japanese under secretary at the United Nations tonight, Mr. Ben Hari. It should be an interesting evening—I'd like you to come with us.''

Ali nodded. ''Thank you, Mr. Cunningham, I'd be delighted to come.''

''Wonderful. Miss Jordan will pick you up at a quarter to eight. We'll have dinner and then go on to the reception.'' He turned to the Englishman. ''We'd like it if you could come, too, Mr. Matthews.''

Rupert looked from Ali to Genevieve. With the same slightly amused look he'd had all during the meeting, he said, ''That's kind of you, Mr. Cunningham, but I have a great many things to do this evening. Perhaps another time before we leave.''

"Yes, of course," Cunningham said with a nod. "Mr. Ben Hari is at the St. Regis," he told Genevieve. "I'll make dinner reservations at Lutece."

And though Cunningham had smiled, there was a firmness in his voice that Genevieve knew from experience meant, this is serious business, Gen. This is the way it's going to be. No argument.

Kashkiri was a million-dollar account. She would do as she was told.

Ali saw her the minute he stepped off the elevator. She had stopped at the front desk, apparently to ask the clerk to ring his room. She stood sideways to him, beautifully regal in an asymmetrically designed white Grecian-style dress that draped across one shoulder. The other shoulder was bare, and in the lobby light her skin looked like pale polished ivory.

She turned, appraised him head to toe, then said, "I have a limo waiting."

Her perfume, faint but exotic, drifted like a wisp of smoke in the interior of the limo. Her voice, when she said, "I hope you'll like the restaurant," was softly musical and totally impersonal.

He wondered if she had a lover. What kind of a man could break through that regal poise and make her sigh with ecstasy? he asked himself as he studied her profile. In his mind's eye he saw her supine on satin sheets, her golden hair unbound and spread upon the pillow, her body bathed in the silver light of the Kashkiri moon.

Unexpectedly his body tightened. Silently he cursed ancient Kashkiran curses. He didn't approve of the woman beside him—he didn't even like her—yet the thought of possessing her sent a fever of excitement racing through his body.

He watched her all through dinner, watched those long, slender fingers close around the stem of her wineglass, the red wine stain her lips. She was opinionated and bossy, everything he detested in a woman, yet every time he looked at her, he found himself wanting to nibble on her bare shoulder.

Damn the woman! He turned away from Genevieve and concentrated on what Mrs. Cunningham, a pretty redhead with a gentle voice and demeanor, was saying. She had been to Egypt, she said, and she'd loved it.

"Then you must come to Kashkiri some day," Ali said. "My country, though small, is beautiful. I think you would like it."

"Do you have many tourists?" Genevieve asked.

"Very few."

"The women who come to the conference with their husbands will very likely want to travel around a bit. How are accommodations outside the city?"

"Sparse."

"Even in the beach areas?"

"I'm afraid so."

"What about the desert? Are there any hotels in the desert?"

Ali shook his head. "I have a lodge at the edge of the Sahara. It has ample space."

"How ample?"

"Thirty rooms."

"That ought to take care of the wives. We'll have to arrange something."

"I told you Genevieve was the one to go to Kashkiri," Cunningham said with a smile.

That was impossible. Kashkiri was a man's country. His father would have apoplexy if he returned with a woman executive to handle the conference. And yet... Ali almost smiled, because the thought of Genevieve Jordan in Kash-kiri was an amusing one. Almost without realizing it, he said, "If she comes to Kashkiri, I would expect her to follow the same rules all Kashkiri women follow. Naturally she would have to live in the harem with the women of my father's house."

"In a harem?" An expression of horror crossed Cunningham's face. "You'd expect Genevieve to live in a harem?" The look of horror faded, and Cunningham chuckled. "What an interesting idea."

"She'd have her own quarters, of course," Ali said.

Cunningham darted a look at the now-furious Genevieve, who said, in a voice chillier than the ice cubes in Rosemary Cunningham's drink, "I couldn't possibly live in your—" she almost choked on the word "—harem." She straightened her shoulders and, looking first at Cunningham, then at Ali, said, "I will *not* live in a harem, Mr. Ben Hari."

"That's where the women of my father's house live," Ali said in a coolly autocratic voice.

"I prefer to stay in a hotel."

"And I prefer that you reside in the harem while you're in Kashkiri." His dark eyes were fierce, his chin thrust forward belligerently.

Genevieve tried to stare him down. Green eyes clashed with dark eyes. "I will not live in a harem," she repeated.

She didn't remember ever being this angry. Ali Ben Hari was an impossible man, right from the top of his midnight-black hair all the way down his lean, hard, narrow-hipped and impossibly long-legged body. He came from a totally male-oriented society, a society where women kowtowed to men. Where they lived in a harem!

Well maybe *they* did, but she'd be damned if she would. She'd stay in the hotel.

"The two of you can work the living arrangements out once you arrive in Kashkiri," Cunningham said. "After all, it's only for two months." Then, because he knew Genevieve was angry and because he wanted to tie the deal up, he said, "Well, then, that's settled. Genevieve will go to Kashkiri."

And she knew that she'd better start packing.

The room in which the reception was being held was filled with glittering lights and glittering people. Rosemary and C.J. preceded Genevieve and Ali in the reception line. When they moved away, Genevieve paused in front of the Japanese under secretary.

"May I present Prince Ali Ben Hari of Kashkiri, sir," she said. "Prince Ben Hari, this is Mr. Yoshiro Sumoto."

"I will be in your country in October, Prince Ben Hari," Sumoto said. "I am looking forward to my visit." He turned to the attractive woman beside him. "May I present my wife. She will accompany me to Kashkiri, and I know she looks forward to seeing something of your country."

Ali bowed over Mrs. Sumoto's hand. "It will be our pleasure to show you around."

"I told you wives would be accompanying their husbands to the Kashkiri conference," Genevieve murmured when they moved away from the reception line. "I most definitely believe that it's important for your father's wife . . . for at least *one* of his wives, as well as for the wives of his cabinet ministers, to take an active part in the conference." She paused to lift two glasses of champagne off a proffered tray. She handed a glass to Ali, and when she had taken a sip from her glass, she looked at him over the rim and asked, "How many wives do *you* have, Mr. Ben Hari?"

"I have not yet decided to marry, Miss Jordan."

"When you do, how many wives will you take?"

"We are allowed four by our religion."

"And will you take four, Mr. Ben Hari?"

He was tempted to tell her that if the women in Kashkiri were as opinionated as she was, he would never marry. Instead, he said, "It is my personal belief that one wife is enough for any man to handle. When the time comes, I will marry. But only once."

Ali glanced around the room, where people of all nationalities mixed and chatted. Observing one attractive couple, he nodded his head toward them and said, "I can see that in certain cultures it might be an asset for a wife to accompany her husband."

Genevieve smiled. "That's Mrs. Buhrani, the Prime Minister of Kafistan. Her husband is accompanying her."

"*He's* accompanying *her*?" Ali shook his head. "The world is changing, and I do not approve of the changes."

A small orchestra began to play at one end of the room, and a few couples began to dance as Ali led her to a cushioned loveseat. Genevieve sat down and looking up at him she said, "Tell me about your mother. Was she your father's first wife?"

Ali nodded. "She died giving birth to me."

"Oh, I'm sorry." She touched his hand. "Forgive me for asking."

He gazed at the pale hand that had touched him so briefly. For the first time since he had been introduced to her this morning, there was a softness in her voice, concern in her wide green eyes. It startled him to think that the ice princess could melt.

"And your father remarried?" she asked.

Ali took a sip of his champagne. "He remarried a year after my mother's death. His wife Melita gave my father six girls before she died. They're all married, one to an Egyptian, the others to Saudis. He married three times after that, and I have five other grown sisters, an eight-year-old brother and two-year-old twin sisters."

The slightest of smiles curved Genevieve's lips. "Your father must be quite a man," she said.

"As are all Kashkiri men." Ali put his glass down and said, "I would like to dance with you." Before she could reply, he brought her up beside him, and with a hand against her back he led her to where other couples were dancing.

When he put his arms around her and drew her close, a shiver ran down Genevieve's spine. She had known that he was a powerful man, but she had not realized how overwhelmingly masculine he was. She was too intensely aware of him, of the feel of his body against hers, the warmth of his hand against her back, the brush of his cashmere jacket against her cheek.

They moved to the rhythm of the music, line of body, line of hip joined in this brief space of time. She looked up at him, and her breath caught because his eyes, so deep and dark and mysterious, gazed into hers with an intensity that frightened her. She tried to look away, but she was held by his eyes and bound by his arms.

The blood beat hot through Ali's veins. All others disappeared from the room; there were only he and this woman, this one woman who looked up at him with eyes the color of the sea of Kashkiri.

He tightened his arms around her. The press of her breasts against his chest, the feel of her long slender legs against his, became an exquisite kind of torture. Yet he did not relinquish his hold. A smothered sigh escaped her lips when he rested his face against her golden hair.

He didn't approve of her, and he wasn't sure he wanted her to come to Kashkiri, but for a reason he could not explain, she set him on fire.

He thought then how exciting it would be to mold her into the kind of woman she should be: quiet, submissive, loving.

Yes, loving.

He turned his face and because he had to taste her, he caught her earlobe between his teeth and ran his tongue across her ear.

He heard her indrawn breath. He felt her tremble.

Then she stepped away from him. Her face was flushed, and her eyes were angry.

"I apologize," he said. "Perhaps it was the champagne. I'm not accustomed to drinking."

But Ali knew it hadn't been the champagne; it was Genevieve Jordan who had made him behave in so uncharacteristic a manner.

He thought of the months ahead, when she would be in his country, living within his reach in the harem of the government palace. And as he followed her across the room to where the Cunninghams waited, he smiled a secret smile. She would be in his country, on his turf. All things were possible.

Chapter 2

The phone call from his father came in the middle of the night.

"There's trouble," Turhan Ben Hari said. "Sheik Omar Haj Fatah has staged another uprising. You must return immediately."

"Yes, of course." Ali switched on the bedside light. "Have the troops been called out?"

"This morning. They're holding the rebels back." His father swore. "Word of this cannot get out, Ali. Nothing must spoil the conference—it's too important."

"I agree, Father. I'll leave New York tomorrow."

"Good. I'll feel better once you're here. Have you arranged things with the public relations company? Are they sending someone?"

"Yes, I've taken care of it."

"Were you able to get Randall?"

"No. He's on a leave of absence. The company is sending someone in his place. Someone by the name of Jordan."

"Bring him with you tomorrow. Be sure he's on the plane with you."

"Very well, Father."

When they said goodbye, Ali put the phone back on the receiver and picked up the telephone book. When he found G. Jordan, he dialed Genevieve's number.

She picked it up on the second ring, and when she said, "Hello?" her voice sounded fuzzy with sleep.

"This is Ali Ben Hari. I'm sorry that I woke you."

"What time is it?"

"A little after three."

"What in the world ...?" Her voice sounded more alert now. "What do you want, Mr. Ben Hari?"

"I've just had a telephone call from my father in Kashkiri. There's trouble at home. We will have to leave tomorrow."

"That's too bad. There are still a lot of things to talk about."

"We can talk about them on the plane."

"I had planned to..." He heard her gasp. "What did you say? About the plane?"

"I said we could discuss things on the plane."

Ali heard her shift in the bed and he pictured her arranging the pillows behind her back and reaching out to switch on a light. He wondered what she wore to sleep in and had a sudden and clear picture of her in a revealing satin-and-lace gown.

He tightened his hand on the telephone.

"I couldn't possibly leave tomorrow," she said in a breathy voice.

"Why? Surely you have a passport."

"Yes, but I have to pack. I have things to finish up at the office. Papers I need to take with me. We need airline reservations—"

"My plane and pilots are standing by at Kennedy Airport. We can take off with an hour's notice."

"Your own plane?"

"Of course." He was surprised that she would ask such a question. "It is most urgent that I return to Kashkiri as soon as possible. Do what you have to do at the office tomorrow, and I'll have you picked up there at five. If we leave at six, we should be in Rome by midnight."

"Rome?" Genevieve lay back against the pillows. This was all happening too fast. She had matters to attend to at the office, dozens of things to coordinate for the trip. She had to shop, pack, get her hair done. She needed a manicure.

"Look," she said. "I'll be in Kashkiri for two months. I can't just leave on a moment's notice."

"Of course you can," he said impatiently.

"I need to shop."

"You can buy anything you need in Rome."

"I could follow you at the end of the week."

"But I want you to come with me tomorrow."

Damn the man! Genevieve smacked the mattress with her fist. If he was like this now, what would he be like once they got to Kashkiri? The thought unsettled her. She'd be in his country, subject to his rules.

"I have to call Rupert," he said. "He'll be the liaison between your New York office and Kashkiri. He can finish the details with Cunningham and come on to Kashkiri next week. Try to get some sleep—it's going to be a long trip."

Genevieve put the phone down and silently cursed the day that Ali Ben Hari had walked into the offices of Cunningham, Tabler. She wasn't looking forward to the next two months of being under his autocratic thumb. He was every-thing she disliked in a man: domineering, opinionated, chauvinistic and so sure of himself that he set her teeth on edge. In addition to that, his overpowering masculinity un-settled her. Certainly he'd unsettled her tonight when he'd nibbled on her ear.

With the thought of the whisper of his breath against her ear, Genevieve scooted down in the bed and pulled the sheet up to her chin as though to shield herself. She rubbed her earlobe between her thumb and first finger to try to erase the memory of his caress. But the flame that had kindled her body then, kindled now. She could not deny the fact that Ali Ben Hari was one of the most attractive men she'd ever met. But he wasn't a man she could ever be seriously interested in because of who he was and where he came from.

She had a job to do and she couldn't let anything get in the way of that job. Ali Ben Hari was as much of a chal-lenge as his country, and she'd never yet turned her back on a challenge.

It was exactly six o'clock, New York time, when the big 747 lifted into the air over Kennedy Airport. Genevieve, never a happy flier, pressed the small of her back against her chair and closed her eyes.

Last night after Ben Hari had called, she'd packed two suitcases and a flight bag. She'd phoned Cunningham at six-thirty to tell him she was leaving today, and as soon as she'd arrived at the office, she'd given her secretary instructions on how to handle her personal mail and to take care of pending appointments. She cleared her desk and gathered most of the papers she'd need in Kashkiri and shoved them into her briefcase. Cunningham could send whatever else she needed.

She had her hair and nails done, and at four-thirty she'd changed into a two-piece red wool crepe suit and high-heeled black pumps.

She had been ready when her secretary knocked to say that Rupert Matthews had come to collect her, and calling out last minute instructions, she'd run for the elevator.

Now here she was, clutching the arms of a beautifully upholstered chair in the most luxurious plane she'd ever seen.

"Are you a nervous flier, Miss Jordan?" Ali smiled at her from across the aisle. "I assure you, there is nothing to worry about. Salim and the rest of the crew have been with me for almost five years. He's a most capable pilot, so please try to relax and enjoy the trip. Dinner will be served in a little while. Perhaps when the seat belt sign is turned off, you'd enjoy a cocktail or a glass of champagne."

Genevieve wet her lips. "Yes, thank you, I would like a glass of champagne."

"We should be in Rome a little after midnight, New York time. I'll phone my father from there, and if the situation in Kashkiri has not worsened, we will spend tomorrow in Rome and go on to Kashkiri the next day. Have you ever been to Rome?"

"Once, a year ago. But it was a business trip, and I'm afraid I didn't see much of the city."

"I'm sorry we can't stay longer. I'd enjoy showing it to you."

That was the polite thing to say, but suddenly Ali found himself wishing that they did have more time in Rome because he would have liked showing her around. She was really a most attractive woman and she looked very pretty in her red suit, although he in no way approved of the length of the skirt, which came just to the top of her knees and displayed her shapely legs.

An exciting warmth spread through his loins, and for a moment he was angry because she made him feel this way, and because he knew that any man, seeing her as he did now, would feel the same. Why didn't the Western world understand the Arab point of view that a woman's body should be concealed from all except the man she belonged to? The idea of a woman as attractive as Genevieve Jordan walking unprotected among men in any of the cities of Arabia was preposterous. Certainly it would be unthinkable in Kashkiri.

Ali's eyes narrowed in thought. He looked at the two suitcases stowed toward the back of the aircraft and wondered if all of her clothes were as enticing as the red suit. If they were, they would never do. He would have to see that while she was in Kashkiri she was properly attired.

As soon as the plane leveled out, Ali took Genevieve's arm and led her to a salon nearer to the front of the plane. When she had been seated in a white leather sofa, he took a comfortable chair next to her and gestured to one of the white-jacketed attendants. In a few moments the man brought an ice bucket with a bottle of Dom Perignon, and after he had opened it and filled both their glasses, he set a silver plate of caviar, finely chopped onions and sour cream, along with a dish of crackers, in front of them.

Genevieve, though used to a modicum of luxury, couldn't help being impressed. When she leaned back against the sofa and sighed, Ali said, "There are comfortable beds in both of the staterooms if you'd like to rest before dinner."

"Perhaps I'll rest later," she said. "I only had three hours' sleep last night."

"I'm sorry I disturbed you, but I'm afraid it was necessary." He took a sip of champagne. "I like champagne, but I only drink it when I'm not in Kashkiri because it is forbidden by our religion." He set the goblet down on the table in front of him.

"You said last night there was trouble in Kashkiri. Is it serious? Something that might interfere with the conference?"

"I hope not." Ali stared out of the window at the gathering darkness. "There is a man in Kashkiri, a sheik who is an opponent of my father's. His name is Omar Haj Fatah. In the last two years he has tried to cause trouble." Ali spread caviar on a cracker and handed it to Genevieve. "I know that you think my country is backward, Miss Jordan, but believe me, it would sink back to the barbarism of the Dark Ages if Sheik Haj Fatah overthrew my father. He has no regard for human life. He would kill my father and his ministers, and what women he didn't kill, he would sell into slavery. He would sacrifice his own men, his own family if need be, to get what he wants." His fingers tightened around the stem of his goblet. "And he wants Kashkiri."

He closed his eyes and pinched the skin above the bridge of his nose, wondering if it was a mistake to take this American woman into his world. He had not thought of what danger she might be in when his father had called last night, but now he knew he'd been hasty in obeying his father's orders that she come on the plane with him. A woman like Genevieve would bring a king's ransom in the few existing slave markets in the world, if Omar Haj Fatah ever got his hands on her.

"I'll phone Kashkiri tonight," he said. "If things have not settled down, it would be better for you to wait in Rome until they do."

"But the conference is in two months," Genevieve protested. "There's so much to do. I can't—"

"You will do what I say, and if I say you stay in Rome, then you will stay in Rome...." Ali stopped. He ran a hand through his thick black hair and with a shake of his head said, "I'm sorry. I didn't mean to snap at you. But I have a responsibility to you and to your company. If any harm came to you while you were in Kashkiri, I would be responsible."

He took her glass and refilled it before he handed it back to her. "I'm sorry," he said again.

He was a strange man, an undeniably forceful man, yet there was an air about him, a commanding presence that Genevieve admired. And though his ideas of a woman's place in the scheme of things seemed primitive, he was obviously sincere in wanting his country to make a good impression on the rest of the world.

Dressed as he was now in a white crewneck sweater, dark brown trousers, and brown loafers, he seemed more a man of the Western world than of the Middle East. It was hard to picture him in a society that was so vastly different from her own.

She had read about both Ali and his father when she'd known that the firm would be handling the Kashkiri account. His father, Sheik Turhan Ben Hari, had been one of the richest playboys in the 1950s, and his son, known to columnists as the Lord of the Desert, had followed in his father's footsteps by dating most of the socially eligible women in Europe.

He was an impressive man, both in stature and manner, handsome in a rugged, masculine way that a certain type of woman would undoubtedly find attractive. She, of course, had too much sense to let herself be attracted to him, even if he was the Lord of the Desert.

Genevieve found herself more relaxed by the time the dinner of chateaubriand and a fresh garden salad was served. She asked questions about Kashkiri, and Ali told her about his family.

"Do the smaller children live in the harem with their mothers?" she asked.

Ali nodded. "There are many children, of course, so my two-year-old twin sisters, as well as my little brother Ismail, have many playmates. It's a pleasant life for them, and for the women."

"I can see where it would be for the children," Genevieve said as she put a slice of brie and a small cluster of green grapes on her dessert plate. "But I should think it would be a terrible way for women to live."

"But why?" Ali looked honestly puzzled. "They have no responsibility other than caring for their children. Everything else is done for them."

"But they live in a harem," Genevieve protested. "They're virtual prisoners. They—"

"Of course they're not prisoners," Ali said indignantly. "They go out shopping, and occasionally a woman accompanies her husband on a trip. You'll see for yourself how pleasant it is there."

"I've already told you, Mr. Ben Hari, I prefer to stay in the hotel when I'm in Kashkiri. I absolutely refuse to live in the harem."

His dark heavy brows knit together in a frown. "We shall see."

And they finished the rest of the meal in silence.

When the dinner table had been taken away, Ali said, "Why don't I show you to a bedroom so you can rest until we arrive in Rome?"

"All right." Genevieve stood up. "Perhaps I will for an hour or two. Wake me before we land."

He put a hand on her arm to guide her toward the rear of the plane, and when he paused in front of one of the stateroom doors he said, "Sleep well, Miss Jordan."

"Thank you, Mr. Ben Hari."

"Please." A slight pressure on her arm delayed her. "We're going to be together for two months. I'd like you to call me Ali."

She nodded. "My name is Genevieve."

"Jahn-vi-ev," he said slowly, giving it the French pronunciation. "Does anyone call you Genny?"

A slight smile curved her lips. "My father does."

"Then with your permission, that is what I will call you." He raised her hand to his lips. "Good night, Genny."

When she closed the door, she kicked her shoes off and lay down. "Oh, my, " she whispered, looking up at the ceiling. "Oh, my."

The Eternal City was a blaze of color in the hour before sunset. Genevieve and Ali had paused at the Piazza Barberini to admire the arc of water from the conch shell at the Triton fountain there before they made their way up the Via Venetto to a sidewalk café. When they ordered an espresso, Ali looked at her and said, "You must be tired, Genny."

"I'm too excited to be tired. It's been a lovely day." She took off the straw hat with the jaunty pink feather— "It matches my dress," she'd said when she'd bought it that morning—and placed it on the empty chair beside her.

A man at the next table smiled at her, and Ali turned to glare at him.

More than one man had smiled at Genevieve as they'd traversed the streets of Rome today. A man had whistled at her on the Spanish Steps, and a youth in his early twenties had reached out to pinch her just as they started into the Roman forum. Ali had grabbed the youth's wrist. "Don't!" he'd said quietly, and the young man had uttered an oath and sprinted away.

Genevieve settled back in her chair and crossed her legs. Two men passing by on the sidewalk turned to stare at her.

When one had the effrontery to whistle, Ali found himself thinking that if Genevieve belonged to him, he would see that she was properly covered. From head to toe, he thought, so that only her sea-green eyes would show.

"You're frowning," she said. "What is it? Are you worried about the situation in Kashkiri?"

Ali shook his head. "No, I spoke to my father last night when we arrived. There was still sporadic fighting on the outskirts of Kashkiri, but he said the situation was well in hand. Fatah's forces will regroup, of course, and one of these days he'll make another try at overthrowing my father."

"I'm sorry. That must be a worry to both you and your father." She looked out at the busy street. "What time will we leave tomorrow?"

"In the early afternoon. That will get us into Kashkiri before nightfall." He flexed his broad shoulders. "It will be good to get home."

His home. She wondered what it would be like.

They had dinner at the Trattoria Romolo, a garden restaurant set in the courtyard of a Renaissance home near the Aurelian wall. The biggest and best antipasto Genevieve had ever seen was followed by cannelloni, then roast baby lamb with wild asparagus and artichokes. And though she said she simply could not eat another bite, she ate every mouthful of the creamy zabaglione.

"You have a good appetite," Ali said approvingly. Which was amazing because she did not seem to have an ounce of fat on her curvaceous body. Tonight she'd worn a deceptively simple black velvet sheath. Once again the skirt came just to her knees to display the length of her black-silk-stockinged legs and high-heeled black pumps. Her hair, as it had been since the first day he'd seen her, had been pulled back into a chignon and fastened with a black velvet bow.

"How do you stay so slim?" he asked after he had taken a sip of the hot, rich coffee.

"I work out."

"I beg your pardon?"

"I do aerobic exercise at a health club four or five times a week, and after the exercise I swim for thirty minutes."

Ali nodded. "There is a pool in the section of the harem that you will be assigned to."

Genevieve's face tightened. "But I won't be in the harem— I'll be at the hotel."

"We will need to confer on the conference. That would be an inconvenience if you were at the hotel."

"Nevertheless, that's where I'm going to stay."

His heavy dark brows drew together in a ferocious frown. "You will be more comfortable in the harem."

"My staying in your harem with your wives and concubines is quite impossible."

"We have no concubines. The women in the harem are wives, sisters, daughters, relatives of our family and the families of the ministers. They all live very well, I assure you."

"But wives are separated from their husbands."

"Not all the time. The wives spend time with their husbands."

"At night?" Genevieve's green eyes sent sparks of anger his way.

His lips twitched in a smile. "Of course at night," he said. "When they are sent for."

He thought then how it would be to send for her, to have her come into his chambers after the day's work had been completed. To hold her, to undress her, to...

With a smothered oath Ali put money on the table, and getting quickly to his feet, he said, "Come, it's a lovely night. Let's walk for a while."

And though he knew she was angry, he took her hand and brought her arm through his. They were in Rome, and for tonight at least they could walk arm and arm through this beautiful and ancient city.

As they neared the Trevi Fountain, they heard the sound of mandolins. When Genevieve paused, Ali said, "Do you like the music?"

"Yes, I like it very much. It seems..." She smiled. "It seems very Italian."

"Shall we have a brandy and listen for a little while?"

And when she said yes, he led her up a flight of stairs into a café. "Do you prefer to sit in here or would you like to sit outside?" he asked.

"Outside," she said. And they followed a waiter with a red jacket out onto a balcony that overlooked the Trevi Fountain.

"It is said that if you throw a coin into the fountain, you will return to Rome." Ali gestured to the cascading waters below. "When we leave here, you must remember to throw a coin, that is if you wish to return."

"I wish to return." Her earlier anger forgotten now, Genevieve looked out over the ancient and mysterious city and the beautiful fountain below. And it seemed to her that she could almost see it as it had been in the days when Caesar's legions had ruled over half the world.

They sat quietly for a while, and when they had finished their brandy they left the café.

The streets of Rome were still now, and the only sound was the rush of the water from the Trevi Fountain, where sea horses pranced next to the figures of Neptune. Though eroded by time and pollution, the fountain was as beautiful as when it had been built almost three hundred years ago.

"I wonder if it's true, the legend about returning to Rome," she murmured.

Ali placed a few coins in her hand, then he took her by the shoulders and turned her around so that her back was to the fountain. "Now," he said with a smile, "to be sure that you will return one day."

She raised her arm over her head and tossed the coins, but before she could turn back, Ali put his hands on her shoulders again. He looked at her, a question in his eyes, and with a sigh he brought her close and kissed her.

For a moment Genevieve stood still, too surprised to move. Then she put her hands flat against his chest to try to push him away.

He tightened his hands on her shoulders. "Genny," he whispered against her lips, and his arms came around her, holding her close in his embrace.

Her mouth trembled under his. She heard the rasp of his breath, and the kiss deepened. He kissed her again and again, soft questing kisses, his mouth warming hers, sampling, tasting, savoring.

Suddenly, without warning, her body caught fire and her lips softened against his. The hands that had tried to push him away crept up around his neck so that her fingers could stroke the soft hairs that curled there. When he pressed one hand against the small of her back to urge her closer, she didn't protest. Instead, she molded her body to his, loving the feel of him close to her this way, excited by the warm moistness of his mouth.

He whispered her name against her lips and held her away from him for a moment. Then he brought her close again, and this time his kiss was fierce with desire. He urged her closer, and she felt the power of his manhood press against her body.

"No!" She tried to struggle out of his arms. "No," she said again, and her breath came fast, as though she'd been running.

Ali stared at her. "Genny...?" His voice was a soft caress against the cascading water. His eyes were deep and dark and warm. "Genny," he said again. Then he straightened his shoulders and let her go.

"I'm sorry. I didn't mean to do that." He took a deep breath. "It won't happen again."

Genevieve nodded and tried to slow her racing heart. "It's the romance of Rome," she said, hating the tremble in her voice. A sudden chill ran through her body. She shivered and hugged her arms.

"You're cold," he said, and before she could stop him he took off his jacket and placed it over her shoulders. His hands lingered for only a moment, then he let her go and said, "Let's try to catch a taxi, shall we?"

And when they had found a cab and settled into the back seat, Ali talked about the coming conference and the work that had to be done. And tried to pretend that his insides were not trembling and that his body was not on fire with wanting her.

He leaned back against the seat and closed his eyes. He knew that he had never wanted a woman as much as he wanted Genevieve Jordan.

Chapter 3

When they left Rome the next afternoon, Genevieve gazed down at the shining domed cupolas, the church spires and the rooftops. As the plane dipped low over the city and sunlight shone on the water bubbling from fountains, it seemed to her as though she could see that one special fountain where Ali Ben Hari had kissed her last night. And she knew that if she closed her eyes, she would be able to hear, instead of the roar of the jet engines, the rush of the water from the fountain, and that she would feel once again the press of Ali's mouth on hers.

She had gone to sleep still shaken by the warmth of his embrace and by the sure knowledge that what had happened must never happen again. Ali Ben Hari was an enormously attractive man, a physically appealing man. But theirs was a business relationship, and except for a business luncheon or dinner, she had never, in all of her working life, had any kind of a personal relationship with a client. Over the years she had been barraged with flowers and phone calls from some of the men she had worked with, but she had never succumbed because personal involvements did not make for good business relationships.

For the next two months she would be working in a country far different from her own, working closely for a man whose cultural beliefs were as different from hers as night was from day. Last night she had let herself be carried away by the magic of Rome, and yes, by the warmth of Ali's kiss. She mustn't let that happen again.

This morning when he had met her downstairs in the hotel, he had been wearing a conservative business suit. He looked like any other Italian businessman, and for the barest fraction of a second she had wished that that's what he was and that they could stay here in Rome and not go on to Kashkiri.

Ali had been pleasant but withdrawn when he had greeted her, and she'd known that he, too, realized that last night had been a mistake. She glanced now to where he sat, his back to her, papers spread out on the desk in front of him, and with a sigh she opened her briefcase and began making notes of all the things she would have to do as soon as she arrived in Kashkiri.

Several hours went by before her concentration waned and her head began to nod. Finally, no longer able to stay awake, she leaned back in her chair and closed her eyes.

It was late afternoon when she awoke. She opened her eyes slowly, trying to adjust to her surroundings, and when she looked out of the window of the plane, she saw that they were flying over an endless expanse of desert.

The Sahara, she thought, that ancient and barren land of sand and stone that extended from the Atlantic Ocean to the Red Sea, land of the Tuareg, Tibesti Massif and Berber. She closed her eyes as a feeling of anticipation ran through her body.

When she opened her eyes, she saw Ali coming down the aisle toward her. But it was not the Ali she knew. This was a different man, a strange and foreign man who had cast aside his conservative business suit and wore instead a gray *djellaba*, the Arabian robe, and a *howli* around his head.

Genevieve stared at him, and suddenly, vividly, she saw him in all his primitive manhood, a man from another place, another time.

He met her gaze. Look at me, Genny, he wanted to say. For this is who I am, Ali Ben Hari, son of Turhan, heir to the Sheikdom of Kashkiri. I am not one of your pale Western men, I am Arab. My blood is the blood of the bedouins, my roots are in the desert that I love, with the people I come from.

Because of all that he felt in this moment, defensive of his world, hurt by the shock that he thought he saw in her eyes, his voice was harshly cold when he said, "We'll land in Kashkiri soon. Do you still insist on staying at the hotel?"

Genevieve wet her lips. "Yes. Yes, I prefer being in the hotel."

"Very well. I'll arrange for a suite."

"Thank you." Her throat constricted. Where was the man who had held her in his arms last night? The man who had kissed her and whispered her name there by the Trevi Fountain?

When he turned away, she told herself that the sting of tears in her eyes came from the reflection of the sun on the plane's silver wing and had nothing whatever to do with anything she might be feeling.

The chauffeur of the air-conditioned Rolls-Royce drove smoothly through the streets of the walled city, past minarets and mosques, down the palm-lined boulevard and gardens where flowers bloomed in the late-afternoon sun.

The weather had turned cool the day Genevieve had left New York, but the temperature was in the nineties here. She wondered what it must be like in the desert that lay less than two hundred miles to the east.

There were many men on the street and in the sidewalk coffee houses, but only one or two robed and veiled women. Genevieve looked at the grilled or barred windows of the houses they passed and wondered about the women there. Women who waited patiently for their husbands to return.

It hadn't been like that in Morocco or Tunisia, especially in the last few years that Genevieve had lived in those countries. By the time she had left, there were many professional women, as well as all the young women who attended the universities. It hadn't been unusual to see women in Western dress in those countries. But this was not Morocco or Tunisia; this was Kashkiri.

At last they came to a broad avenue lined with stately royal palms, and when they passed through a tall iron gate, Genevieve saw the hotel: a modern steel-and-glass building, banked by beautifully terraced gardens.

As soon as they entered the circular drive, two young men in clean white robes rushed from the glass doors out to the limousine.

The chauffeur helped Genevieve from the car, and the two young men took her suitcases. "I'll see you inside," Ali said.

The man behind the front desk bowed when they entered. Ali spoke too rapidly for Genevieve to understand. The man said, "Yes, *sidi*. As you wish, Prince Ben Hari," and darted nervous glances toward Genevieve. Then, with the two white-robed young men ahead of them, they crossed the lobby to the elevators.

"I'll see you to your rooms," Ali said, ignoring the men who turned to stare at them. "I suggest you have dinner in your room tonight and that you not leave the hotel until I or one of my men call for you at noon tomorrow.''

"But . . ." Genevieve hesitated, stopped by the sudden flash of anger in Ali's dark eyes.

"It isn't the custom here for women to stay unescorted in a hotel," he explained.

"So I'm to be secluded in my rooms unless you send for me?" As angry as he was now, she stopped and faced him. "I might just as well be secluded in your harem."

"You would have more freedom and certainly you would be safer there than here." One dark eyebrow raised in question. "It's not too late for you to change your mind."

"I won't change my mind," she retorted as she turned to follow the two young men down a long red-carpeted corridor.

They stopped in front of a heavy carved door with an engraved gold disk the size of a dinner plate in the middle of it. One of the men swung the door open, and Genevieve stepped inside. The room, decorated in white and rose, was as beautiful as any she had ever seen. With a smile she crossed the thick white rug and dropped her purse next to the bowl of oranges on the coffee table in front of the white sofa.

The same young man who had ushered her in opened a door at the far end of the room. "The sleeping chamber, madam," he said, and when Genevieve went in she gasped, for the bedroom, decorated in the most delicate shade of blue she had ever seen, looked like something out of a movie set. A crystal chandelier hung over the canopied king-size bed. Talisman roses had been placed on the white-and-gold dresser and the bedside stands. There was a television set, a radio and a gold satin chaise that had been placed in front of the windows.

When she went back into the sitting room, the two young men were gone and she walked out on the balcony to stand beside Ali.

Kashkiri lay before her, ancient and venerable, golden-domed mosques shiny in the afternoon sun, graceful palms and blossoming flowers blooming along the boulevard. Genevieve raised her eyes to the mountains. Beyond lay the sea to the west, the desert to the east. A faint and plaintive call drifted out over the city. The muezzin, she thought, calling the people to prayer.

She had heard it often when she'd been growing up, and it had never failed to move her. In a voice softened by memory, she said, "I've never forgotten that sound."

"It's the first sound I remember hearing." Ali, his hands resting on the balcony railing, looked out over the city of Kashkiri. "It's good to be home," he said.

He turned to look at her. In the last rays of the sun, her face was so classically beautiful that for a moment it was all he could do not to touch her. He wanted to cup her face between his hands, to hold her there while he kissed her eyelids, her cheeks, that tempting indentation between her nose and her lips. And the mouth that had trembled beneath his last night.

With the thought of it, of the way she had felt in his arms, he tightened his hands on the railing, afraid that if he touched her now, if he kissed her now, he would be unable to stop himself. He would pick her up in his arms, carry her into the bedroom and lay her on that wide soft bed. And when she lay naked before him, he would kiss every inch of her lovely body. Then he would take her, fiercely, deeply. And with the thought of it, of her softness closing around him, his heart began to pound and his breath grew ragged.

He turned away. "My father is waiting for me," he said. "I must go. If there's anything you need, ask the clerk at the front desk or phone me at the government palace."

"Very well." Genevieve followed him into the sitting room. "Thank you," she said formally. "For the rooms I mean. They're really quite lovely."

Ali nodded. "I'll see you tomorrow." As his hand closed on the knob of the door, he hesitated as though about to speak. Then he shook his head. "Tomorrow," he said, and went quickly out the door.

Genevieve, as she had been told to do, phoned down for dinner. And after it had come, she went into the bedroom and switched on the television. There was news in Arabic on one channel and a French film on the other that she settled down to watch. When it ended, she undressed and went to bed.

But though the bed was comfortable, she couldn't sleep. She felt strangely alone and isolated. If she had been in any other city, she would have taken a walk after dinner. She would have...but no, she thought with a smile, she wouldn't have walked alone at night in New York or Chicago, Los Angeles or Detroit or any other large city in America. Perhaps Kashkiri wasn't so different after all.

Tomorrow she would go to the government palace with Ali. She would meet his father and the ministers and with them she would begin to lay plans for the coming conference. She wondered about Sheik Turhan Ben Hari, and whether or not he was anything like his son. How many children did he have? She tried to remember the one brother and all of the sisters Ali had told her about, but she couldn't—there were too many of them. She smiled, remembering that when she had said that Ali's father must be quite a man, Ali had responded that so were all Kashkiri men.

If they were all like Ali... Genevieve closed her eyes and turned her face into the pillow. Like Ali. What were the words that had formed in her mind this afternoon on the plane when she'd first seen him in his robe? Primitive masculinity? Yes. He was primitive and masculine, and so physically appealing that it was all she could do to keep her hands off him.

Genevieve smacked the pillow. Then with a sigh she closed her eyes and vowed not think about Ali Ben Hari for the rest of the night.

But she awakened in the morning with a smile on her lips and the half-remembered dream of a man in a flowing gray robe who had carried her off into the desert on a stallion whose coat was the same midnight black as Ali Ben Hari's eyes.

When she came out of the shower, she pulled the drapes back and looked out. The day was beautifully sunny and much too nice to stay inside, and she decided that she would go downstairs to the dining room for breakfast.

She dressed in a jade-green suit and white high-heeled pumps, changed some of her things from her travel purse into a white purse, put in a list of things she wanted to discuss with Turhan Ben Hari and left the suite.

A different desk clerk was on duty this morning. He said a perfunctory "*Sabbah al khair*, good morning," and when Genevieve responded with *"Sabbah annour,"* he asked, "Is there anything I can do for you, madam?"

"I'm looking for the dining room."

"It is at the other end of the lobby. Is madam meeting someone there?"

"No, I'm alone." With a nod she turned and started off in the direction he had indicated, uncomfortably aware as she crossed the lobby that she was the only woman. But that didn't matter; a hotel was a public place, and she had as much right in the lobby or the dining room as anyone else.

When she entered the dining room, a waiter with a white jacket led her to a corner table where two places were set. "Do you wish to wait for your husband before you order?" he asked.

Genevieve said no, that she was alone, and his bushy brows rose half an inch. He frowned, and Genevieve stared straight at him. "I will have orange juice, scrambled eggs and flat bread," she said. And because his lips were pursed in disapproval, she added, "I'd like my coffee now, please."

She looked over the list of things she wanted to discuss today and made a few notes while she ate breakfast, all the while aware that she was the only woman in the room. Some of the men were staring at her, but she refused to be intimidated.

By the time she finished her third cup of coffee, most of the men had left the dining room. She asked for the check, signed it, and gathering up her papers and her white purse, she left.

When she glanced at her watch, she saw that she still had an hour before Ali came to pick her up and so she went to the front door of the hotel and looked out.

The street was crowded with people. There were a few robed and veiled women among the men this morning. Shops were open, and a number of cars and buses whizzed by, directed by a traffic policeman on a raised platform in the center of the busy street.

She wouldn't go too far from the hotel, Genevieve decided as she stepped out onto the busy sidewalk. She'd have a look in the shops and maybe buy a few souvenirs before she had to leave for the government palace.

The sun was shining, and the temperature was in the eighties. She turned to her right out of the hotel and walked toward the corner. A man in a dirty *djellaba* said something to her. She paid no attention to him. He grabbed her arm and she whirled around. *"M'shee!"* she said. "Go away!"

He laughed and put his arm around her waist.

Other men stopped to watch.

Genevieve shoved against her captor's shoulder, but all he did was laugh and tighten his hold. Before she could free herself, he shoved her farther down the street and pulled her into the entrance of an alleyway.

Frightened as well as angry now, Genevieve struck out at the man and in a loud voice cried, "Let me go! Let me go!"

A man peered into the alleyway, shrugged and continued on.

The man holding her ran a hand over her breasts. She hit him across his face. He said something she didn't understand, grabbed both her wrists, shoved her hands behind her and with his free hand began to fondle her.

She brought her knee up, but he dodged out of the way, laughed at her and snaked his hand down her body. She screamed. The traffic policeman turned to look, and she went weak with relief because he'd seen her.

"Help!" she cried. "Help me!"

He looked in her direction for a moment, then he turned his back, blew his whistle and signaled for cars coming from the other direction to proceed.

This couldn't be happening. It was eleven o'clock in the morning. There were people on the street. Someone had to help her. Someone . . . She struggled wildly against her captor, tried again to stab him with her knee, and when he dodged she kicked him as hard as she could in his shins.

"Zfftt!" he cried, and struck her across the face with the back of his hand. *"Haram!"* he shouted. "You are bad woman. You—"

Genevieve turned her face toward the wall, trying to shield herself from another blow. But suddenly her captor spun away from her, skidded and slipped and went flat on his back, legs akimbo, yelping in terror.

She turned back just as Ali hauled the man to his feet and slammed him hard up against the side of the building. The man tried to speak, but Ali hit him before he could. Then he fastened his hands around the scrawny neck. The man's eyes bulged, and his knees began to buckle.

Ali let him go, but before the man could fall, he grabbed him by the scruff of his neck and sent him skittering and stumbling down the alley.

Only then did Ali turn to Genevieve and ask, "Are you all right?"

"I think so." She pushed her tumbled hair back off her face. "My God," she said, still in shock. "My God! It's broad daylight. I screamed for help but nobody would help me. Even the policeman. He heard me. He saw me. But he didn't try to stop the attack. He just stood there directing the damn traffic!"

"Because it was your fault."

Genevieve stared at him. "What? What did you say?"

"It was your fault. You had no business leaving the hotel. I told you to stay there until I came for you." So angry now that he wanted to shake her, Ali clenched his hands to his sides. "What did you expect, dressed as you are?"

"Dressed as I am? I'm wearing a suit, for heaven's sake."

"With a short skirt, displaying your legs for every man in Kashkiri to see. Your face is uncovered, and you're wearing makeup."

Genevieve glared at him, so furious she couldn't speak. Then she whirled away and started back toward the hotel. But she'd only gone a few steps when Ali grasped her arm. He propelled her ahead of him into the hotel, and when they entered he went to the elevator with her.

"You needn't come up with me," she said, trying to free herself from his grasp.

But he only tightened his hold on her arm, and when the elevator doors opened he shoved her inside. At the door of her suite he demanded her key. "Pack your things," he said when they were inside. "You're coming with me."

"No, I'm not!"

"You're checking out of the hotel and coming to the palace harem, where you won't be able to get into trouble."

Genevieve turned to face him. "And if I refuse?"

"You'll be on a plane for New York this afternoon. And I'll phone Rupert and ask him to engage another public relations firm."

She stared at him and knew by the anger in his eyes and the set of his jaw that unless she obeyed, he would do exactly what he had said he would do.

"It will take me a few minutes to pack," she said, turning away from him. "My suit is torn— I'll have to change."

Ali nodded. His anger had begun to fade. "I'm sorry I shouted at you before, but when I saw you with that man, when I saw his hands on you..." He put his hand on her arm and gently turned her around. "My father has many enemies. Omar Haj Fatah will do anything he can to prevent the conference from taking place. Once he finds out that you're here in Kashkiri to assist us with the conference, he might try to do something to you. To have you kidnapped or—"

"Kidnapped?" Genevieve stared at him. "You can't be serious."

"Believe me, I am. If you insist on staying here at the hotel, you'll be a virtual prisoner in these rooms. I could send a guard to be posted outside your door, but even then you might not be completely safe."

He looked down at her and without knowing that he did, he drew her closer. "I'm responsible for you, Genny. If anything happened to you . . ."

His dark eyes seemed to burn into hers. For a moment neither of them spoke. Then he said, "Change your clothes, Genny. You're coming to the palace with me."

Chapter 4

The government palace lay at the edge of the city, a fortressed bastion of stone and mortar, stark against the rugged hillside.

Genevieve pressed her hands together in her lap and wished that she were back in New York. But it was too late. The limousine passed over a bridged moat and came to a stop in a walled courtyard.

Ali took her hand to help her out of the limo. "Come, let me show you the palace," he said, and led her across the patio and through the arched Moorish entrance.

It was as though they had stepped into another world, for the inner patio rivaled the beauty of the Alhambra. Palms and flowering plants circled a pool where water lilies floated, as pure white as the clouds reflected on the smooth, clear water. The only sounds to break the silence were the birds that scolded and sang from the branches of a lemon tree.

"This way," Ali said, and led Genevieve across the patio and through the intricately carved archways there.

They passed through the arches into a long tiled corridor and other patios, some larger than the first, some smaller. There were pools with stone-carved fountains from which water sparkled in the sunlight, and flowers: bright red hibiscus, carnations, gardenias and roses.

White-robed male servants bowed as they passed, and though Ali greeted each one, he did not pause.

"I'll take you to the harem," he told Genevieve. "When you've rested and are properly attired, a servant will bring you to one of the dining salons. Tonight you'll have dinner with my father and some of his ministers."

"Will you be there?"

"Of course, Genny." He grinned. "I wouldn't ask you to face my father alone."

She smiled uncertainly, not sure if he meant that his father was an ogre or a Kashkiri male on the lookout for another wife. It didn't occur to her to ask what he meant by "properly attired."

He stopped before a fifteen-foot copper door, opened it, ushered Genevieve into a red-and-gold-tiled foyer, then up a short flight of stairs. "This is the entrance to the harem," he said.

A Persian carpet covered most of the tiled floor. Velvet drapes hung on either side of latticed doors.

Genevieve looked at the doors and pressed her hands to her sides so that Ali wouldn't know they were trembling.

"I know this is strange to you," he murmured, "but you'll be safe and cared for here."

"I have to be free to do what I came to Kashkiri for," she said. "I can't spend my time locked away."

"You won't be locked away. You have only to pick up the phone in your chambers when you want to speak to me or to leave to go into the city. I'll take you there or anywhere else you want to go." He put a finger under her chin and raised her face. "This isn't a prison," he said softly. "You mustn't be afraid."

"I'm not afraid. It's just—"

"Different," he said. "I know, Genny, and I understand. But while you're in Kashkiri, you'll have to abide by our customs."

He wanted to kiss her, but when he saw the slight tremble of her lips, he made himself step away; he knew this was strange for her and that in spite of what she said, she really was frightened.

He pulled the gold cord that hung beside the velvet drapes.

The latticed doors opened.

Genevieve's heart beat hard against her ribs. She had heard stories of Western women who had done what she was about to do and who were never heard from again. She had to get away from here. She had to...

A robed woman appeared. She looked at Genevieve, then at Ali and said in English, "Greetings, madam. Good afternoon, Prince Ali Ben Hari. I have been expecting madam."

"Has everything been prepared?"

"Yes, my lord."

"Tonight at seven you will bring her to my father's salon. She will dine with us there."

"As you wish, *sidi*."

"This is Haifa," he said to Genevieve. "She'll take care of you. If there's anything you need that isn't provided, tell her and she will attend to it."

Genevieve nodded.

"I'll leave you now." But still Ali hesitated, reluctant to leave her, wanting to do something, to say something to quiet that look of apprehension in her eyes.

But because he had no choice, he turned away and started down the corridor. He'd taken only a few steps when she said, "Ali?"

He stopped. "Yes? What is it?"

"Nothing. I…" She shook her head. "Nothing," she said again, and followed the woman named Haifa into the world of the harem.

She was not sure what she had expected: odalisques in flowing gossamer, sad-eyed veiled ladies reclining on velvet chaises. But the ladies here were neither sad nor veiled. Dressed in colorful kaftans, chattering and laughing, with children in their arms or clinging to their long skirts, they clustered around Genevieve, crying, "*Marhaban, marhaban*, welcome, welcome."

A small boy swaggered to the front of the gathered women. "I am Ismail," he said. "Second son of my lord, Turhan."

Genevieve looked down at the little boy, and offering her hand, she said, "*Labas*, Ismail. How do you do."

He pumped her hand. "You're very pretty," he said, "for an infidel."

Genevieve bit back a smile. "Is that what I am?"

He looked up at the woman standing beside him. "She is, isn't she, Mother?" And before the young woman beside him could answer, he grasped the hands of two little girls and brought them forward. "She's an infidel," he told them.

"Ismail!" His mother, who looked to be no more than twenty, shook her head and said, "You're being rude to our American guest. Your father would be most displeased." To Genevieve, she said, "I am Tamraz, lady, third wife to my lord, Turhan. Forgive my son. He means no harm."

"He did no harm." Genevieve ruffled the boy's black curly hair. "He's a handsome boy, Tamraz. You must be pleased with him. Are these your daughters?"

"Yes, lady. They are Zora and Shbelia and they are two years old."

Genevieve took each little girl's hand and said, "My name is Genevieve and I'm very glad to meet you."

"Genevieve," several of the women murmured, and one, a beautiful young woman with wide dark eyes, said, "You are the lady from New York in America."

"Yes, I am."

"I am Zuarina." The woman offered her hand. "You are truly welcome, madam."

"Please call me Genevieve, or Genny, if you prefer."

"Genny," Zuarina said shyly.

Haifa took Genevieve's hand. "Come, madam," she said. "I will show you to your quarters."

Her quarters. Wide-eyed with wonder, Genevieve looked around. This is a dream, she thought, for it was as though she had stepped from the twentieth century back through the pages of time into the illusionary beauty of the *Arabian Nights*.

This was a room unlike any other she'd ever seen, a room with snow-white pillars and billowing chiffon, of deep satin sofas and a carpet of pile so thick that it was difficult to walk with her high heels. There was a white-and-gold desk with a matching chair in one corner of the room, hanging lamps, hassocks and ornately carved tables. A white-and-gold cage held a pair of turquoise-feathered love birds.

"Prince Ali ordered that these rooms be prepared before he left your country," Haifa said. "We had less than a week to arrange them, madam. I hope they meet with your approval." And before Genevieve could reply, she said, "Come this way, I will show you the bedroom."

Genevieve followed the other woman through a carved arched doorway into the bedroom, and gasped. It was one of the most beautiful, the most feminine rooms she had ever seen. In the middle of the room, on a raised dais, there was a round bed, canopied with gossamer in a delicate shade of apricot.

A small table and two chairs had been placed beneath latticed windows, and a satin chaise sat near latticed doors. There was a bouquet of pink roses on the dresser.

Haifa opened the doors and, motioning to Genevieve, led her out into a walled garden. There were flowers everywhere, orange and lemon trees, ferns and potted palms. And a swimming pool in which hundreds of gardenias floated.

"This is your private garden, madam," Haifa said. "No one will bother you here except for the gardener, who comes before dawn to put fresh gardenias in the pool."

It was like a dream, a slice of paradise in a desert oasis. Too stunned to speak, Genevieve followed Haifa back into the bedroom.

"The bath is through here, madam," Haifa said, and leading Genevieve behind a screen, she opened a door to reveal the bathroom. The rose-tiled sunken tub was banked by bamboo and fern. An array of perfumes and bath oils was displayed on a pink table, and a pink terry cloth robe had been placed over a chair.

"I will run your bath in a moment, madam." Haifa motioned Genevieve back to the bedroom. "But first perhaps we should select something for you to wear this evening."

"Then I'd better unpack," Genevieve said.

"I'll do that while you bathe, but Prince Ben Hari has instructed me that you won't wear the clothes you have brought from America while you're here."

"Then what am I supposed to wear?" Genevieve, hands on her hips, frowned at Haifa.

The other woman ignored the frown as she moved across the room and slid back the mirrored closet doors. "These are the clothes you'll wear while you are in Kashkiri," she said.

Genevieve stared at the array of gowns: kaftans of every color and material, sheer overgowns to be worn over Arabian-style cotton gauze blouses and trousers, plain white robes, gray and black robes, vividly hued gowns that sparkled with sequins, braidwork and appliqué.

"The shoes you will wear are here." Haifa indicated the racks of jeweled slippers in another part of the closet. She selected a pair, then reached up and took out a blue crepe-de-chine gown patterned with gold thread and sequins. From one of the drawers in the closet, she chose a blue chiffon scarf patterned with the same gold thread and sequins.

It was a beautifully exotic outfit, but one Genevieve did not want to wear.

"I prefer my own clothes," she said.

"While you are in the house of Ben Hari, you will dress as a Kashkiri woman." Haifa hung the dress outside the closet. "It has been so ordered. You will obey."

With that, she turned and went into the bathroom to run Genevieve's bathwater.

Genevieve took a deep breath. She was so angry that she wanted to throttle Haifa, pick up her suitcases and go storming out of the palace. But she knew that defying Haifa wouldn't help; the woman had been given her orders, and she would follow them. When Genevieve left her chambers, she would be dressed Kashkiri-style.

And though she was still angry, Genevieve admitted to herself as she went into the bathroom and lowered her body into the fragrant water of the tiled tub, that the dress Haifa had chosen was lovely and feminine. It would be like playing dress-up, she told herself. She'd wear the harem clothes while she was in Kashkiri, but never for a moment would she forget who she was or why she was here.

A slight smile curved the corners of Genevieve's lips as she lay back into the perfumed water. What would it be like to live her days in this exotic setting? To never again have to whistle down a taxi, make a mad rush for the subway or try to eat a sandwich at her desk in between telephone calls? What would it be like to awake when she chose? To sun and swim, to have someone draw her bath and prepare her for the evening to come?

What would it be like to be sent for by a man like Ali Ben Hari, to go silently down the long corridors to his chambers? To have him come to hers at night, when the air was scented with orange blossoms and jasmine?

She closed her eyes. What would it be like to bathe with him, to make love with him? To...?

Genevieve's eyes snapped open. What in the hell was wrong with her? Ali Ben Hari was a client, a man from a world far different from her own, different from the men she dated, danced with, flirted with. Men who expected no more than a casual kiss on the cheek when they took her home.

Ali had kissed her last night in Rome, but it hadn't been a casual kiss; it had been deep, intense, hot. She'd felt his desire and it had frightened her. It frightened her now because she knew he wouldn't be an easy man to say no to. He was a man used to taking what he wanted. If he wanted her...

Genevieve slipped farther down in the water. For the next two months she'd be living in the harem, subject to both Ali and his father's rules. She had to be careful.

Ali Ben Hari was an attractive man. If she had met him anywhere else, she would have been very interested. But Ali wasn't from her world; he was a Kashkiri man, a man who would some day become the sheik of Kashkiri.

This wasn't make-believe. Ali wasn't Valentino, and she wasn't a frightened female quivering at his feet. She was Genevieve Jordan from Ann Arbor, Michigan, vice president of one of the most prestigious public relations companies in New York. A today woman who could hold her own with any man anywhere in the world.

She had to remember that, though she must live in a harem with other women, this was a world that she wanted no part of.

But it was hard to remember that this was make-believe when she stepped out of the bath and Haifa handed her the pink terry cloth robe and said, "Come, madam, I will do your nails now."

She had a manicure and a pedicure, then Haifa brought a luncheon tray with a steaming bowl of couscous, flatbread, tea and cream-filled dates. When Genevieve finished eating, Haifa pulled back the apricot spread and said, "You should rest now, madam. I will wake you when it is time to dress for dinner."

The bed was soft, the satin cool against her skin. Chiffon curtains billowed out from the open French doors that led to the garden, where the singing of sparrows was the only sound that broke the afternoon quiet.

With a sigh Genevieve closed her eyes. Make-believe, she thought, and then she slept.

Ali had known that she was beautiful, but now, as she came toward him, the breath caught in his throat and his hands felt hot with the need to touch her. Her skin looked paler, her eyes more exotic, and she moved with a swaying delicacy.

The other men were as aware of her as he was, and as she drew nearer he saw his father's eyes narrow in appraisal.

There had been a scene this afternoon, when he'd told his father that the Jordan of Cunningham, Tabler, Randall and Jordan was not a man but a woman.

"A woman!" His father's voice had reverberated through the corridors. "You've brought a woman to Kashkiri to handle the conference?"

While Ali had explained that Genevieve was knowledgeable in the ways of the Arab world, that she had lived in both Morocco and Tunisia, his father had paced up and down.

"I don't give a camel's tail where she's lived or how knowledgeable she is," he'd roared. "A woman has no place in the business of men."

But now, as Ali rose to take Genevieve's hand and lead her to his father, he saw the obvious appreciation in the way Turhan looked at her.

"May I present Miss Genevieve Jordan from the United States," Ali said. To Genevieve, he said, "Miss Jordan, this is my father, Sheik Turhan Ben Hari."

"Sheik Ben Hari." She touched her forehead and slightly bowed. "I am honored, sir."

Turhan smiled.

"I have come from the United States to represent my company, offering my poor services to help make the coming conference a successful one."

"Come sit next to me." Turhan motioned to the silk pillow at his side. "First we will eat, then we will discuss the conference."

Genevieve settled herself next to the sheik as her gaze quickly swept the room. A beautiful Oriental rug covered most of the polished floor. The white walls were softened by silken drapes in shades of rose, pink and coral. The faint scent of incense perfumed the air.

There were ten men around the low table, all of them dressed in flowing white robes. One by one, Ali introduced them to Genevieve: the minister of finance, the minister of trade, of foreign affairs, all of Sheik Turhan Ben Hari's cabinet. She tried to remember their names and the offices they held, and when she knew she couldn't, she resolved to ask Ali to get her a list so that she could begin to associate faces with names and positions.

Several of the men were close to Ali's age, but most of them were in their fifties or sixties. Turhan, she thought, must be in his middle fifties. He was a handsome man, shorter than his son but of a broader build. His neatly clipped hair showed only faint traces of silver, as did his mustache and goatee-type beard.

She tried to remember the number of children he had fathered. Ali had said that some of his half sisters were grown and married. Did their mother live in the harem along with Tamraz, the mother of Ismail and the twins? And what about the second wife? Did she live in the harem, too? Tomorrow she would begin to know the women and try to sort out Turhan's wives, as well as the wives of his ministers, to see who could best represent their husbands at the conference.

The dinner course arrived: *mahshikusah*, zucchini stuffed with fried ground meat, spices and pine nuts; a salad of tomatoes, cucumbers, and lettuce; *kabsah*, a dish made of lamb mixed with rice and tomatoes; stuffed grape leaves; artichokes cooked in a saffron sauce; fried eggplant; and pita bread topped with a thin layer of finely ground meat and onions.

When the main meal was finished and the dishes had been cleared, servants brought in *baklava*, cherry bread, stuffed dates and hot mint tea.

"Now we will talk," Turhan said. "What are your ideas on the conference, Miss Jordan?"

"I've studied the agenda of the meetings, sir, and it appears that you and your capable ministers have everything in order. I'll help set up your meetings, of course, but it seems to me the main part of my work will be to make sure that the wives are entertained while their husbands are attending the meetings. I'll also help in arranging dinner parties, of course."

"Quite so," the minister of foreign affairs said.

"In addition to the Arab countries, I understand that delegates and their wives will come from the United States, England, Germany and Japan." Genevieve smiled at the men seated around the table. "I'm sure some of the other men will also bring their wives."

"That is expected," Turhan said.

"Then of course your wives will participate in the conference."

"I don't understand what you mean by 'participate,'" Turhan said with a frown.

"I mean your wives and the wives of your ministers will take an active part in the conference." And seeing the look of consternation on all of their faces, Genevieve quickly added, "In the dinners you will give, and in whatever social activities are planned."

For a moment there was only silence. Then Sheik Turhan said, "That's quite out of the question."

It was Genevieve's turn to frown and say, "I beg your pardon?"

"Out of the question," Turhan repeated. "Our women do not mingle in the affairs of men."

"The affairs of men?" A smile curved the corners of Genevieve's mouth. "I'm not suggesting they attend the business meetings, sir. I'm only suggesting they appear at the dinner parties and that they participate in showing the foreign ladies around your beautiful country."

"Impossible!" the minister of trade said.

"May I ask why?" Genevieve kept her smile in place.

"It is not our custom," the minister said.

"I see." Genevieve steepled her fingers as she gazed at the men around the table. "Perhaps I've been mistaken, gentlemen. I had the impression that Kashkiri wanted to become part of the twentieth century."

"We *are* part of the twentieth century!" Turhan banged his glass of mint tea down on the table.

"Perhaps you are, sir, but it appears your women are still in the Middle Ages. At least that's the way it will appear to the men and women of the more—" she hesitated "—advanced countries."

Every one of the minister's heads jerked toward Turhan Ben Hari, waiting for him to speak.

When he did, it was with barely controlled anger. "Kashkiri is not like other countries, Miss Jordan. We have our traditions, our own way of doing things. Our women are revered, cherished and protected from the uncertainties and cruelties of the outside world. They are childlike in their simplicity."

"Because they're treated as children, Sheik Ben Hari, not as women." Genevieve looked him square in the eye. "Certainly not as human beings who are equal in every way to a man."

There was a communal gasp. Then silence.

Turhan rose and glowered down at Genevieve. "You are excused, madam. Ali will take you back to the harem, where you belong."

Ali came beside her, but before he could lead her away, Genevieve said, "I'm sincerely sorry if I've upset you, Sheik Ben Hari, but if I'm to help Kashkiri make a good impression at the coming conference, then I must be allowed to express my opinions. I believe that your women would be a great asset to you."

"They know nothing of protocol," he said.

"My job would be to teach them, sir. To help them be comfortable with women who are a little more worldly than they are."

Turhan tugged at his goatee.

Genevieve lowered her head. If she had overstepped, if she had angered him so that they could not talk again, then she had failed before she had even begun.

"Well . . ."

She raised her head.

"I will think about what we have discussed tonight," he said. "Perhaps we will speak again tomorrow."

"I look forward to it, sir."

"You may go now. My son will see you to your quarters. I hope they're acceptable."

"More than acceptable, Sheik Ben Hari. They're quite beautiful and I thank you."

The barest suggestion of a smile appeared. Then Turhan waved his jeweled fingers and said, "Until tomorrow, then."

And Genevieve knew that although she had not won, neither had she lost.

Chapter 5

"My father isn't used to Western ways," Ali said as he guided Genevieve through one of the patios that led to the harem. "He was educated at the University of Beirut back in the days when that school had the reputation of being one of the finest in the Middle East. He's been to Madrid and to Paris, but always with an entourage so that he was surrounded by his own people, his own customs."

He paused beside a fountain and turned to look at her. Though he had been angry when she had argued with his father, he had nevertheless felt a sense of pride when she'd stood up to Turhan. He himself had many times, but other people rarely did. Even the most trusted men of his father's cabinet rarely dared to disagree with him. Yet Genny had; she'd refused to back down, and Ali admired her for that.

So he smiled and said, "The idea of women in business is strange to my father. You angered him, but I'm sure he'll forgive you when he cools off a bit."

"His forgiveness isn't important, Ali, but his respect is. Unless he respects my opinions, we can't work together." Genevieve trailed her fingers through fountain water silvered by the light of the moon. The night was soft with the scent of the lemon trees, and for a moment she felt a sense of sadness because it was so beautiful here, and because she knew that she didn't belong in a world in which men ruled and women were second-class citizens.

"Perhaps you were right about what you said back in New York." She sighed. "Perhaps a man should have come in my place. It isn't too late, Ali. You could call New York tomorrow and tell them your father objects to working with a woman. They can send Joe Tabler. He doesn't know a great deal about the Middle East, but he's a good man. You can arrange a flight for my return—"

"No, Genny, I don't want Tabler, I want you." He slipped the jeweled scarf back from her hair and, cupping her face between his two large hands, he said again, "I want you."

Half in fear, half in anticipation, Genevieve looked up at him. The night seemed to still. The only sound was the gentle splash of water from the fountain. They were alone, and she was more aware of Ali Ben Hari than she'd ever been of anything or anyone in her life. His eyes were as velvet black as the night, his lips sensuous and full, and his shoulders were broader than any man's shoulders had a right to be.

The hands that cupped her face were strong, the eyes that gazed so compellingly into hers held both a challenge and a promise.

Without even knowing that she did, Genevieve swayed toward him. Then she was in his arms, and it was as it had been that night in Rome. She was enfolded by him, held close to him. His mouth possessed her mouth, and her lips parted when he whispered her name and trailed hot, moist kisses over her face and her throat.

She sighed against him, and he took the lobe of her ear between his teeth to lap and to tease. He found and cupped her breasts.

A soft moan of need escaped her trembling lips when he ran his fingers across the rigid peaks that pressed against the sheer blue gown. She whispered his name, and he took her mouth again, whispering, "I want you, Genny. You must know how much I want you."

"Ali, please. Let me go. Let me..."

But even as she said the words, her arms tightened around him, for she knew that if he let her go she would surely fall. Her body was on fire, her breasts feverish. She pressed against his chest, and now it was she who sought his mouth and touched her tongue to his.

The blue scarf drifted down and off her shoulders. Ali kissed her eyes, her nose, her mouth. Before she could stop him, he unfastened the clasp and the pins that held her hair, and threading his fingers through it, he shook it loose around her shoulders.

"You're glorious," he whispered as he held her away from him so that he could look at her. "You're so beautiful you take my breath."

"Ali, I—"

"Let me come with you now, Genny," he said huskily. "Let me hold you and kiss you. Let me make love to you." He kissed her lips and against them, he murmured, "I want to bury myself inside you. To—"

With every ounce of her remaining strength, Genevieve pulled away from him. She mustn't let this happen, mustn't allow herself to give in to the sweet languor that made her yearn to return to his arms, for if she did she would be lost.

"I can't," she whispered brokenly. "No, I can't."

Before he could stop her, she turned and ran across the moonlit patio to the corridor that lay beyond.

For a moment Ali didn't move. Then he bent and picked up the chiffon scarf and held it to his lips.

"Genny," he whispered. "Genny."

It seemed to her as though her heart would surely burst. It beat like a frightened bird's against her breast as she ran through the patios and the corridors, back to the safety of the harem.

She had wanted Ali as badly as he had wanted her. In another moment, with another kiss, another caress, she would have yielded.

And she knew, in that part of her brain that still functioned, that it would be madness to give in to all of the feelings Ali had evoked. He was a man from a world so different from her own that the thought of becoming involved with him terrified her.

She reached the door of the harem. Out of breath and trembling, she pulled the cord. "Hurry," she whispered. "Let me in. If he comes after me, if he touches me . . ."

The door opened, and Haifa led her inside.

"You came alone?" the woman asked. "Unescorted?"

"Yes, I . . . I don't feel well."

"Then come." Haifa took Genevieve's arm and led her into the quiet patio toward her quarters. "I will help you undress," she said.

But Genevieve shook her head. "No, but thank you. I want to be alone."

Before Haifa could insist, Genevieve closed the door to her rooms, and stood, leaning against the door, willing her breathing to even, her heart to slow.

When she went into the bedroom, she pulled the gown over her head and, clad only in the blue teddy she'd worn underneath, she went to the French doors and looked out into her garden. The pool was clear and shining in the moonlight. She leaned her head against the cool windowpane, and because she knew that she could not sleep, she went back into the room and put a short robe on over the teddy and went out into the garden.

It was so quiet here, so peaceful. She breathed in the sweet night air and paused at the edge of the pool. Then she took off the robe and eased herself down into the gardenia-scented water.

It lapped like a soft caress over her body, like his hands, she thought, the feel of his hands on my breasts. A soft groan of need escaped her lips, and though the water was cool, her body burned with remembered passion. The potent scent of gardenias drugged her senses. She rubbed her face against the fragrant petals and began to swim in slow, lazy strokes so that she could feel the brush of the flowers against her breasts, her belly, her thighs. She shivered with the need to be touched by him, to be covered and possessed by him.

With a sob she rolled onto her back and looked up through the palm fronds at the star-filled sky. It was a night made for love, and her body cried out with the need to be loved. It would be so easy to let herself be seduced by the beauty of this place, by Ali Ben Hari.

She began to swim, fast and hard, back and forth across the water, and when at last her body began to relax, she lifted herself up to the edge of the pool and sluiced the water off her body.

She stood there for a few moments, pale in the moonlight, looking up at the sky, until at last, with a sigh she turned and went back through the French doors into her bedroom.

But Ali did not move from his place in the adjoining garden.

He had not meant to spy on her; he'd only wanted to walk a bit in this quiet place, to try to cool the heat of the blood in his veins. But he had heard that quiet splash when Genevieve had slipped into the pool, and because he could not help himself, he had moved closer to the trellised wall that separated them.

He had seen her there, swimming among the gardenias, and he had watched when she came up out of the water to stand in the moonlight. She was unbelievably, classically beautiful. The garment she wore clung to her body. Her breasts were high and full. She was slender and shapely, and her legs... Ali's breath caught in his throat as he pictured them encircling his back.

His body had tightened with renewed desire, and it had taken every bit of his willpower not to go to her. As he watched her, he'd thought how it would be if he slipped through the gate that connected their gardens. He would ease her down on the cool grass and cover her body with his. He would kiss her moonlit breasts and take her, slowly, deeply, and feel her softness close about him. Would she whisper his name in the quiet of the night? Would she caress him as he longed to caress her?

With a strangled cry Ali tore at his clothes and dove headlong into the pool. He swam as hard as he could, his muscled arms slashing through the water, strong legs pushing him forward, his body taut and hard with desire.

He drove himself on, faster and faster through the water, until at last, exhausted, his passion spent, he lifted himself out of the pool, and as he had seen her do, he gazed up at the star-filled night.

"Genny," he whispered into the silence. And he knew that before she left Kashkiri, he would have her.

Genevieve spent the next few days getting to know the women of the harem: the wives, mothers, sisters, aunts and grandmothers of Turhan and his cabinet. Since some of the men, like Sheik Turhan, had more than one wife, Genevieve found it difficult to sort out who belonged to which family, which wife belonged to which husband and in what order. Who was wife number one or two or three or four?

As for the twenty or so children, the only ones whose names she remembered after the first two or three days were little Ismail and the twins, Zora and Shbelia.

Ismail, though as autocratic as his father, was an irresistible little boy. He found it fascinating that there was an infidel in their midst, and he asked Genevieve endless questions about herself and where she came from. Though his mother, Tamraz, softly chastened him, he followed Genevieve wherever she went in the harem. At times, when she sat on one of the hassocks surrounding the communal bathing pool, he came to lean against her knee.

Why was her hair the color of gold? he wanted to know. Why was her skin so light, her eyes so green? Did she have children? Why didn't she have children? Would she stay here with him and the other women forever? The questions went on and on, and Genevieve, because she liked the little boy, patiently answered all of them.

The women, too, were eager to talk to her when they discovered she spoke a little Arabic. They were unfailingly pleasant, and just as curious as little Ismail. How was it, they wanted to know, that she had come to Kashkiri alone? Hadn't her family objected? Why was she here? And though Genevieve told them she had come from New York to help set up a conference in Kashkiri, she knew from the looks that passed from woman to woman they could not believe that was the reason she was here.

"You came because of Ali Ben Hari," a woman named Sarida said. And though Genevieve shook her head, the others only giggled and exchanged knowing looks.

"Every woman in Kashkiri is in love with Ali," a woman named Zaida said. "But he has brought you all the way from your country. That means he intends to make you his wife."

"It is time," one of the older women said with a nod. "Ali is thirty-six and has no children. By the time Sheik Turhan was that age, he had fathered eight of his fifteen." She gave Genevieve a sharp jab in the ribs and with a knowing wink said, "If Ali wishes to do half as well, it is time to begin."

"That is true," Tamraz agreed, and with a note of preening smugness said, "I am but twenty, madam, much younger than you, and already I have three and another on the way. It's best not to delay these things. Ali Ben Hari is the handsomest and the most virile of men. You are indeed fortunate that he has chosen you."

Seferina, who Genevieve had learned was the second wife of Sheik Turhan, touched Genevieve's hair. "Ali is dark and you are light. Together you will make many beautiful children."

Make children. Something fluttered in Genevieve's midsection. Three days had passed since she had seen Ali, three nights since she had been in his arms. She had lain alone in the round bed, longing for his kiss, trying not to think about him, trying to deny the warmth that spread through her body when she did.

Embarrassed by the knowing looks of the other women, she made herself smile and say, "I've come to Kashkiri to help Ali Ben Hari and Sheik Turhan with the conference. When the conference is over, I'll return to my own country."

With as much dignity as she could muster, she rose from the hassock near the pool. "I'm sorry to disappoint you," she said, "but there really is nothing romantic in my relationship with Ali Ben Hari." Then, as quickly as she could, she excused herself and hurried to the safety of her own quarters.

She had just started into the bedroom when there was a soft knock, and when she opened the door she saw the young woman whose name was Zuarina.

"I'm sorry that we have embarrassed you, madam," Zuarina said. "Tamraz and Seferina meant no harm."

Genevieve hesitated, then she opened the door and said, "Please, won't you come in?"

"*Shukran*, thank you."

"I was just going to order some tea. Won't you join me?"

Zuarina nodded shyly, and Genevieve picked up the phone, as she had been told to do when she wanted anything, and asked Haifa to bring her some tea. "English tea," she said, because while she liked the hot mint tea occasionally, it was often too sweet for her.

When she turned back to her guest, she saw that Zuarina had gone to stand by the French doors that looked out into the garden. She stood in profile, slim and lovely in a pale pink kaftan that seemed to bring out the warm honey tones of her skin. Her wide dark eyes had been outlined in kohl, and her lips had been touched with coral. Her heavy black hair, with only the slightest suggestion of a curl, hung halfway down her back. Genevieve guessed her age to be in the late twenties. She didn't know whether or not Zuarina was married.

"Why don't we have tea in the garden?" Genevieve opened the French doors. "It's lovely there this time of day."

And when they were seated at the round table beside the pool, Genevieve asked, "Do you have children, Zuarina?"

"No, madam." Zuarina dropped her gaze. "That is why my husband, Ahmed Baraket, divorced me."

"Baraket?"

"The minister of finance, madam. He wanted me to leave the harem and go back to my parents' home, but my lord, Turhan, knowing that I would have been in disgrace, said that I must stay here."

"I see," Genevieve said. She waited until Haifa had served their tea, then asked, "Are you happy here?"

"Yes, madam."

"Please call me Genny."

Zuarina smiled shyly, then, lowering her head asked in a low voice, "I would like to ask you something, madam…Genny. Do you think it is true, what Tamraz said about you and Ali Ben Hari having beautiful children? I mean do you think if one is dark and one is light, the children would be a combination of both?"

"Yes, I suppose that's true, but I have no intention of…" Genevieve paused because Zuarina's face was flushed with color. What was it? Was the other woman in love with Ali? Was that why she was asking? Was she afraid that what the women had said about her and Ali was true?

Jealousy tightened her body. Zuarina was one of the most beautiful young women she had ever seen. Of course Ali would be attracted to her.

Genevieve sipped her tea in silence, so caught up in her own thoughts that she was startled when Zuarina asked, "Is Mr. Matthews still in New York?"

"Mr. Matthews?" Genevieve nodded. "Yes, he stayed behind to gather more of the things we'll need for the conference. I should imagine that he will arrive in a day or two."

Genevieve took another sip of her tea. "I didn't spend too much time with him, but he seems to be very nice."

"He is."

The words, though quietly spoken, were said with such feeling that Genevieve stopped, cup poised in midair.

"Do you...?" Genevieve hesitated and tried to frame her words as carefully as possible. "Do you and Mr. Matthews know each other well?"

"We have met a few times at family gatherings. He is a most kind gentleman."

"Yes, he seems to be." Genevieve waited.

"He will take part in the arrangements for the conference?"

"Yes, I'm sure he will."

"You will see him?" She looked at Genevieve through lowered lashes.

"Yes."

"Then perhaps you could...could relay a message for me."

Genevieve put her cup down carefully. "I'd be happy to."

Zuarina took a small white envelope from the folds of her kaftan and handed it to Genevieve. "If it is possible, give it to Mr. Matthews when no one else is there. If that is not possible, then return it to me." Zuarina's dark eyes held a hint of fear. "And please, do not tell Ali Ben Hari."

Genevieve swallowed hard. So there was something between Ali and Zuarina. But why had she asked about Rupert Matthews?

Hands clenched together in her lap, Genevieve said, "Are you and Ali Ben Hari...? Is there an arrangement? An engagement?"

Zuarina's eyes widened. "An arrangement? Between me and Ali Ben Hari?" The young woman shook her head.

"The arrangement is with Ali's father, Sheik Turhan. He wishes to make me his fourth wife, madam. He..."

Suddenly Zuarina's lips quivered, and she began to cry. "I know it is a great honor," she said between sobs. "I know I should feel the most favored of women and that I should thank Allah because my lord, Turhan, has found me desirable. But I do not love him. I love..." She covered her face with her hands. "I am wicked," she said. "I should not speak so."

Very gently Genevieve pulled Zuarina's hands from her face. "You're in love with Mr. Matthews," she said softly. "That's it, isn't it?"

"Yes." Tears ran down Zuarina's face. "I know it's bad of me, but I cannot help myself, madam. I—"

"Genny," Genevieve said. Then carefully she asked, "Has Mr. Matthews ever said anything? I mean has he ever indicated how he feels about you?"

"Once, at the last family gathering we both attended. He said..." Zuarina's lips trembled. "He said, 'Though I know it isn't possible, I wish we could to be alone today. I would like to walk in the garden with you. I would like to hold your hand and tell you how beautiful you are.'"

"Does he know that Turhan Ben Hari has asked you to become his wife?"

"I think so, Genny. Before he left to go to your country with Ali Ben Hari, he sent me a letter, telling me that he was leaving. Inside was a poem by a countryman of Mr. Matthews, a Mr. Walter Savage Lan—"

"Landor," Genevieve said. "What was the poem, Zuarina? Do you remember?"

"Yes, Genny, for there was only one verse." Zuarina bowed her head and in a trembling voice began to recite:

"Proud word you never spoke, but you will speak
Four not exempt from pride some future day.
Resting on one white hand a warm wet cheek
Over my open volume you will say,
'This man loved me!' then rise and trip away."

For a moment neither woman spoke. We're the same, Genevieve thought. I am of the West, she of the East. Yet we are the same. We're both attracted to men who are different from us.

She took Zuarina's hand in hers. "I'll give your note to Mr. Matthews, Zuarina," she said.

And because Genevieve did not know how else to comfort Zuarina or how to quell her own sadness, she sat there in the garden with the other woman until long after the evening shadows fell and the birds came to roost in the lemon trees.

Chapter 6

Genevieve looked at herself in the mirror. The veil tickled her nose. Only her eyes, outlined with the kohl that Haifa had insisted on, showed. The rest of her, from head to toe, was covered with a dove-gray robe. She felt strange, like a mysterious Middle Eastern Mata Hari who had a rendezvous in the casbah with an equally mysterious tall, dark stranger.

But today her rendezvous wasn't with a stranger; it was with Ali Ben Hari.

"I've talked to my father," Ali had said when he'd phoned yesterday. "He's agreed that you will stay in Kashkiri and handle the conference. He's also agreed to at least think about the advisability of allowing a few of the women to participate. You are to select certain wives of the ministers and tutor them on how to behave with foreign women."

Foreign women, Genevieve had thought. Like me.

"Tomorrow we'll go out into the city," Ali had gone on. "I'll show you the university, the library and the hospital, and we'll discuss an itinerary for the diplomats' wives. Since it wouldn't be proper for you to go out unchaperoned, you can ask Haifa to accompany us.''

''I've made friends with a young woman whose name is Zuarina. Would it be all right if she accompanied me instead of Haifa?''

''Yes, of course, whomever you like. Just as long as we...'' She'd heard the hesitation in his voice before he finished, ''Just as long as we're not alone.''

Now she stared in the mirror at the stranger with her eyes. ''Ali,'' she whispered, and her heart raced in anticipation at the thought of seeing him again.

When Haifa escorted Genevieve and Zuarina to the main entrance patio of the palace, it was not Haifa or the other woman Ali saw as they approached; it was Genny. Though the gray robe covered all of her feminine shapeliness, his body stirred with remembered passion, for he had seen her half-naked in the moonlight. He knew what glories lay hidden by the folds of cloth.

In his mind's eye he saw the rise of her full breasts, the slender waist, the flaring hips and the ivory loveliness of her legs. He rubbed his suddenly damp palms against his robe, and in a voice roughened by all that he was feeling, he said, ''*Sabbah al khair*, good morning.''

Genevieve raised her head and looked at him, and for a moment he couldn't breathe. The veil covered all but her wondrous green eyes, eyes that set him on fire. And though he thought of himself as a more modern man than his father, there was a part of him that made him want to hide Genny away from any eyes except his own. No other man should look upon such beauty and speculate upon the body that lay hidden by the folds of cloth. No other man should look upon the glory of her face.

Once both women had been helped into the long black limousine by his chauffeur, and he had taken the center seat facing them, he said, "We'll go to the university first, if that's all right with you."

"Yes, of course. I'd like to see it." Genevieve smiled at Zuarina. "Have you ever been there?"

"My husband, Mr. Baraket, took me there shortly after we were married. It is a wonderful place where men can study many subjects. My father, before Mr. Baraket asked for me in marriage, had promised that I could attend the Sorbonne in Paris. I was disappointed, but of course I understood that my father could not refuse a man like Mr. Baraket."

Genevieve's lips tightened. "It's never too late for an education. Perhaps you could still persuade your father to send you to Paris."

Zuarina shook her head. "I have been promised in marriage to my lord, Ali Ben Hari's father. I must not think of Paris but of the honor that has been bestowed on me by Sheik Turhan."

"That is as it should be," Ali said with a nod. "You will make my father a lovely wife."

"And what of his other lovely wives?" Genevieve asked sharply. "What of Tamraz and Seferina?"

"They will be as they were, beloved by my father, cared for as always." His dark brows drew together in a warning scowl. "It is the tradition."

Genevieve glared at him, then turned her attention to the passing scene. Tradition! It was archaic, unjust and unthinkable that in the 1990s a woman could still be forced into a marriage she didn't want. Zuarina was in love with Rupert Matthews, and Rupert was in love with her. It was Rupert she should be marrying.

Turning back from the window, Genevieve asked, "Has Mr. Matthews returned from New York?"

"Yes, he got in last night," Ali said.

"I'm sorry he couldn't have come with us today."

"He had many things to attend to."

"Then perhaps tomorrow." Beside her Genevieve felt Zuarina tense. "I'd enjoy seeing him again."

"Then I'll arrange it. We can visit the museum tomorrow afternoon."

Genevieve smiled at Zuarina. "Won't that be nice," she said.

After the university, a splendid old building that had been built in the late 1800s, they went to the four-hundred-room municipal hospital. Located in the center of town, it was a modern building, complete with well-equipped operating rooms, coronary-care and intensive-care units, a maternity ward, a children's ward and a separate wing for elderly and indigent patients.

"Most of our medical staff have received advanced training in either Zurich or Paris," the doctor who showed them around said. "If any of the diplomats who attend your conference become ill, they will receive the very best in medical aid. We even have a skilled woman doctor, an Egyptian, who attends all female patients."

"*All* female patients," Genevieve asked.

"Of course, madam. Unless there is an extreme emergency, it would not be proper for a male doctor to attend a female."

Genevieve raised her eyebrows and remained silent during the rest of the tour.

It was after twelve-thirty when they left the hospital, and because Genevieve wanted to see some of the guest rooms and suites in the hotel, Ali suggested they have lunch there.

"Lunch?" she said. "How can I eat when my face is covered?"

"It is not difficult, Genny. You lift the veil with one hand and eat with the other." Zuarina demonstrated. "You see? It isn't difficult at all."

"But it won't be necessary," Ali said. "You may remove your veils when we enter the dining room."

You may remove your veil. You may take two giant steps. I will permit you. I will not permit you. It is not allowed. It is the tradition. Good Lord, how could the women of Kashkiri stand to live in such a totally male-oriented, male-dominated society? How could they spend day after day doing nothing but preparing for the evening to come? Giving each other pedicures and manicures, doing each other's hair, helping each other select a gown that would please a husband, *if* said husband chose to send for them that night?

Genevieve had talked with the women, had listened to their conversations, to their gossip and their giggles. The frankness with which they teased each other had surprised her. Zaida, the fourth wife of the minister of education, had received good-natured jibes and jokes when she'd returned sleepy and smiling from a night with her husband. Old Tamara, the minister's first wife, had also been teased a few nights later, when she, too, returned tired and smiling.

How could these women share their husbands? How could Tamara have joked about Zaida, or Zaida about Tamara, when they both slept with the same man?

Children were also the subject of many conversations, and it soon became obvious to Genevieve that the women were more concerned about their sons than their daughters.

"Ismail will go to a fine university," Tamraz had told her. "Perhaps it will be Cambridge in England, like his brother. Or perhaps he will go to France, or even to your country."

"And what of Zora and Shbelia?" Genevieve had asked. "Where will they go?"

"Go?" Tamraz had looked at her as though she were a stupid child. "They will go nowhere, madam, unless, of course, a marriage with a foreign diplomat is arranged."

"But what about their education?"

"They will be taught to read and write, how to make themselves attractive and how to select the clothes and the colors that best suit them. These are the essential things that a girl should know, madam."

And though Genevieve had to bite her tongue to keep from speaking up, she told herself she must not. It wasn't up to her to judge, nor was it her business to try to change things. Even if she wanted to, there was little she could do in two months.

Two months. She would leave Kashkiri and return to her own country. She would leave Ali Ben Hari and never see him again.

The thought made her feel hollow inside, but she tried not to think about it as she entered the hotel.

The suites they saw there were all as luxurious as the one Genevieve had so briefly occupied. Genevieve spoke to the manager to make sure that the proper number of rooms had been reserved for the conference and asked to see meeting rooms. She checked menus with the head chef, and arranged with the concierge for flowers and fruit baskets to be delivered to the guest rooms.

In the beginning the manager was coolly aloof, the chef surly, the concierge amused. Eyebrows raised, they had looked at Ali. Ali hadn't spoken; he'd only looked back at them. With much clearing of throats they had become almost obsequiously attentive.

"Everything will be attended to, madam," they assured Genevieve. "Just as you wish, madam. Our only desire is to please."

And all the while they sent nervous glances Ali's way.

At last the three of them were escorted into a small private dining room, where, because no other men except Ali and the waiters were present, Genevieve and Zuarina were permitted to remove their veils.

Zuarina, like a beautiful bird who had been let out of her cage, sparkled with excitement. "What a beautiful hotel," she said. "What lovely rooms. Isn't this a perfect little dining salon?"

The stuffed grape leaves were wonderful, the couscous the best she had ever eaten, the *baklava* the richest.

And because of her new friend's enthusiasm, Genevieve found herself smiling and enjoying her own meal.

It seemed to Ali that her smile filled the room. Was it because, like Zuarina, she was glad to escape for a day? Was it so difficult for her in the harem? Was she so unhappy there? He himself had ordered that her rooms be luxuriously prepared and that she have her own private garden and swimming pool. He knew she enjoyed that, for he had seen her, night after night, strolling about her garden. But while he had watched her in the garden, he had never again allowed himself to observe her in the pool. It had been voyeuristic and ungentlemanly of him to have done it that one time, and he had vowed never to do it again.

And while he told himself he did not because it was not what a gentleman should do, he knew the real reason was that if he ever saw Genny like that again, he would not be able to control himself.

He watched the curve of her mouth as she said something to Zuarina, and thought of that same mouth framed to whisper love words to him. Now, as she had in New York, she looked poised and in control. But for a few minutes that night in the patio, she hadn't been in control. Her body had trembled against his, and he had known that she had wanted him just as much as he had wanted her. It had taken every bit of his willpower to let her go. The next time, he knew he would not let her go.

He began then to plan a trip out of Kashkiri, to somewhere where he could be alone with Genny, where she could not run back to the safety of the harem.

I will have you soon, my love, he silently vowed. Soon, my Genny.

"How did you manage this?" Rupert Matthews asked the next day at the National Museum. He and Genevieve had stopped in front of a display of Islamic sacred writings, and she had taken advantage of the moment to hand him the letter Zuarina had given her several days earlier.

"The only time Zuarina and I have seen each other has been at a family gathering." He slipped the note in the pocket of his robe as he looked over at the young woman. "She's really quite beautiful, isn't she?" he said in a low voice.

"Yes, she is," Genevieve answered softly. "Perhaps it's none of my business, Mr. Matthews, but are you in love with her?"

"Desperately." Rupert ran a hand through his pale blond hair. "Hopelessly."

"Then why don't you do something about it?"

"How can I, Miss Jordan? Zuarina is going to marry Sheik Turhan, and there's nothing I can do about it. Ali is my friend. He trusts me. How can I betray that trust by running away—even if I could—with the woman his father plans to make his fourth wife?"

"Have you tried to talk to Ali? Have you told him of your feelings for Zuarina?"

Rupert shook his head. "I don't think you understand how strongly the Kashkirans feel about mixed marriages. They take great pride in their culture, Miss Jordan. It's both their strength and their weakness that they want no interference from outsiders."

He glanced at the centuries-old exhibits. "Theirs is an ancient civilization of sultans and sheiks, of desert tribes that roamed the Sahara centuries before any kind of advanced civilization reached Europe. They were nomads, lords of the desert who made war with their enemies and took what they wanted without thought of the consequences. There were no laws, no restrictions. They did as they wanted then—they do as they want now. While foreigners like you and me might be called upon to help from time to time, we could never be a part of the Kashkiran world."

Rupert attempted a smile. "Well, perhaps you could because you're a woman, but I don't suppose harem life would suit you."

"You're damned right it wouldn't." Then, seeing his smile, Genevieve laughed and said, "Please call me Genevieve or Genny. We're going to be working together for the next two months. There's no need to be so formal." She glanced over to where Ali and Zuarina stood in front of a display of ancient weapons. "How long have you known Ali?" she asked curiously.

"For almost fifteen years. I was in graduate school when he came to Cambridge, and because his English wasn't as good as it is now, I was hired to tutor him." His lips quirked in a smile. "That first year was a difficult one for Ali. He'd never been out of Kashkiri before and he barely spoke English. As the first-born son of Sheik Turhan, he'd had only to ask for whatever he wanted and of course he was used to having his own way. But it wasn't like that at Cambridge— he was a foreigner, a student like everyone else.''

Rupert shook his head and, with a chuckle, said, ''He'd never seen women mixing with men before, and it was something of a cultural shock. The first time one of the young women in his class spoke up to disagree with him, he was outraged. 'Today a woman told me I didn't know what I was talking about,' he said that night when he came to my rooms. He was absolutely horrified that a woman had had the audacity to speak up to him.''

Genevieve laughed because she suddenly had a mental picture of Ali at eighteen: handsome and arrogant, used to having his own way, the son of a sheik, abruptly thrust into a society foreign to his own, a society where women were equal to men.

''I wonder if he's changed that much from those early days,'' she said thoughtfully.

''The inbred ideas are still there. You could see it yourself in New York, couldn't you? He was almost as shocked when he discovered you were a vice president of your company as he was that first day at Cambridge when a girl told him he didn't know what he was talking about. I could see his hackles rise every time you voiced an opinion.''

''Which was often, as I remember.'' Genevieve grinned. ''I caught you smiling a couple of times during that meeting, Rupert. I think you were enjoying yourself.''

''I was, enormously. It does Ali good to have someone speak up to him.'' Rupert hesitated. ''I don't quite know how to say this, but—'' he shook his head ''—it really isn't any of my business.''

''What isn't?'' She could see him debating with himself, and she said, ''Please, Rupert. What is it?''

"Ali's more than a little attracted to you, Genevieve. I don't know how you feel about him, but I think you should be careful. He's a headstrong man, used to having what he wants, to taking what he wants. I wouldn't like to see you placed in a compromising position. I . . ."

He stopped. Ali had turned away from the exhibit to watch them. A look of anger darkened his face. He said something to Zuarina, and the two of them started toward Rupert and Genevieve.

When he reached them, he took Genevieve's arm and, frowning at Rupert, said to her, "Come along, there's something in the other room I want you to see."

And though he didn't speak of it, she knew that he was jealous of her show of friendliness to Rupert.

Whoever had said "East was East and West was West and never the twain shall meet" had undoubtedly known what he was talking about. She was in a world very different from her own. Rupert had said that Ali was attracted to her, and though he was Ali's friend he'd warned her to be careful. Careful of what? Of Ali or of her own feelings?

As she had so many times in the past few days, Genevieve tried to remind herself that she was in Kashkiri only because of the conference. When her work here was finished, she would return to New York.

A little while later, when she said that she would like to speak to the curator, Ali escorted her to the museum director's office.

She spent a little over half an hour working out the arrangements for a tour of the conferees' wives, then went back to the salon where the others were waiting. Because they were absorbed in a display of costumes, she stopped to look at the exhibits of desert life. Next to the exhibits there was an elaborately gilded mirror. She started to pass by without pausing, then glanced up, saw the woman there and murmured a greeting.

She stopped, hand to her lip, staring at her own reflection. Dressed as she was in a robe, with a scarf covering her hair and a veil covering her face, she had barely recognized herself.

This is what it would be like if I were his woman, she thought. If I were Kashkiran. If . . .

He appeared in the mirror behind her. Without a word he placed his hands on her shoulders. They stared at their reflections, the tall Kashkiran man and the veiled woman with the green eyes.

"Look at us," he whispered. "What do you see, Genny?" He tightened his hands on her shoulders.

She stared as though hypnotized.

"Are we not handsome together? Does it not seem as though we belong together?" His voice, so sensuously soft, held her like the hands on her shoulders.

"Genny," he whispered. "Don't you know how much I—"

"Genny! Come look!" Zuarina hurried over to them. "There's the most beautiful display of jewelry over here. You must see it."

Ali let her go.

"Come along," he said in a low voice, and taking her arm he followed Zuarina.

The man who had been watching waited until they passed into the other room before he stepped from the shadows.

He ran a hand across his whiskered face and smiled. So the rumors of the American woman and Ali Ben Hari were true. She was, as it had been rumored, very beautiful. That would please Omar Haj Fatah.

This was what they had been waiting for. The woman would be the means to bring Sheik Turhan and Ali Ben Hari to their knees.

Chapter 7

The two limousines followed closely, one behind the other. Ali and Genevieve occupied the first; Haifa, a manservant and three bodyguards rode in the second.

Two days had passed since their visit to the museum. The evening after they had returned, Ali had phoned Genevieve in her rooms. "I've arranged for you to visit the family home at the desert," he'd told her. "You said it might be an interesting excursion for the visiting wives."

"Yes, I think it would be."

"Then you should see it. We'll leave the day after tomorrow."

When she'd put the phone down, she thought, this is business. That's all it is, just business. And told herself that her heart was racing because she'd had too much coffee that morning.

They had left at dawn, and for the past two hours had followed the shoreline of the Sea of Kashkiri. The day was sunshine perfect, the sea a turquoise-green.

"Do you mind if I open the window?" Genevieve asked. "I want to smell the sea."

"Of course." He pushed one of the buttons on his door, and the window slid open. "It's good to be out of the city, isn't it?"

Genevieve nodded, then turned toward the open window to sniff the sea air. For the first time since she had moved into the government palace, she felt free.

"What time will we arrive?" she asked.

"Before dark. The villa is just at the edge of the desert. I hope you'll like it, Genny."

For two days he'd thought of nothing except the trip and spending time alone in the desert with her. Tonight they would be together in the place he loved most in the world, away from the confining restrictions of the presidential palace. There would be no harem here, no rules of protocol, no government duties. He would be alone with her.

Ali took a deep breath and, leaning forward, he tapped on the window that separated them from the driver and said, "We'll stop for lunch now. There's a place just up ahead where you can pull over. Signal the other car, please."

The driver nodded, then switched his radio on and gave instructions to the second limousine. When they came to the turnoff and parked, the drivers and one of the bodyguards carried robes and the picnic lunch down to the beach. A place was prepared for Ali and Genevieve, then another, farther down the beach, for Haifa, the manservant and the two drivers.

The three bodyguards did not sit down, but stood at attention, gripping their automatic rifles as they watched the highway.

"Aren't they going to eat?" Genevieve asked curiously.

"They can eat later."

Her eyebrows came together in a questioning frown. "But why are they here? Why did you bring them?"

"My father has enemies." Ali looked out toward the sea. "I don't think we were followed when we left the city, but I prefer not to take any chances."

"Is there still a problem with the rebels?"

"There's always a problem. Omar Haj Fatah won't rest until my father and I are dead. When we are, he'll go after Ismail." Ali's voice hardened. "He's been in hiding since his last attempt to overthrow my father, but one of these days he'll make another move. When he does, we'll be ready for him."

"If there's any danger, you'll have to call off the conference."

Ali shook his head. "I'd hate to do that, Genny. My father has been planning it for a long time. The conference will enhance our standing in the Arab, as well as the Western world. Haj Fatah knows that and he'll try to stop it. We can't let him. We—"

A truck came toward them down the highway. His men tightened their hands on their rifles. Ali tensed. He waited, ready to thrust Genevieve down on the sand.

The truck slowed. He put a hand against her back. She turned, startled. "What...?"

The truck passed. "It's all right." Ali let out the breath he didn't know he'd been holding.

She looked at him, concern written on her face because for the first time she realized that the danger Ali spoke of was real; there were men who wanted to kill him. Without conscious thought she clasped his hand.

"I won't let anything happen to you," he said because he thought she was frightened. "Don't be afraid."

"I'm not afraid. Not for myself." Her eyes were wide with concern. "It's you, Ali. Something could happen to you. You could be . . ." She shook her head, unable to go on.

An emotion Ali had never felt before welled up inside him—she cared what happened to him. "There's nothing to fear," he said. "I'm well protected."

But because she still looked frightened, and because he wanted to touch her, he took a date from one of the silver dishes and held it to her mouth. Her lips parted. He touched her lips with the date and, when she bit into it, he felt the brush of her tongue against his fingers.

He whispered her name, and a flush of color rose in her cheeks.

He knew that before they returned to the city, he would make her his.

They turned away from the sea an hour later and began to pass through small villages. When they came to a village where it was market day, Ali tapped on the window and asked the driver to stop.

The other limousine stopped behind them, and as soon as Ali and Genevieve stepped from the car, the three body-guards took up a position close to them. They carried no rifles this time, but Genevieve was sure there were automatic pistols hidden in their robes.

Ali took her arm to lead her through the crowded marketplace. His manservant followed.

Ali was so big, so powerfully built, and he had such a commanding presence that without saying a word or making a gesture, people stepped aside for him. They whispered to each other when they saw Genevieve, for though her hair was covered, her face was bare.

A bare face. The idea amused her. And though she would never have admitted it, there had been times when she'd felt an odd kind of comfort in hiding her face from the world. With a veil on she could smile or frown or purse her lips without anyone being any the wiser.

Many of the women here were without their veils, but their faces were tattooed and their hands and feet were hennaed. They wore earrings in their ears and rings on their fingers. With their hands shielding their mouths, they nudged one another and exchanged whispers as they pointed to her.

But Genevieve paid little attention to them. Everything fascinated her, the sights, the smells, the sounds were all intoxicating.

The stalls held an intriguing assortment of goods. Figs and dates, apricots and oranges, papayas and mangoes were displayed in symmetrical designs of stars and triangles.

Other stalls displayed robes for women and *djellabas* for men, sequined veils, lacy veils, and plain black veils, belts and jeweled slippers. Brass pots and urns hung from hooks; gold and silver glittered in glass cases.

Incense permeated the air, and with it there was the smell of lamb cooking over an open fire, of crushed mint, exotic perfumes and camel dung. Her senses reeled. She stood gazing about her, trying to absorb everything, mesmerized until Ali took her arm and led her to a display of gold jewelry.

"We must buy you a present so that you will remember your trip to the desert," he said, and when she protested, he pointed to a heavy gold chain. "Do you like it?" he asked.

"It's lovely," Genevieve said. "But really, Ali, I can't—"

"We'll take it," he said.

The seller held up matching earrings and a gold chain bracelet.

Ali nodded. "Yes, those, too."

Genevieve shook her head. "I can't accept such an expensive gift," she said.

But Ali refused to listen. The seller quoted a price. Ali nodded to his manservant and took Genevieve's arm to lead her away while the servant paid.

"It's only a small gift," he said, "but it makes me happy to give it to you. Perhaps you'll wear it tonight."

The "small" gift had cost well over three thousand dollars. She started to shake her head, but he cupped her hands around the package and said, "It's a token of my appreciation for the work you're doing on the conference, Genny."

And because she knew he would not take it back, she said, "Thank you, Ali. And yes, I'll wear it tonight."

He thought of that night all through the long afternoon. The closer they got to the desert, the more aware he became of her, of the shape of her face, the curve of her mouth, the delicacy of her hands. Her faint but exotic perfume.

Soon, he told himself. Soon.

When they reached the edge of the desert, she said, "Oh, just look," and it thrilled him to know that she found the desert as beautiful as he did.

"Once, when I was fourteen, my father and I took a trip into the desert," she said. "I didn't like the camels but I loved everything else; the endless miles of rolling dunes, the sunsets, the smell of food cooking over a camp fire."

She leaned back against the seat and closed her eyes. She and her father had grown very close on that trip. On their last night out he had told her about her mother's illness. "I need you to help me be strong," he'd said. "I'm counting on your strength, Genny."

She'd remembered his words a year later, when her mother had died, and she'd tried as hard as she could to be strong for him.

"What is it?" Ali covered her hand with his. "Why are you sad, Genny?"

She brushed the tears away with her fingertips. "I was thinking about my mother and father," she told him. "About the trip into the desert."

"Perhaps before you leave to go back to New York, we can arrange a trip. I haven't gone into the desert in years. It would be a treat for me, too."

"I'll have to go back right after the conference." She shook her head and with a smile said, "This isn't supposed to be a vacation, Ali, but thank you for suggesting it. If there's time..."

The words hung in the air. If there's time.

There will be time, he thought. Time to take you into the desert with me, Genny. Time to be alone with you, to do all of the things I have dreamed of doing with you.

They passed a small village a little before sunset. Ten minutes later they reached the villa.

As large as a country inn, Ali's home stood at the edge of the desert in an oasis of palm trees, its ochre color in perfect harmony with the dunes that lay beyond.

To one side of the villa there was a stable and a corral. Half a dozen tents were scattered near the corral, and at the very edge of the desert was a large black nomad tent.

"That's where I stay when I'm here," Ali said, indicating the tent. "It's as close to the desert as I can get. I like it because it gives me a feeling that I've stepped back in time, that I'm a part of the desert, as my ancestors were." He looked out toward the rolling dunes as the limousine rolled to a stop. "My grandfather was a bedouin chieftain. To hear my father talk, he was a combination of Attila the Hun and Mohammed. I wish I had known him," he said quietly. "I wish I had known the desert the way it was in his time."

With a sigh he turned back to her. "Haifa will take you to your room," he said. "It's been a long day—perhaps you'd like to rest. We'll have dinner at eight." He brushed the scarf back from her face. "There's no need to cover your hair here, Genny. This is my home, and I want you to feel that it's also your home. Tomorrow I'll show you around, and you can decide if it will be a suitable place to entertain the wives of the conferees."

"I'm sure it will be, Ali. It's beautiful here."

Genevieve looked toward the other limousine and saw the bodyguards spreading out, rifles at the ready as they checked the area.

"Is that necessary?" Her eyes were troubled. "Surely there's no danger here."

"My men are only doing their job, but I'll see to it that while you're here they won't interfere with you." And to Haifa he said, "Show Miss Jordan to her room. Dinner will be at eight."

He brought her hand to his lips. "Until tonight," he murmured. And his desert-dark eyes were warm with promise.

The foyer, richly carpeted in Persian rugs of a deep red color, led into a gardenlike patio where gardenias and aza-leas bloomed fragrant in the early-evening sun. Water spar-kled from a central fountain, and orange trumpet vines brightened the surrounding walls.

Haifa led her through the patio, up a short flight of red-carpeted stairs, into a small salon and beyond to a circular staircase that led up to the second floor. The staircase, as well as the walls, were tiled in blue-and-gold mosaic.

The suite of rooms that Haifa led her to, while not as el-egant as her chambers in the palace, was quite beautiful. The silken drapes and the chiffon hangings over the bed were a delicate shade of gold, the walls a pale ivory.

Haifa drew back the drapes to reveal French doors leading to a balcony. "I'll run your bath, madam," she said, "and while you bathe, I'll unpack and lay out a gown for you to wear tonight. Then you must rest, for it has been a long day and you are tired."

Genevieve smiled at Haifa, then she crossed the room and stepped out onto the balcony. Before her lay the Sahara, and as she watched, the sun began to sink below the distant dunes. The perfume of gardenias and orange blossoms wafted up from the gardens below, and with it the scent of the desert. She watched the twilight settle over the land, then went back inside. When she had undressed, she got into the marble tub and lay back in the aromatic water.

Again, as she had when she'd first arrived in her quarters at the government palace, she could feel herself becoming seduced by the luxury of her surroundings. She loved her life in New York, her apartment overlooking Central Park, her job and her pleasant circle of friends. She didn't want to change her life, yet she knew that in spite of all the things she objected to here in Kashkiri, it would be difficult to leave the sybaritic luxury of the country.

And, yes, it would be difficult to leave Ali Ben Hari.

She had to be careful. She had to remember that she was here in Kashkiri for only a short time.

When at last Genevieve left her bath, she saw that the bed had been prepared, and though she was sure she would not sleep, it seemed only a moment before Haifa touched her shoulder and said, "It is time to dress, madam."

A pale green chiffon caftan had been draped across the white velvet chaise. Her makeup had been laid out on the dressing table, along with her perfume, hairbrush and comb. Haifa asked if she could help her dress, and when Genevieve answered, "No, but thank you," the woman left, saying she would return at eight to escort Genevieve to the dining room.

She applied her makeup with more care than usual and, when she had faintly outlined her eyes, she touched the lids with pale green shadow and her long lashes with mascara. When it came time to do her hair, she started to pull it back into her usual chignon, then decided that tonight she would let it hang loose about her shoulders. After she had dabbed perfume behind her ears and in the hollow of her throat, she stepped into the green caftan and the matching jeweled slippers. Then she opened the package of jewelry that Ali had bought for her. She put the gold chain over her head, fastened the earrings in her ears and the bracelet around her right wrist.

When Haifa knocked, Genevieve followed the other woman down the blue-and-gold-tiled stairway to the first floor and into the dining room.

Ali, who had been standing at the window gazing out into the desert night, turned when Haifa said, "Madam is here, *sidi.*"

"*Shukran*, Haifa. That will be all." He looked at Genevieve, but it was a moment before he spoke.

She touched the heavy gold chain that fell between her breasts. "Thank you for the jewelry," she said. "It's lovely."

"So are you." A slight smile curved his mouth. "You really are an incredibly beautiful woman, you know." And before she could reply, he turned to the sideboard and poured a glass of sherry for her and a mineral water for himself. "Perhaps you'd better tell me what kind of refreshments we'll need for the foreign diplomats. The Japanese drink sake, don't they?"

Genevieve nodded. "But most of them prefer Scotch. It's terribly expensive in Japan, so it would be a special courtesy to offer it." She glanced at the liquor cabinet. "One of the representatives from the United States is a Texan, so you'd better have some bourbon. You'll want several good wines, of course, cognac and beer, and a few cases of vodka for the wives."

"Is that what women drink?"

"Some of them." She smiled. "I do."

"Then by all means we must have vodka. And vermouth for martinis. Yes?"

Genevieve nodded. "But don't forget the olives."

"Olives, of course." He looked up as a servant entered and said, "Dinner is ready to be served if you and madam are ready, *sidi*."

The dinner, as with every meal Genevieve had had since she'd been in Kashkiri, was delicious. Rich lentil soup was followed by a heart of palm and artichoke salad, and that by a rack of lamb.

They chatted during dinner, and because Ali was curious about her life in New York, he began to ask questions. He wanted to know where she lived and if she liked her job. What did she do for entertainment? he asked, but what he really wanted to know was whether or not there was someone special in her life.

Genevieve answered his questions. She went to the theater, she said. And she enjoyed opera.

Ali drummed his fingers on the table. "Are you seeing someone? Someone special, I mean?"

For a moment Genevieve hesitated. She knew that it would be safer to tell him that yes, there was a special man in her life. She wanted to say yes, but instead she found herself shaking her head and saying, "There's no one."

And as she looked into his eyes, his pupils widened and the irises grew as velvet black as the desert sky. She tried to look away, but she was trapped by the sensuous intensity of those eyes. Then slowly her gaze drifted to his mouth. She studied the curve of his lips, the way the upper lip met the full lower one. It was a good mouth, a curiously gentle mouth. A mouth made for kissing a woman.

"Don't look at me like that," he said hoarsely.

A flush of color crept into her cheeks, and she lowered her eyes.

"Come." He took her hand. "Let's take a walk."

Without giving her a chance to decline, Ali pushed his chair back and got to his feet. "Come," he said again.

The night was silent except for the whisper of the wind through the palms. And the air was fragrant with the scent of desert flowers. He took her hand and led her away from the oasis to the very edge of the desert.

"Out there is where time began, Genny. It's as unchanged today as it was centuries ago, as it was before we discovered the oil that has made Kashkiri so rich. It's still hundreds of years removed from the civilized world of jets and computers, of pollution and chemical waste, of all the terrible weapons that can destroy the earth as we know it." He sighed. "When we do destroy it, only the desert will remain. And somewhere out there the bedouins will still roam free."

She heard the longing for a world far removed from his own in his voice, and for the first time since they had met, she began to have a sense of Ali the man. She closed her eyes, and it seemed to her that she could see him riding across the drifting sand on a strong black stallion, his robe blowing in the wind, a look of pure joy on his face.

He tightened his hand around hers. "I've been away too long," he murmured, and gesturing to the black tent, he said, "That's why I stay there when I come. The top of the tent is open, and I can look up and see the stars." His voice softened to a whisper. "Look up, Genny. Have you ever seen so many stars? Have they ever been so close before?"

She looked up at the stars that seemed almost within reach, then she looked out at the path of silver moonlight over the dunes. The breath caught in her throat because she knew there'd never been a night as beautiful as this one, and because she was sharing it with Ali Ben Hari.

His face was shadowed by moonlight. She touched it, then with a sigh she rested her head against his chest and felt the brush of his lips against her hair.

"Genny?" he said, and kissed her.

It was like coming home, like finding that one particular place where you belonged. It was warmth and tenderness, exciting yet strangely comforting, for there was a sense of rightness to it.

Her lips parted under his, and she could feel the thud of his heart against her breasts. He rained kisses across her face, her closed eyelids, her cheeks, her mouth. He followed the line of her jaw to her throat. She tilted her head back, and he captured an earlobe between his teeth and began to circle her ear with his tongue.

"Genny," he whispered. "Oh, Genny."

When he cupped her breasts, she whispered, "No, don't." But her arms crept up around his neck, and a soft moan escaped her lips.

He brushed his fingers across her nipples, and they rose hard against his fingertips.

He knew he couldn't wait much longer. The need to feel her close was too strong. He put his hands on her bottom, pulled her against the swell of his need and gasped aloud because she was so warm, so soft, so pliant.

She moved against him. She pressed closer, her mouth seeking his.

Ali's body caught fire. "My tent," he said hoarsely against her lips.

"I...I can't," she whispered, and stepped away from him.

"You want this as much as I do."

"Ali, please, I—"

He took her mouth again, and though she whispered, "No, don't," he wouldn't let her go. Never before in his life had he wanted a woman as much as he wanted Genny. Never before had a woman refused him.

Heat unlike any he'd ever known surged through his body. He had to have her. He would have her. She wanted this as much as he did. If she struggled at first, she would yield in the end.

His big body began to shake because he knew how it would be, knew that it would be better than anything he'd ever experienced, that together they would climb the heights of ecstasy.

He brought her back into his arms, his mouth covering hers, and when her lips parted under his, he felt strong and powerfully male.

"Come with me now," he whispered against her lips.

Flame surged through her, and yet somewhere in her brain a warning cried out, No, don't, you mustn't do this. For if you do, there'll be no turning back. You'll never be able to leave him if you do this now.

With every ounce of her strength, Genevieve drew away. "Ali, I..." Hands flat against his chest she gazed up at him. "No," she said brokenly. "I can't. I just can't."

He tightened his hands on her shoulders, and his mouth thinned to a cruel, hard line.

Fear shot through her, and something else, a shiver of an excitement unlike anything she'd ever known. He was going to take her. It didn't matter that she said no; he was going to take her. There wasn't anything she could do. He was more powerful than she, stronger...

He dropped his hands to his sides, and Genevieve stepped back.

"I'm sorry," she whispered. "Sorry..."

Before he could speak, she turned and ran back toward the villa.

Chapter 8

The promise of the night had faded; he was alone.

He lay with one arm across his eyes and tried to quell the hunger that raged through his body. He'd been a fool to let her go, to yield to that desperate entreaty of her eyes. He remembered the stories his grandfather Youssef had told him. If he had been a desert man and she a desert woman, he would not have let her go.

"The tribes were always at war in those days," the old man had said, and there'd been a look of unholy joy in his eyes. "We raided them, and they raided us. If there was a woman we wanted from another tribe, we rode in and took her.

"Can you imagine the thrill of riding into an enemy camp to take the woman you wanted? Of lifting her up onto the saddle in front of you, holding her there while you raced through the night with her struggling against your body until you were so excited you wanted to rein in your horse and take her there on the sand? Can you imagine . . . ?"

Ali closed his eyes and thought how it would be if time turned back. If he were bedouin...

There was no moon that night. He rode with a dozen of his men and, as they neared the encampment, he raised his hand to caution them to silence. He could barely see the heavy black tents; he wasn't sure which one was hers.

Quietly his men fanned out to encircle the perimeters of the camp. He waited until he knew they were in place, then raised his arm and screamed his war cry into the darkness.

They attacked, driving their horses into the camp, shouting as they rode. Men ran from the tents. He pushed on, intent on finding her as he fought his way with slashing sword to where the women were huddled together. At last he saw her, saw the fear and the recognition on her face an instant before she turned to run.

He spurred his horse after her. She looked back just as the moon slid from beneath a cloud, then turned and ran on as though the devil himself were after her. He reached down and with one arm swooped her up onto the saddle in front of him. She half turned, striking out, raking his face with her nails, struggling hard against him. But he held her tight to his body and laughed because now she belonged to him.

When they reached his camp, he jumped from his horse and lifted her off the saddle. He slid her down the length of his body and felt the softness of her breasts and the curve of her thighs. She tried to fight him, but he picked her up and carried her into his tent and laid her down upon the thick carpets. She looked up at him, and her eyes were as green as the Sea of Kashkiri.

She was his, the prize of his conquest. He said, "You're mine now— I'll never let you go because you belong to me. You..."

Ali groaned. "By Allah," he muttered angrily. "I'm losing my mind."

He cursed the day he'd met Genny Jordan. He wished by all that was holy that he'd never set foot in New York, had never sat across the table from her in the offices of Cunningham, Tabler.

She was a woman from a world far different from his own, but Allah help him, he wanted her. His body ached with wanting her, but if she didn't want him . . .

But she does want you, a voice inside his head whispered. You feel it, you know it. Take her. Keep her with you here in Kashkiri. No one will ever know. You can tell them in New York that she disappeared on a flight between Kashkiri and Rome. Or you could say that the villa had been attacked and that she had been taken by bandits.

Yes, he could keep her here in this desert home. Or in the harem, where he would need only to call for her. She would be his. He could . . .

No, he could not, for after all, he was a civilized man. He didn't take what did not belong to him. He wanted Genny as he had never wanted a woman before, but he wasn't a brute, he couldn't force her to be his.

And after all, no matter how much it hurt, he didn't blame her for leaving him tonight. She was wiser than he; she knew that though there was something between them, the fact remained that they were from different worlds. There could be no permanency, no lasting relationship.

But oh, he wanted her. If he could have her, just once. If he could cover her body with his. If he could . . .

He stilled. There was a whisper of sound. Through the midnight shadows he saw someone standing in the opening of the tent. The breath caught in his throat, and his heart began to pound hard against his ribs. Almost afraid to say her name, he whispered, "Is it you?"

She came forward through the darkness and stood above him, silent, waiting.

"Genny?"

She knelt down before him. Her eyes were luminous in the moonlight that shone down from the opening at the top of the tent. She touched the side of his face.

He dared not move.

She said, "Ali?" and then she was in his arms, holding him as he held her.

He kissed the top of her head and whispered to her in his language, "My sweetness, my precious one."

At last he held her away from him and, tilting her face to his, he kissed her. A feeling he had never known before came over him then, a feeling of such tenderness, of such caring, that it was almost as though a hand had squeezed his heart.

Passion waited; it was enough to hold her. He lay with her against the cushions so that he could feel the whole length of her body against his. He began to stroke her back, easing the tremors of nervousness that ran through her. She touched his face again, and he took each fingertip between his lips to kiss.

He felt the heat of her body through the fabric of her gown, and though he wanted her, he made himself wait. Only when her body yearned toward his did he begin to ease the gown up. And when he had tossed it aside, she whispered, "Now you, Ali."

He pulled his robe off and then, holding her with his gaze, he hooked his thumbs in his briefs and pulled them down.

Her eyes didn't waver. She reached out behind her and unfastened the wisp of silk and lace that covered her breasts. He saw the trembling of her lips.

He brought her back against the cushions and slid the satin panties down over her hips. Her body was bathed in moonlight, and she was so beautiful that for a moment tears clogged his throat.

She lay motionless when he leaned to kiss her breasts. She threaded her fingers through his hair. "Yes," she murmured. "Oh, yes, like that."

His mouth was so warm, his lips so unbelievably tender. He took a nipple between his teeth to carefully scrape and tug, and all the while his tongue soothed and excited her.

She brought him closer. Their bodies touched. His hand moved down to the apex of her legs. He cupped her there, then began to caress her.

"Please," she whispered as shiver after shiver ran through her. She reached to touch him and played her fingers along the length of his rigid manhood. She stroked lightly and loved the velvet feel of him against her fingertips.

He moaned low in his throat, and the sound excited her as nothing ever had because she knew she was pleasing him. His body began to tremble, and he closed one hand over her wrist.

"No more," he rasped. "No more."

He kissed her again, and his mouth was warm and moist and sweet on hers. "Genny," he said against her lips, and with a fierceness that took her breath, he joined his body to hers.

She was filled by him, one with him, part of him. He plunged against her, offering no quarter now in this moment of terrible urgency. He withdrew, he surged back, withdrew, then surged again. She cried out, not in fear but in eagerness, and lifted her body to his. She moved against him, frantic in a need that was equal to his.

Her senses reeled, and she sought his mouth and took his lips to bite and to suckle.

But soon, too soon, she began to spin out of control. She tried to hold back, but she couldn't.

"Yes!" The breath rasped deep in his throat. "Oh, yes!" His body surged over hers, and he tightened his arms around her.

With a low and passionate cry Genevieve looked up at the stars. And the stars merged to one great blinding light that spread in a shining brightness across the night sky, then broke and fell in diamond shards as her body soared.

"Genny. My Genny." He covered her face with kisses. He told her how lovely she was and how she made him feel. And held her until her breathing evened and she was still and pliant in his arms.

He had never known, had never even imagined, that anything could be as wonderful as what he had just shared with her. He looked up at the sky and said a prayer of thanks to Allah for this wondrous gift.

"I didn't know . . ." she whispered, and unable to go on, she kissed his chest.

His heart swelled because he knew it had been for her as it had for him. And he knew as he lay there and held her close to his heart that from this moment on there could never be another woman for him. For as long as there was breath in his body, there would be only Genny. She was his now; he would never let her go.

For a long time they lay without speaking. Finally she said, "I should go."

But when she made as though to move, Ali tightened his arms around her.

"Stay with me," he implored. "I want to go to sleep with you. I want to awaken with you." He kissed the side of her face. "Do you have any idea how much I've wanted you?" he asked. "From almost the first moment I saw you, I've thought of nothing else, Genny. I've wanted to hold you like this, to touch you like this."

She smiled. "Even when I disagreed with you?"

"Even then." He ran a thumb over her nipple and, when it peaked, he gently squeezed it. Her response, as it had been only a few moments before, was instantaneous. It pleased him more than he could ever say that she was so warm and loving, so totally responsive.

His body began to tighten with renewed desire, but because he didn't want to press her, he said, "It's been a long day for you, Genny. Try to sleep now."

Genevieve leaned her head against his chest, and with a sigh she closed her eyes. Earlier tonight she had run away from Ali. She wasn't sure, even now, why she had come back. She'd only known that she had to, that if she had not she would have been sorry for the rest of her life. Because of who they were, there could be nothing lasting in their relationship, but she wanted this brief time in the desert with him. When they returned to Kashkiri, she would throw herself into the work she had come to do, and when her work was finished, she would go home to New York.

Genevieve buried her face against his chest and, when his arms came around her, she snuggled close to him.

Ali, she thought. My love. And then she slept.

A touch as light as the brush of a feather caressed her breasts. Without opening her eyes she leaned into it, and a fine liquid warmth began to coil and grow. She sighed and moved closer into his embrace.

He began to stroke her back, down from her shoulders, around to her bottom, slowly, gently urging her closer with each stroke. He kissed her eyelids. He found her mouth and, when her lips parted under his, he sighed with pleasure and sought her tongue, stroking as he stroked her back, giving a loving notice of what was soon to come.

Eyes still closed, Genevieve began to play her fingers across his broad shoulders. She threaded them through his hair, caressed the back of his neck, the tender skin behind his ears, then down across the width of his chest to curl her fingers through the matt of chest hair before she moved lower.

Ali's breathing became faster, shallower. Her fingers splayed across his stomach, and she felt his muscles tighten. She moved to his inner thighs, then lightly stroked his throbbing manhood. He groaned into her mouth and began to caress her as she caressed him.

An electrifying spasm streaked through her body. She turned her head and began to lick the skin of his shoulder while she stroked and soothed him.

"No more," he whispered against her lips, and with a muffled cry he rolled her beneath him.

He plunged against her, and all the while he covered her face with his kisses.

Genevieve lifted her body to his. She murmured small cries of pleasure and with each cry, she sent Ali closer to the edge.

"Ali," she whispered. "Oh, darling."

Lost in an ecstasy of passion, he gripped her hips and thrust himself harder, deeper.

And she said, "Yes, oh, yes."

"Now?" He reached to suckle her breasts. "Now?"

So out of control that she was unable to answer, she tightened her hands on his shoulders, afraid if she didn't, she'd be lost in this spinning vortex of a feeling so strong it frightened her.

He cried aloud as spasm after spasm racked his big body. It went on and on, and he clung to Genevieve, tightening his body over hers, holding her close until he collapsed, spent and replete over her.

"You're mine now," he whispered in an Arabic dialect she didn't understand. "I'll never let you go."

The sun shone through the top of the tent the next time Ali awoke. It seemed to him at first that last night had been a dream, then he looked at Genny sleeping so quietly beside him and knew that it hadn't been. She'd slept all night in his arms and now she lay curled against him, one arm thrown over his waist, her golden hair in tangled disarray across his chest.

He wanted her again with an urgency that surprised him, but because it had grown warm inside the tent and because he thought the daylight might embarrass her, he kissed the top of her head and said, "Genny?"

Her eyes drifted open. She looked up at him through her long lashes. "Is it morning?" she murmured. Then a blush spread across her cheeks and she dipped her head against his chest.

Ali put a finger under her chin and raised her face. "Don't be embarrassed by what has happened between us, Genny."

"I'm not." The blush remained. "It's just..."

He kissed her. "That this between us is so new?" He ran his fingers over her breasts and down her body, down to the apex of her legs. Very gently he began to soothe her there. "Was I too rough last night?" he asked. "I tried to hold back, but when I touched you..." He drew in a breath. "Did I hurt you?"

She rubbed her face back and forth against his chest, then raising up to look at him, she said, "No, Ali. It was..." Her shoulders lifted as she sought for the words to tell him what their lovemaking had meant to her. "It was wonderful," she said at last. "It was more...so much more than I thought it could be."

Ali gazed into her sea-green eyes, and his throat tightened with all that he was feeling: relief that she could be so honest, joy because it had been as good for her as it had been for him.

Because he knew she could feel the pressure of his swelling against her thigh, he said, "It's too warm in here now. I don't want you to be uncomfortable. We shouldn't—"

Genevieve stopped his words with a kiss, and, when the kiss ended, she whispered, "Yes, we should," and her hands slipped down to the small of his back to press him closer.

Ali closed his eyes. Surely there had never been a woman like his Genny. Surely no other woman had such tender hands, such honeyed lips. Surely no other breasts were so sweetly rounded, no nipples such a delicate color.

Without opening his eyes he bent his head and took one rosy peak to kiss and tease. Never before had he known a woman of such warmth and passion. Never before had a woman responded to him so openly, so without shame. She set him on fire with every touch, every whispered word.

He circled his tongue around and around her nipple and, when she whimpered and her body trembled, he eased into her, bonding her to him as her softness closed around him.

They moved with exquisite slowness, gently caressing each other all the while. He stroked her breasts, and she massaged his shoulders. They kissed and told each other how good this was, how fine this felt. And when at last their bodies began to tremble and yearn toward that climactic final moment, she whispered, as she had last night, "Oh, Ali. Oh, darling."

And his heart trembled with an emotion so new, so deep, that he knew he would never be the same again.

There had never been so glorious a sunset. They reined in their horses and Ali said, "It's magnificent, isn't it?"

The sky to the west was a fire of brilliant color: red, streaked with flamingo, orange shot with bright patches of blue. As they watched, the sand turned to gold, then amber as the sky slowly darkened.

Let me remember this, Genevieve thought. Let me imprint this memory on my mind so that when the nights are cold I can remember the way it was.

Tears flooded her eyes and blurred her gaze.

"What is it?" Ali pulled his horse closer. "Why do you cry, my Genny?"

"Because it's so beautiful," she said. "Because I love..." She'd almost said, because I love you. But since she was afraid that if she said the words she would never be able to leave him, she said, "Because I love the desert."

"I hoped that you would." He hesitated as an idea began to form. "If I arrange it, would you like to take a trip into the desert?"

"Yes." She brushed the tears away. "Oh, yes, I'd love to."

"I'll phone Rupert tonight. He can manage until we return." He looked out toward the east. "There's an oasis less than a day's ride from here. We'll have to take the camels because it's too long a trip for the horses, and we'll be camping out. But if you wouldn't mind that—"

"I wouldn't mind."

"We'll leave tomorrow at sunrise. I'll have Haifa prepare the proper clothes for you to take. It will be hot, but we'll stop often to rest." He grinned. "I don't want you too tired when we get there."

Genevieve grinned back. "I may be saddle sore."

"If you are, my hands will soothe you."

A trickle of flame shot through her body.

He tightened his hand around hers, and she knew that the same kind of heat burned through him.

"Don't look at me like that," he whispered, "or I swear by Allah I will take you here on the sand."

"That would be..." A smile tilted the corners of her lips. "Gritty," she finished.

Some of the tension eased out of him. "You're a wicked lady," he said, loving thât unexpected show of bawdiness. "And just for that, tonight I'm going to love the living hell out of you."

Her green eyes shone with laughter. "Promises, promises," she said with a mocking laugh, and before he could stop her, she wheeled her horse and galloped off into the dark desert night.

Ali raced after her, but she bent low in the saddle, riding fast, her hair blowing free, the wind in her face, beautiful and wild and free, a creature of the desert night.

He caught up with her and laughed aloud at the look of pure joy on her face when she turned her head. They raced on until finally, when their horses' sides were heaving, they reined in.

Ali swung off his mount and, reaching up, he pulled her down beside him. Before she could get her breath, he put his arms around her. Holding her close, he covered her mouth with his and kissed her with all the hunger and excitement he'd held in check all that long afternoon.

Her knees went weak, and she clung to him. He nibbled the corners of her mouth and sucked hard on her bottom lip. He made small love bites against her throat and her ears, then healed the bites with his tongue.

Genevieve swayed in his arms, so overcome by the heat that spread through her body that she could barely stand when he held her away from him.

"Gritty be damned." Ali swore under his breath as he pulled the white robe off over his head and spread it on the sand a few feet from the horses. Then he yanked off his briefs and stood, splendidly male, there in the darkening night.

He was magnificent, broad and muscled of shoulder and chest, narrow of waist and hip. Larger than a man had a right to be.

Her throat clogged with desire. He held out his hand, and when, in a daze she went to him, he pulled her so close that the power of his arousal pressed hard through the thin cotton material of her robe.

"I want you," he whispered hoarsely. "Here! Now!" He pulled her down to the white robe and began to undress her. When she was naked, he held her away from him, narrowing his eyes as he studied her. With a hoarse cry he covered her body with his and buried himself into her soft, moist warmth.

Too excited to hold back, he grasped her hips and thrust hard against her because he knew with a certainty that she wanted this as much as he did.

And oh, she did. She clung to his shoulders to urge him closer and lifted herself to meet him thrust for thrust. She was lost in the sweet agony, too soon near completion.

It came, shattering her body into a million pieces, and she cried aloud with a pleasure so intense she came perilously close to fainting.

He said her name over and over again, as shattered, as spent, as she.

They lay on their backs and watched the stars come out. He took her hand and brought it to his lips.

Genevieve had never known such peace, such utter and complete fulfillment. She wanted to stay here on the desert with him forever. She wanted to live with him, grow old with him.

He raised himself on one elbow and looked down at her. Gently he smoothed the tumbled hair away from her face and leaned to kiss her brow. "Genevieve, my Genevieve."

"Ali," she said, and touched his face.

They held each other close for a little while. And finally, by the light of the moon, they dressed and rode back to the villa.

Chapter 9

Ali objected when the guard whose name was Kamil insisted on going into the desert with them.

"Sheik Turhan ordered us to protect you," Kamil said. "We cannot do that if you ride out alone on the desert as you did last night. If anything had happened to you and the lady, sir, your father would have had me shot."

Though it angered Ali, he knew that Kamil was right; his father most certainly would have all three of the men shot if anything happened to him or to Genevieve. He didn't think they were in any danger here on the desert, but Omar Haj Fatah had spies everywhere—he had to be careful.

They left at dawn, he and Genny in the lead, the three bodyguards behind them leading four pack camels. Genny was dressed in white cotton pants and a long-sleeved shirt. A white *howli* covered her hair and protected at least part of her face from the sun.

At ten o'clock, when the sun was already high in the sky, they stopped to rest and have a cool drink. The men put up a canvas covering, and Genevieve removed the *howli* and wiped her face with a damp cloth. She had almost forgotten how hot the desert was, how unrelenting the heat. She hadn't been on a camel in years, and the awkward rolling motion made her slightly queasy. Though she offered no complaint, Ali insisted she rest for a little while before they went on.

He stopped several times that day, and the sun had already started to sink below the dunes when at last they caught sight of the oasis.

"There, Genny," Ali said as he reined in his camel. "A little to your right."

She raised herself in the saddle and, shielding her eyes, she gazed out beyond the dunes. And there it was, a paradise of sheltering palms and a welcome stretch of green.

It had been a long day, and she was tired. But as she gazed out at the oasis, her fatigue faded and she said, as she had the night before, "Race you!" With a shouted *"Yala, yala!"* she whacked her camel across his flanks with her riding crop and galloped off toward the oasis.

Ali laughed with pleasure, for she rode like a bedouin, hell-bent across the desert sands. Then with a whoop he dug his heels into his animal's sides and raced after her.

Genevieve drew back on the reins at the edge of the oasis and waited for Ali and the bodyguards to reach her and for one of them to bring her camel to his knees so that she could dismount. It was beautiful here. There were date palms, thatch and tall coconut palms. There was a well, and beyond, sheltered by fan palms, she saw a pond.

"You can bathe while we set up camp," Ali told her. "The pool is hidden from view, so you'll have all the privacy you need." Lowering his voice, though he knew the guards spoke no English, he said, "Later tonight I'll bathe you, but for now I have to let you go alone."

"I'll think about tonight," Genevieve said, and with a wicked grin she took the small travel case he gave her and headed for the pool.

A breeze rustled through the palm fronds overhead as she made her way toward it. By the time she reached the pool, the sky had begun to darken. Soon night would fall, and she and Ali would be alone.

As she lay back in the cool, clear water, she began to think about Ali and to ask herself how it was that he could move her to a depth of passion unlike anything she'd ever known before.

She was thirty-three years old; there had been other men in her life. She'd had an affair with a young man in her senior year at college, and another affair that had lasted almost two years. But with neither man had she experienced what she'd felt these past few days with Ali. She wondered as she looked toward the dunes why, of all the men in the world, she had fallen in love with Ali Ben Hari.

They were very different people, from very different worlds. He would never be able to adjust to her kind of life in New York, and certainly she would never be able to adjust to life here in Kashkiri. It was an impossible situation, and yet the thought of leaving him, of never again sharing the kind of rapture they had found together last night, made her feel empty inside.

At last she bathed, and by the time she returned, the camp had been set up, complete with a folding table and two chairs in front of the tent she and Ali would share.

"The guards will sleep beyond the dune," Ali said, indicating a rise of sand that separated the two sections of the oasis. "They won't disturb our privacy but they'll be close by if we need them." He handed Genevieve a glass of sherry. "Your aperitif, madam," he said with a smile.

"You don't drink when you're in Kashkiri, do you?"

Ali shook his head. "No, only when I'm away." He touched his glass of mineral water to her sherry. "It will be dark soon," he said.

Her lips parted, and a flush of color rose in her cheeks.

"The steaks are ready, *sidi*," Kamil said.

Ali took Genevieve's arm and led her to the table, which had been set with silver plates. When she was seated, Kamil placed one of the steaks on her plate and passed the other to Ali.

"I will return later to clean up," he said, but as he turned to go, Genevieve said, "There's no need, Kamil. I'll take care of clearing the things tonight."

The bodyguard frowned.

"Madam will take care of things," Ali said. "We'll see you in the morning."

"One of us should stand guard, *sidi*."

"You can guard from the other side of the dune. If riders approach, we'll see the cloud of dust long before any riders reach the camp."

"But your father—"

"Is not here," Ali said.

Kamil's face tightened, and he turned on his heel and strode away.

"Was it wrong of me to have spoken up?" Genevieve asked.

"Not wrong, just something he isn't used to. You gave him an order, and that's not something women do here."

"Oh?" She raised one eyebrow.

"I'm glad you did, Genny. Kamil means well but he tends to hover."

"I suppose he's just trying to do his job." She took a sip of her sherry. "Is there any danger, Ali? Even out here?"

"I don't think so, Genny. When Haj Fatah attacks, it will be in the city, not out here in the desert. Besides, it's my father he wants, not me."

"But you're your father's successor." Which meant, she thought sadly, that when his father stepped down, Ali would become the sheik of Kashkiri. In time he would marry a Kashkiri woman—women. Maybe he'd even have as many children as his father had.

She pushed her plate away.

"What's the matter?"

"Nothing."

"Aren't you hungry?"

"No."

"Tired?"

Genevieve shook her head.

"Then what is it?"

She shrugged. "I don't know."

"You've suddenly become unhappy, Genny. Why?" He laid his knife and fork across his plate. "Are you sorry you came?"

"No."

"Then tell me. What is it?"

"For the first time I realized that one day you'll be the Sheik of Kashkiri. I guess that makes me a little sad." She tried to smile. "You'll marry—maybe as many times as your father—several nice Kashkiri women who'll make you proper wives. You'll have multitudinous children and grandchildren, and you'll—"

"*Grand*children!" He looked horrified.

"And maybe some day, when you're very old, you'll tell them about the lady from New York." No longer able to smile, she bowed her head so that she would not have to look at him.

For a long moment Ali didn't speak. "My father's still a young man," he said at last. "It well may be that by the time he steps down, Ismail will be old enough to rule in his stead. Lord knows I have no wish to become the next Sheik of Kashkiri. As for several wives—" his lips quirked in a smile "—I told you in New York that when I marry it will be only once, that in my opinion one woman is more than enough for any man to handle. I meant it then, and I mean it now."

He stood up. "I'm going to bathe. How'd you like to wash my back?"

"How'd you like to wash my front?" Before Ali could answer, she got up and said, "I've got to clear up here. Why don't you go on? I'll join you as soon as I'm through."

He hesitated, then he ducked into the tent, grabbed a bar of soap and a towel and headed for the pond. "I'll be waiting," he said over his shoulder.

He was glad to be alone because he needed some time to think about their conversation. Genny had said that when the time came, he would marry a proper Kashkiri woman. That's what was expected of him. He had told her that perhaps Ismail would rule one day, but he knew the chances of that were slim. He was his father's oldest son; it would be up to him to take over the reins when the time came. If he married a foreign woman...

Ali sucked his breath in hard.

Genny was a foreigner, an infidel. The people of Kashkiri would never accept her.

Nor would Genny ever accept the kind of life she would lead as his wife. She'd fought him tooth and nail before she'd agreed to stay in the harem for two months. He could only imagine how she'd feel about spending the rest of her life there.

She was a Western woman; she'd never be able to adapt to life here in Kashkiri. He would not ask her to.

Then what the hell was he going to do? He wanted her, not just for a day or a week or a month, but forever. In the beginning, when he'd first realized how intense his attraction to her was, he'd thought that if he could have her just once he'd be able to get her out of his system. But once hadn't been enough. After last night a thousand times a thousand would never be enough.

He went into the water and, when it reached his thighs, he rolled onto his back and looked up at the stars. He floated motionless, thinking about her and about the way it had been with her last night. When at last he heard a rustle of sound, he looked toward the bank and saw her coming toward him through the palms. She stopped at the water's edge, there in a circle of moonlight, and while he watched, she pulled the white robe over her head and started into the pond.

His response was strong and immediate. Jolts of electricity ran down his spine and spread heat to his loins. He swelled, throbbing with a desire so intense he wasn't sure he could control himself.

She came slowly toward him, her pale hair loose about her shoulders. It took all of his willpower to stand where he was and wait for her to come to him.

She took the bar of soap from his hands. "I've come to wash your back," she said.

"Genny..." His throat clogged with desire.

She reached up and took him by the shoulders. "Turn around," she said.

When he turned, she put her arms around his waist and leaned her face against his back. She held him like that, as though to quiet all of the tension running through him, then let him go and, soaping her hands, she began to lather his back.

"Take the soap," she said. She started at his shoulders, massaging slowly, rotating the palms of her hands down his spine to the small of his back. Then she began to wash and to knead his firm buttocks with both of her hands.

Her soapy hands were smooth against his skin as she caressed him, around and over skin so sensitive that it felt as though his nerve ends were exposed and raw.

"Now turn around," she murmured.

When he did, he reached for her. But though her lips were parted and her eyes were smoky with desire, she shook her head and with the faintest of smiles said, "But I haven't finished, Ali."

She came closer, so that her body barely touched his, and reaching around behind him, sluiced water off his back. He put his arms around her then and pulled her up against him.

"Do you know what you're doing to me?" he asked through clenched teeth.

"I know." She took the soap from his hand and began to lather one of his arms. She started at the shoulder and worked her way down to his hand. And when she had washed it, she brought his arm up, shoulder high, and rested his hand against her breast.

He curled his fingers over it as she began to wash his other arm. When she had finished, she took his hand and brought it to her other breast.

She began to soap his chest. "Enough!" he growled.

"But I haven't finished." She lathered his chest, then moved lower across his stomach. And down.

Her hands began to tremble. Her eyes drifted closed.

Ali stood, legs apart, panting through his mouth, trying to hold back, trying...

But suddenly it was too much. He grasped her arms and, raising her up, he pulled her legs around his hips and with a cry he thrust himself into her, deep and hot and hard.

Genevieve moaned. Her head went back, and she tightened her legs around his hips. He took a nipple between his teeth to tug and scrape and lap, and her body began to shake. He held her there and surged against her, again and again, until, unable to hold back, she cried his name into the silence of the night, and her body quivered as shudder after shudder coursed through her.

He dug his fingers into the flesh of her bottom. He sought her mouth in a frenzy of desire, and the world exploded with a force that staggered him.

She wouldn't let him go. Her legs were tight around his hips, her arms around his neck, and she held him there because she wanted it to go on and on. Just as he did.

But at last her legs slipped away, and she stood, trembling with reaction against him.

He let her rest for a moment, then he raised her face to his so that he could look into her eyes. "What miracle has brought us together?" he asked. "We come from different worlds—we worship different gods. Everything I believe in, every idea I've grown up with, is so vastly different from yours. Yet when we're together, none of those things matter. In you I've found my other self, the other half of *me*, the better half of me."

He drew her closer into his embrace. "I don't know what will happen to us, Genny. I only know that I don't want to let you go."

Genevieve's throat closed with pain. Everything he said, every word he uttered, echoed all the things that were in her heart.

She raised her face and looked into his dark desert eyes. "I love you," she said.

But when he made as though to speak, she rested her fingers against his lips. "Let's enjoy what we have, Ali. Let's not think about tomorrow or next week or next month. This is our special time, our memory, our—"

"I can't live the rest of my life on a memory." The words were wrenched from the center of his being. "How can I let you go now?" His expression changed; his mouth grew cruel. "I could keep you here," he murmured. "I could tell Cunningham that you were lost in the desert. I could lock you up in the harem. I could—"

Genevieve shook her head. "No, you couldn't, darling." She rubbed her face against his chest and felt the tension and the cruelty leave him. And she wanted to weep because she loved him and because there was a part of her that wished she could live as Kashkiri women lived and be content to wait for the night when he beckoned her to come.

But she couldn't. That's not who she was; that's not who she could ever be.

When at last she stepped out of his embrace, he began to bathe her, but not as she had bathed him. He touched her tenderly, reverently, and let his passion wait.

Finally they came up out of the water and stood, hand in hand, there in the moonlight, on the edge of their desert oasis.

There was a dreamlike quality to the next few days. They talked often because it seemed important to learn everything about each other. Genevieve told him about her growing-up years in Morocco and Tunisia.

"The cultural shock came when we moved to Washington," she said. "I'd been accustomed to one way of life, and suddenly I was transplanted into one of the busiest cities in the United States. I was sixteen and I'd never seen snow, that kind of traffic, that kind of rushing about. My mother died a month after we moved there, and that was hard."

Ali took her hand. "Did you go to school there?"

Genevieve nodded. "But that was different, too. I'd been used to the small American school in Rabat. The high school in Washington was so big that I felt lost all the time. But after a while I adjusted. Six months after we were there, I began acting as my father's hostess. I liked that."

Ali smiled, and it seemed to him he could picture her as she had been then: a rather serious teenager, her hair pulled back to look older, wearing a proper dress, high heels and stockings, welcoming her father's guests, supervising a luncheon or a dinner party. He wished he had known her then.

"When did you go to New York?" he asked.

"After college." Another look of sadness crossed her face. "Dad died when I was in my sophomore year at William and Mary. After I graduated, I went to New York and got a job as a junior secretary at Cunningham and Tabler."

"Where did you live?"

"In an apartment on West Fifty-Seventh Street with two other women." Genevieve smiled. "There were three beds in the bedroom and one closet. It was terrible and it was fun. I wouldn't trade the time I lived there for a mansion on Park Avenue, but I'd never do it again." She laughed. "We ate spaghetti four times a week and hot dogs the other three days."

A frown drew Ali's brows together. "But didn't you have money? Hadn't your father provided for you?"

"My mother's illness had taken a lot, Ali. There was some money left when Dad died, but I still had two years of college to finish. When I went to New York, I took night classes at Columbia, and that cost money, too."

"You were on your own? You had no one to protect you? How old were you?"

"Twenty-one."

Ali swore under his breath. The thought of a young Genevieve on her own in New York enraged him. "A thing like that would never have happened in Kashkiri,'' he said. ''Here a woman is protected by her family until she marries.''

''But I had no family.''

''Surely there were male relatives.''

Genevieve shook her head. ''There was no one.'' She drew herself up. ''I managed all right. I was as capable of taking care of myself then as I am now.''

''You Westerners think the way we take care of women is archaic,'' he muttered. ''But at least our women are protected.''

''By protection you mean they're shut away in a harem.''

''Where they are safe.''

''Where they are prisoners.'' Genevieve glared at him. ''I'd rather live in one room and eat spaghetti for the rest of my life than live like that.''

''The women in my father's harem are happy. They live a life of luxury, and they have everything they want.''

''Except their freedom.'' She took a step forward so that she stood almost nose to nose with him. ''They're virtual slaves.''

''Slaves!'' So angry now he could barely speak, Ali clenched his hands to his sides.

''They're ruled by their men, unable to do as they choose, ordered about, forced to marry—''

''That's not true.''

''It is for Zuarina.''

''Zuarina? What in the hell are you talking about? Zuarina's going to marry my father. She knows what an honor that is. She—''

''She's in love with Rupert.''

''Rupert?'' Ali stared at her.

''And he's in love with her.''

''Where did you get an idea like that?''

She wished now that she hadn't started this. In her anger she had betrayed a confidence—no, two confidences. There could be terrible repercussions.

"Well?" Ali demanded.

"I shouldn't have said anything."

"Is that why you arranged for them to go to the museum with us?" He glared at her. "Dammit, Genny, I want to know what this is all about. Zuarina is betrothed to my father. This could be a deadly serious situation. Rupert is my friend. If he's touched her, if—"

"I'm sure it's nothing like that," Genevieve protested. "They've only seen each other at family gatherings. I don't think they've even held hands."

"I hope to Allah that's true." Ali ran a hand through his thick black hair. "How did you find out?"

Genevieve hesitated, then decided the truth wasn't nearly as bad as what Ali might be imagining. "Zuarina told me," she said at last. "The women in the harem had been teasing me about you."

Ali raised an eyebrow. "Go on."

"They said . . . they joked about the . . . the kind of children we'd have."

Something clutched at his insides.

"Because you're dark and I'm fair."

Children, he thought. Genny's children.

"Zuarina came to see me, I guess because of that, because that's the way she'd thought about Rupert. I mean because he's so fair . . ."

Embarrassed now, wishing she didn't have to go on but knowing that she did, Genevieve said, "Zuarina knows what a great honor it was to have been chosen by your father, but she'd fallen in love with Rupert. She showed me a poem he'd sent her. It was a love poem, Ali. He loves her, too."

A muscle jumped in his cheek. Didn't Rupert realize that a love like that was hopeless? Didn't he . . . ? And suddenly Ali was overcome by his own feelings of hopelessness. Rupert and Zuarina were worlds apart, just as he and Genny were. Zuarina could never be a part of Rupert's world, as Genny could never be a part of his.

If it were true that Rupert had fallen in love with Zuarina, then he sorrowed for his friend.

And for himself.

It would be nice to think that love conquered all, that he and Genny, and Rupert and Zuarina could live happily ever after. But he knew they couldn't. Life wasn't that simple; it didn't always work out the way you wanted it to.

"I'll speak to Rupert when we return," he said.

"I'm sorry I said anything, Ali. I shouldn't have. I was angry."

"I know." He took her hand and brought it to his lips. "So was I, Genny. I'm sorry, too." He forced a smile. "Shall we make an agreement not to talk about Rupert or Zuarina while we're here? This is our time together, our own special slice of paradise."

Paradise she thought, but oh, such a brief paradise.

She stood on her tiptoes and kissed him. "I love you," she said.

Each evening at sunset, while Kamil prepared their evening meal, they rode out a little way from the oasis. It pleased Ali that Genny enjoyed the desert as much as he did, that she took pleasure in the vibrant sunsets.

In the last night of day, when the desert was bathed in a golden amber glow, her skin seemed almost iridescent, and he knew when she left him a part of his heart would go with her and that for the rest of his life, there would be an emptiness in him.

This was their special time of the day, a time of quiet communion with the life of the desert, a time when their passion waited and they were content to look at the sunset, and each other, and know that soon they would come together as lovers.

After dinner, with only the moon and the stars to light their way, they went to the pool to bathe. Ali took a special delight in bathing her, and often he made her stand and wait, as she had made him stand that first night, while he washed her slender body.

Though it was difficult to hold back the passion that touching her brought, he made himself go slowly. As though he had all the time in the world, he lathered her breasts and touched the nipples that pressed against his fingertips.

He delighted in watching her eyes drift closed, her lips part. He loved her small sounds of pleasure when his hands went lower to tease and stroke.

Sometimes when it became too much, when they could not wait to get back to their tent, they made love on the grassy bank of the pond. Once they fell asleep there, naked in each other's arms. And awoke just before dawn to quickly pull their robes over their heads and retreat to the privacy of their tent before Kamil came to prepare their breakfast.

Kamil had grown more dour with each passing day. "We should leave this place," he said again and again. "Sheik Turhan would not like it that we are here."

Finally, when eight days had passed, Ali said, "We will leave tomorrow."

That night, as had become their custom, he and Genevieve rode out to watch the sunset. Because it was their last night, he brought both camels to their knees so that he and Genny could stand hand in hand as they watched the desert sky turn a brilliant rainbow of colors.

"It's been a wonderful week," she said as she leaned her head on his shoulder. "It's been . . ." She looked up at him, puzzled by the sudden tightening of his face. "What is it?" she asked. "What—?"

"Riders." He pointed off to his left. "There, the cloud of dust."

"And on our last night." Genevieve sighed. "I hate to share our oasis with anybody else, Ali, but I suppose we'll have to."

"Get on the camel. We have to get back to camp."

"But—"

"Do as I say, Genny. Quickly." He helped her into the saddle, whacked the beast across the knees so that it would rise, then swung onto his own animal.

The cloud of dust drew closer.

"Hurry!" Ali urged, and smacking her camel across its rump, he raced with her toward the camp.

Kamil and the other two guards were waiting for them. As soon as they dismounted, Kamil tossed Ali one of the automatic rifles.

"What's going on?" Genevieve asked.

"Maybe nothing," Ali said. "We're just being careful."

"The woman should get out of sight," Salim said.

Ali nodded. "Go to the tent," he told Genevieve. "Stay there until I tell you it's safe."

"But—"

"Now, Genny."

She looked out toward the dunes, then at the grim-faced guards.

"If there's trouble, I can help," she said. "I know how to use a gun."

"It's better if you're out of sight." Ali gripped her shoulders. "It's probably nothing, Genny. We're just being careful. Go on now, do as I say."

She worried her bottom lip, then with a nod she turned and hurried toward the tent.

There were seven of them. He couldn't see their faces, but he saw their rifles.

"They will be Omar Haj Fatah's men," Kamil said. He motioned the other two guards down, then dropped to his knees. "We have plenty of ammunition, *sidi*. We can hold them off."

"For how long?"

Kamil raised his shoulders in a gesture that said, Who knows?

A shot rang out. Ali flattened himself against the sand. Leaning on his elbows, he raised the rifle to his shoulder. "Wait," he cautioned. "Wait until they're closer." He snugged the rifle against his shoulder, his eyes narrowed against the advancing darkness. "Now!" he cried, and fired off a round.

One of the riders fell. The others swung from their saddles and ran in zigzag patterns toward the camp.

Beside him Ali heard the steady ta-ta-ta of the guards' rifles.

Kamil crept forward, firing as he went. Another man went down. Kamil rose to his knees.

"Be careful!" Ali called out. "Don't—"

Kamil's body jerked backward. He fell and lay still, arms thrown over his head, his legs bent under him.

Ali swore and kept firing.

There were five of their attackers left. He and the other two guards held them off. Darkness came. The shooting was sporadic. Ali motioned to the two guards to cover him while he inched his way to Kamil. He knelt beside the fallen man and searched for the carotid pulse. But there was nothing.

Grim faced, damning himself because he hadn't listened to Kamil, Ali picked up the fallen man's rifle and slung it over his shoulder.

The shooting stopped, but they were still out there, somewhere in the darkness, waiting for daylight to come. He wanted to go to Genny but knew that he dare not leave. Their attackers could creep up on them. They could...

"Ali?"

"Get back to the tent," he whispered.

"Are you all right? What's happening? The shooting's stopped. Have they gone away?" She grasped his arm. "Who are they? What did they want?"

Ali pulled her down beside him. "I'm not sure who they are, but I've got a pretty good idea. We've managed to hold them off, but they're still out there."

"Let me stay here with you."

"No, dammit. Do as I say. Get—"

"Who...?" She pointed to where the fallen man lay. "Is it Kamil?" she whispered. "Is he...?" Her eyes went wide with shock. "Is he dead?"

"Yes, he's dead."

"Oh, my God!"

She leaned her face against Ali's chest, and he put his arm around her. When he let her go, he said, "Go back to the tent, Genny."

"Shouldn't we...shouldn't we do something about him?"

"Later."

She swallowed hard. "I'm so sorry," she said. Then she touched the side of Ali's face and turned back in the direction of the tent.

The night seemed endless. She paced up and down in the dark, tense, waiting for the sound of gunfire. But there was only silence. At last, exhausted, she sank down on the cushions, and without meaning to she fell asleep.

The sound of gunfire awoke her, and she ran to open the tent flap and look out. It was barely dawn. She tried to see Ali and the guards, and when she couldn't, she left the tent and crept cautiously in the direction of the shots until she saw Ali, flat on his stomach behind a pile of rocks. He was leaning on his elbows, a bandolier of bullets over one shoulder, the rifle positioned against his other shoulder.

There was a guard to his left and one to his right. She couldn't make out the men firing at them, but she heard the splat of their bullets.

Suddenly a terrifying sound split the air, and five dark-robed men, like apparitions from hell, sprang forward, shooting as they came.

Genevieve hit the sand and started squirming as fast as she could toward Ali. He swung around, saw her, then turned back and got off a volley of shots.

One man went down; four others came on.

Genevieve grabbed the other rifle, raised it to her shoulder, took aim and fired. A dark-robed figure fell.

Now there were three.

The guard to the left of her hit one of them, and Ali got another.

The last man threw down his rifle and turned to run. The other guard raised his rifle, but Ali shouted, "No, let him go." He couldn't shoot a man in the back.

He swung around and grabbing Genevieve he shook her. "I told you to stay in the tent," he roared. "Dammit, woman, don't you realize you could have been killed?"

He pulled her against him and held her so close he could feel the rapid beat of her heart. She'd come out of the dawn like an avenging angel, but she'd shot like a man, and by Allah, he was proud of her.

"You're one hell of a woman," he said with a laugh. "And one hell of a shot." Then, not caring that the guards looked on, he kissed her.

"The men and I have some unpleasant work to do," he said when he let her go. "I'd appreciate it if you'd start the breakfast."

She hesitated for only a moment, then, because she knew they were going to bury Kamil and the other men, she took Ali's hand, squeezed it and said, "Yes, of course. I'll let you know when it's ready."

She turned and went back to the tent and began to gather the things she would need.

Chapter 10

As soon as they reached the villa, one of the servants ran out, calling, "Sheik Turhan has been telephoning every day. He has been worried—we have all been worried."

"I'd better call him right away," Ali said as he helped Genevieve off her camel. "Why don't you rest until dinner? I imagine you'd like a hot bath."

"I'd gotten rather used to cool baths," she answered with a tired smile, then turned to follow Haifa toward the stairway that led to the second floor.

And Ali went to place the call to his father.

"Where have you been?" Turhan shouted when he came on the phone. "You were to be gone four days, and it's been almost two weeks. The servants said you took a trip into the desert."

"We arrived back just a few minutes ago."

"We?" His father swore an ancient Kashkiran curse. "It's the American woman, isn't it? She's the reason for the trip into the desert, the reason you're forgetting who you are and where your duties lie? I hope you at least had sense enough to take Kamil and the guards with you.''

"They were with us." Ali pinched the skin between his brows. "There was trouble," he said. "We were attacked."

"Haj Fatah's men! Was anyone hurt?"

"Kamil was killed."

"Killed?" His father swore again, then said, "He was a good man."

"Yes, he was."

"Is the woman safe?"

"Yes."

"Thank Allah for that. We don't need the Americans coming down on us. I suppose she'll be on the first plane out of Kashkiri after a scare like that."

Ali smiled for the first time since he had picked up the phone. "I doubt that, Father. As a matter of fact, she can use a rifle as well as I can. She killed one of them."

"She killed...?" There was disbelief in his father's voice. Then Turhan chuckled. "She is much woman, Ali. I doubt you'll ever tame her."

"I'm not sure I want to."

"Aha! So there is something between the two of you. Do you intend to keep her as your mistress?"

"She'd never agree to that."

"She doesn't have to agree. Shut her away in the harem. When the time comes, you can make a proper marriage and still have the American."

"I couldn't do that."

"*Zfft!*" Turhan exclaimed. "If you're thinking of marriage, forget it. You're my heir. The sheikdom will be yours one day. You cannot rule with an infidel at your side."

"I know that."

"Then get rid of her," Turhan shouted into the phone. "Send her back to New York."

"No." The word, though softly spoken, was hard as steel. "When the time comes, I'll send her away, but for now she stays."

For a moment there was only silence. "There will be no talk of marriage," Turhan said softly. "Remember that." He sighed. "I knew from the moment I saw her she'd be trouble."

"I can handle it."

"See that you do." Shifting the conversation, Turhan said, "How soon can you be here?"

"We'll leave in the morning."

"Then I'll see you tomorrow night. Be careful, Ali. If Haj Fatah finds out that his men failed to get you in the desert, he'll try again."

Ali thought of the man he'd let get away. "I'll be careful," he said.

He wanted to sleep one last night in his tent with Genevieve, but because he didn't want to expose her to danger, he decided to occupy his rooms in the villa.

He'd doubled the guards as soon as he'd arrived, and tonight there were almost a dozen of them posted in different parts of the compound. There was also a guard outside his rooms.

"Is that really necessary?" Genevieve asked.

"Perhaps not, but I don't want to take any chances, Genny." He put his arms around her and brought her closer. "And don't tell me you can take care of yourself," he muttered. "While you're in Kashkiri, I'll take care of you."

And afterward? She put her arms around his waist. She wouldn't think about that now. There would be time later. Time to miss him, time to remember the way it had been.

He whispered a kiss against her ear, and she began to tremble. He found her mouth, and her tongue danced to meet his.

In the minutes that followed she became too absorbed in what was happening to think sad thoughts. It was only later, when she lay in Ali's arms and listened to his regular breathing, that she allowed herself to think of the days ahead.

They couldn't be like this once they returned to the government palace. There Ali had his quarters, and she had hers. They wouldn't be together as they had been in the desert. She had come to Kashkiri to do a job, and she couldn't do it properly if there was any hint of scandal.

She turned her head and kissed Ali's shoulder. We've had all we're ever going to have, she silently told him. It's been wonderful, my darling. These past days with you have meant more to me than you can ever imagine. I love you, Ali Ben Hari. With all my heart I love you.

Though she had done nothing more than whisper a kiss against his shoulder, he stirred. "What is it?" he murmured.

"Nothing, Ali. Go back to sleep."

He put his arm around her and brought her closer. Nuzzling his face against her throat, he said, "Why are you sad?"

"Because I know..." She fought to keep back the tears. "Because when we're back in the palace, I'll be in my quarters in the harem and you'll be in your rooms." She rubbed her face against his shoulder. "We won't be able to be like this again."

He wanted to tell her it would always be like this, that nothing would ever change. But he couldn't. He had responsibilities and so did she. But most of all he didn't want any hint of gossip to hurt her.

"We'll work something out," he said against her hair. But a terrible feeling of hopelessness gripped him. How could he do without her? He'd grown so used to her beside him in the night, to being able to reach out and touch her, to know that she was there.

How could he lose that? How could he lose her?

He urged her into his arms, and with a cry of need he sought her mouth.

They made love again, slowly, tenderly and with an intensity that left both of them shaking in that final moment of ecstasy.

They left at dawn the following morning. This time a guard rode in the front of their limousine with the driver, and four guards rode in the second limousine with Haifa and the servant.

They stopped only once on the way to Kashkiri, but instead of going down to the beach as they had on their way to the desert, they stood next to the two cars to eat the sandwiches that had been prepared for them.

Haifa's face was tense with worry, and when Ali went to speak to his men, she said to Genevieve, "I'll be glad when we're safely back at the palace. Omar Haj Fatah is a dangerous man. Twice now he has tried to overthrow Sheik Turhan. If he ever succeeds—" she gripped her hands tightly together "—it would be a bloodbath," she whispered. "He would slaughter the men and the women he has no use for. The others will be given to his men or sold into slavery."

"Slavery?" Genevieve looked unbelievingly at the other woman. "This is the twentieth century, Haifa. Such things don't happen today."

"Yes they do, madam. Not here in Kashkiri or in other civilized countries, but I have heard of two such countries.

One is Oajdaa, and the other is Jadida. A woman such as you would bring a king's ransom if she were to be put on the block. If Omar Haj Fatah ever got his hands on you…" She stopped because she saw Ali approaching, and hurried back to her own vehicle.

And though Genevieve was tempted to ask Ali if it was true that women were still sold into slavery, she didn't.

When she returned to the palace, Genevieve spent her time talking to the wives of the ministers, and finally some of them agreed that if their husbands requested it, they would act as hostesses to the foreign women.

She telephoned the secretaries of the various delegates and discussed suggested itineraries with them. The representatives in the United States, Japan, Germany and England said that the wives were looking forward to the coming trip to Kashkiri, and that they were especially looking forward to a trip into the desert.

Each evening Genevieve invited Zuarina for coffee and the rich pastries that Haifa loved to prepare. But though the pastries were tempting, Zuarina could not eat them.

She had lost weight during the time that Genevieve had been away. Her face was wan; all of the animation she had shown the day they had spent in the museum had faded.

"The wedding date has been set," she told Genevieve. "It is to take place on the first day of June."

"Have you seen or spoken to Rupert?"

"No, Genny."

And though Genevieve was tempted to say that she would speak to Rupert for Zuarina, she knew that she couldn't. For after all, what good would it do? What good could she do? Perhaps if Ali…

But she had not seen Ali since their return to the palace.

Each evening after Zuarina left, Genevieve undressed. Not bothering with a bathing suit, she would slip into one of the short robes that had been provided as part of her wardrobe and, dimming the lights in her room, she would take a towel and go out through her garden to the pool. Sometimes she sat in one of the chaises looking out at the night; at other times she went directly to the pool and, slipping out of the robe, she would lower herself into the gardenia-filled water.

At times she floated facedown among the fragrant blossoms, reveling in the sensuous touch of the satinlike petals against her skin. Eyes closed, with even the silence of the night blotted out, she would drift until the need for air made her turn and look up at the star-filled night. And she would ask herself if Ali missed her the way she missed him. If he hungered for her as she hungered for him. Did he awake in the night and call her name? As she called his?

When the need for him became past bearing, she would swim as hard and as fast as she could, back and forth, back and forth, until her arms and legs ached and she was panting for breath. Only then, tired enough to sleep, did she leave the pool.

A week after her return to the palace, she was summoned to a meeting of Sheik Turhan's ministers. His secretary, a man by the name of Abdur al-Ahad, called. "My lord, Turhan, and his ministers will see you tomorrow morning at eleven," he told Genevieve. "Your woman servant will bring you to the meeting room."

Ali will be there, she thought when she put the phone down. Tomorrow I'll see him.

The next morning Genevieve bathed in water scented with a faint but exotic perfume. When she came out of her bath, Haifa helped her dress in a royal-blue caftan and matching jeweled slippers.

She took care in applying her makeup and, because she wanted to look more businesslike, drew her hair back in a chignon. When that was done, she fastened the gold earrings that Ali had bought for her in her ears, the bracelet around her wrist, and slipped the heavy gold chain over her head.

"Ali," she said aloud, and holding the chain to her lips, she kissed it.

He greeted her at the door of the meeting room. He said, *"Sabbah al khair,"* and whispered the translation, "It is indeed a morning of gladness" as he brought her hand to his lips. His eyes met hers, then his gaze fell to the heavy gold chain between her breasts.

"Sabbah annour, Ali," she said, and as he had, whispered, "It is also a morning of light."

"Come in, come in," Turhan called out as he stood to greet her.

The other ministers nodded, and Rupert Matthews held out a chair for her next to him.

Genevieve smiled her thanks. "Good morning, gentlemen," she said. "Shall we begin?"

This was what she was good at, what she knew how to do. She spread her notes in front of her and, looking at Sheik Turhan, said, "The representatives from Saudi Arabia, Jordan and Tunisia will arrive on the afternoon of May first. The delegations from Morocco, Germany, England and the United States will be in the following morning. Delegates from Japan will arrive that afternoon.

"Suites have been reserved at the hotel. There are adequate meeting rooms there, too, but I assume you'll want some of the meetings to be held here in the palace."

Turhan, his fingers steepled against his chin, nodded. "Quite so," he said.

"I've talked to the curator of the museum, and he'll arrange a private tour for the delegates' wives. There'll be a luncheon for them the same day, and after lunch I'll take them to the university."

Genevieve glanced around the table. Some of the ministers, while not exactly frowning, obviously disapproved.

"I'd also like to suggest a trip to the desert villa. It's a lovely place. I'm sure all of the ladies would enjoy spending a day and a night there."

The minister of trade, a portly man with a swarthy face and eyebrows that met in one heavy line at the bridge of his nose, narrowed his eyes and said, "How do you know that the wives of the delegates want to do any of the things you're suggesting?"

"I've spoken to their secretaries on the telephone, Mr. Madih. The wives all expressed interest in visiting the museum and the university. The ladies specifically asked if a trip into the desert could be arranged."

"It must have impressed you most favorably during your recent stay," Turhan said slyly. "I believe you stayed longer than you had originally intended to."

Genevieve felt her cheeks flush, but her eyes didn't waver. "As you know, Sheik Turhan, I spent my childhood in Morocco and Tunisia. I've always loved the desert." She glanced at Ali. "I shall never forget the time I spent at the villa."

She wanted so badly to touch him that she forced her hands into her lap under the table and clenched them together. She'd seen the sudden fire in his gaze before she turned away, and she could feel it warming her.

It was a moment before she could go on. When she did, she said, "My only concern is that in view of what happened when I was there, I'm a bit hesitant about taking the ladies to the villa. If there's any threat to their safety, then a trip to the desert would of course be out of the question.''

A muscle twitched in Turhan's cheek. He frowned and said, ''I wouldn't contemplate holding the conference if I thought there was danger, Miss Jordan. You can be assured that security will be tight from the moment the delegates arrive until they leave.''

''But, sir—''

''You're not to worry about such things, Miss Jordan. That is the business of men, not of women.''

''Even though it will be the women's lives that will be in danger?'' she said hotly. ''Are the wives not as important as their husbands? Would you risk them—''

''Genny!'' There was a note of warning in Ali's voice, a note that said, don't go too far. Do not push my father beyond what he will allow.

She drummed her fingernails on the long mahogany table. There was more that she wanted to say on the subject, but perhaps now was not the time to go into it. Instead she referred to her notes and said, ''Shall we discuss the part your women will take in the conference? As you know, there will be two dinners here in the palace, and on the final night of the conference, there will be a banquet.''

''With music and belly dancers,'' one of the ministers said.

''The foreign wives will attend these functions, so of course some of your wives should also attend.''

''This is not our custom,'' Madih said sharply. ''Women do not attend our dinner parties.''

''Perhaps they don't in Kashkiri, Mr. Madih.'' Genevieve tried to keep her voice pleasant. ''But they do—'' she bit back the words *in more civilized countries*, and said instead ''—in other countries.''

"Then they will here," Turhan said. "You will instruct some of our women on how to behave at a mixed dinner party, Miss Jordan."

Genevieve shook her head. "Verbal instructions won't do, Sheik Turhan. The only way the women can become accustomed to dining with you is to dine with you."

Turhan frowned.

"I'd like to suggest that from now until the conference, they dine with you at least two or three times a week."

"Impossible!" The minister of education slammed his fist down on the table. Ignoring Genevieve, he turned to Turhan. "This has gone far enough," he growled. "Surely you're not going to let this American tell us how we must run our lives. She's a troublemaker, an infidel who—"

"Be careful, Ahmed Shahib." Ali's voice was deceptively soft, but his eyes were like the eyes of a panther about to leap upon his prey.

"Do not forget that Miss Jordan is a guest of our government. She's here because she's extremely capable and because she knows more about putting on this type of conference than we do." His gaze swept the other men at the table. "We've engaged her services because we needed help with the conference. We're an oil-rich country, gentlemen, but in many ways we're still a backward country."

There was a rumble of dissent around the table, but Ali went on as though he had not heard. "If we are to give the impression that we've joined the twentieth century, we must act as other countries do. How do you suppose it would look to the other wives if they and Miss Jordan were the only women included in our dinners? Don't you think they would ask why your wives were not attending? Don't you think they'd find our custom of excluding our women just a bit barbaric?"

"That's enough, Ali!" Turhan's face flushed with anger.

"I speak the truth, Father. If you want to increase trade with Western countries, then you have to convince them that we're as modern as they are. If you listen to Miss Jordan, I think you will convince them."

No one spoke. Turhan sat back down in his chair. The other men watched him and waited.

"Very well," he said at last. "You may ask some of our women to join us at dinner tomorrow night, Miss Jordan. You, of course, will attend with them. Warn them, though, to keep silent throughout the meal."

"I'm afraid I can't do that, sir."

"Can't? What do you mean you *can't*?"

"The whole purpose of your ladies being here is that they learn to take part in the dinner conversation."

Turhan drummed his fingers on the table. Then, with a shake of his head, as though to say, I give up, he nodded and said, "Very well, they may speak."

"Which of your wives would you like to participate, Sheik Turhan?"

"Seferina is too old," he said, "and Tamraz is with child." He rubbed his goatee. "Zuarina will soon be my wife. Let her come to the dinner tomorrow night and sit beside me the night of the banquet."

Beside her, Genevieve felt Rupert stiffen. Why doesn't he do something? she thought. Why doesn't he stand up and declare his love? Why doesn't he take Zuarina and run away with her?

She looked at Rupert. Sensing her gaze, his eyes met hers, and she saw his anguish, his desperation. There's nothing I can do, he seemed to say. Ali is my friend; I'm loyal to his father. How can I betray my friendship? My loyalty?

With a smothered sigh Genevieve began collecting her papers. "Until tomorrow then, Sheik Turhan?" she said.

"I shall look forward to it, Miss Jordan."

She glanced across the table at Ali. As she rose he said, "I'll escort you back to your quarters, Miss Jordan."

"That won't be necessary." Turhan signaled to a servant. "The woman Haifa is waiting in the corridor. Tell her that Miss Jordan is ready to leave." He motioned to Ali. "There's something I wish to discuss with you," he said.

The door opened. Haifa beckoned to her. She nodded to Turhan, but her gaze lingered on Ali's face. "Until tomorrow," she said.

Genevieve tried to sleep, but sleep wouldn't come. Restlessly she moved her legs. She closed her eyes and took deep steady breaths—inhale one, exhale two, inhale three, exhale four.

It didn't work. She tried to conjure up a deserted beach. But instead of a beach, she saw Ali as he had been the first time she'd seen him across the table from her in New York. His appearance had been overwhelmingly masculine, and when she'd looked into his desert-dark eyes, her toes had curled. Even then, not sure that she liked him, she'd felt something deep inside her kindle and grow.

These past two weeks had been like heaven. Never before had she experienced the kind of emotion she'd shared with Ali.

With a smothered moan, no longer able to stay in bed, Genevieve got up, drew the nightgown over her head and without bothering with her swimsuit, she slipped into a robe.

Once in the garden, she stood looking up at the sky. She felt more alone than she'd ever felt in her life. Her need for Ali was like a physical ache, not just the need for his lovemaking, but the need to be with him, to talk with him, to share a meal or a cup of coffee with him.

Except for today, she hadn't seen or spoken to him since they'd returned from the desert. Would it be like this until it was time for her to return to New York? How could she bear it? How could she bear being so close yet so far away?

Tears stung Genevieve's eyes and rolled down her cheeks. *Ali*, her heart cried. As though to purge herself of tortured thoughts, she threw off her robe and, arching her arms over her head, she dove into the pool.

She wished there weren't any gardenias. She didn't want their petal-smoothness against her skin tonight, didn't want their fragrance. She wanted Ali, wanted...

She began to swim back and forth, but the swimming didn't help and so she went to the far end of the pool, where the only light was the reflection of the stars shining on the water. She rolled onto her back there and, gazing up at the midnight sky, she thought of the circumstances that had brought her into this world of sheiks and harems, of a richness, and yes, a strangeness of life she hadn't even imagined.

She had lived in Arab countries as a child, but she and her family had been a part of the American community, not of the Arab community. Nothing had prepared her for life in Kashkiri. And Lord knows nothing had prepared her for falling in love with Ali, or for a passion so intense it frightened her.

Perhaps it had started that night in Rome, that night beside the Trevi Fountain when he had kissed her. She closed her eyes and let herself drink in the scent of gardenias. That first kiss, that first embrace. She would never forget the touch of his mouth on hers or the strength of the arms that had held her so firmly yet so tenderly.

Nor would she forget the time they had spent together on the desert. That perfect time that would never come again.

Finally, with a sigh of sadness, Genevieve swam to the ladder and started up out of the pool.

A figure loomed above her, tall and darkly shadowed by the moon.

"Give me your hand," he said.

"Ali?" His name trembled on her lips.

He reached down and brought her up beside him. "You're cold," he said, and drew her close into his embrace.

"Genny," he said against her lips, and with a low cry he picked her up in his arms and started toward her rooms.

"We can't," she whispered.

"To hell with can't."

"Ali, darling—"

He silenced her with a kiss, then hurried across the garden and carried her through the open door. When they were in her bedroom, he put her down. Her arms crept up around his neck, and her body pressed to his.

"I've missed you, Genny," he whispered as he rained kisses on her closed eyelids, her cheeks and her lips.

He let her go long enough to pull the white robe over his head. Then, with a cry that he muffled against her hair, he brought her back into his embrace, scooped her up and carried her to the bed.

"We shouldn't," she tried to say. "We—"

He took her words into his mouth. He kissed her hard and long, and when he let her go, he cupped her face between his hands. "Genny, I want you so much my body aches. I lie in bed at night and all I can think of is you, of how it is when we're together."

"I know," she said. "Oh, I know." She brushed the thick black hair back off his brow. "It's been the same for me, Ali. My body aches, too. That's why I swim at night. Why

I..." She looked at him, puzzled. "How did you get into my garden?"

"My garden is next to yours. They connect." He brought her hand to his lips and began to kiss her fingertips. "Sometimes I watch you swim," he admitted. "I've tried not to, but at night when I can't sleep, I walk in my garden. Tonight I heard you. I couldn't help it, Genny. I didn't mean to spy. I didn't plan to invade your private place, but when I heard you, when I saw you..." He caressed her shoulders and rubbed his face against the softness of her skin. "I couldn't help it, I had to be with you again, Genny. I had to."

"Come over me," she said. "Let me feel your body on mine."

And when he did, she closed her eyes and held him close to her beating heart. This was what she wanted; this is what she had missed. The feel of him, the whole, wonderfully masculine feel of his body against hers.

With trembling hands she caressed his muscled shoulders and the smooth lines of his back. He was so big, so powerful, yet he touched her so gently. She rubbed her face against his throat and breathed in the fresh clean scent of his body.

He brushed the still, damp hair back over her shoulders and ran hot kisses over her skin. He nibbled her earlobe and teased her with his tongue before he moved down to her breasts.

"So soft," he whispered against her skin. "So lovely." He lapped one rigid peak, and she shivered against him.

"I love it when you do that," he said. "I love to feel you tremble. I love to hear the catch in your voice when I touch you." He caught the peak between his teeth and licked hard with his tongue.

"Ali..." she gasped.

"Like that," he said. "Like that, Genny."

His tongue, so honeyed hot and moist, was like a branding iron against her skin. Her body, as though with a will of its own, moved under his. "Please," she begged. "Please, now, Ali."

"Wait, Genny." He moved lower and rubbed his face against her belly. The rasp of a day's growth of beard made her shiver with pleasure.

"Your skin is scented with gardenias," he murmured. "Are you like that all over?" He went lower, feathering kisses on his way.

"Ali? Darling?"

He gentled her with his hands and carefully nipped the tender skin of her inner thighs before his mouth moved upward.

When she tried to move away, he whispered, "Easy, my sweet. Easy, my darling. I need to touch you like this. I need to kiss you like this."

He set her on fire. He teased, he caressed, he loved her as she'd never been loved before.

"Oh, please," she begged, and gripped his shoulders as though to thrust him away. Instead, her hands tightened, and she held him there, held him while he drove her to a peak of ecstasy she'd never before experienced.

Heat flooded her body. She spun out of control, gasping for breath, dizzy with an enormity of feeling that frightened her. And cried his name again and again.

He brought his body up over hers. "Look at me," he said. "Look at me when I come into you, Genny."

And when she looked at him, he joined his body to hers. He rocked her close. He pleaded, "Again, Genny. For me, darling."

His breath came fast and hot. His excitement became her excitement, and suddenly the heat began again. With a frenzied moan she lifted her body to his.

"Oh, yes," he whispered. "Like that, yes."

It was too much, she couldn't . . .

In a voice hoarse with passion, he cried, "Now, Genny. Now . . ."

She rose to meet him, and her body shook with the force of another release. "I love you," she wept. "Always and forever, Ali. Only you."

They lay spent, unable to speak, and when at last their breathing evened and he made as though to move away, she tightened her arms around his shoulders. "Stay," she whispered.

"I'm too heavy for you."

"No." Genevieve kissed the side of his face. "I like your body covering mine. I like you inside me."

He rested his head against her breast and he knew then that, no matter the cost, he would never let her go.

Chapter 11

They sat on cushions around the low table: the ministers and their wives, Sheik Turhan and Zuarina, Ali, Rupert and Genevieve.

The women, their eyes outlined with kohl, their hands hennaed, rings on every finger, jeweled earrings dangling from their ears, looked like colorful but silent birds. Zuarina, who wore a shocking-pink kaftan and a matching head scarf covered with silver sequins, seemed to Genevieve like an exotic princess straight out of the *Arabian Nights*.

The ministers looked uncomfortable; their wives looked terrified. No one spoke.

A servant brought out hors d'oeuvres of stuffed grape leaves, pickled turnips and olives.

The ladies barely touched them, or the chick-pea soup that followed.

"Zuarina and I visited the museum before I left for the desert," Genevieve said, and turning to Zuarina, she asked,

"Was that the first time you had been to the museum, Zuarina?"

"Yes, madam," Zuarina whispered without raising her gaze from her plate.

"It's an interesting place." Genevieve waited and prayed that someone would say something.

"I went there many years ago," Elzakir said. "It was most interesting, and I . . ."

Madih frowned at his wife, and she grew silent.

"Did you enjoy it?" Ali asked, and when Elzakir, with a sideways glance at her husband, mumbled a reply, Genevieve shot Ali a grateful look.

She wanted to reach out and touch him because he was trying to help. He looked incredibly masculine tonight in his white Arab robe, and though the robe covered him, it seemed to her as though she could still see him as he had looked last night: the tautly muscled shoulders, the broad chest, the narrow waist and hips and the strong legs that had bound her to him.

When she had awakened this morning, he had been gone, but on the pillow next to hers there had been a single gardenia, and she had remembered that in the moment of intense passion he had said, "Your skin is scented with gardenias. Are you like that all over?"

Her hand crept up to touch the gardenia she had pinned to the V of her pale green kaftan, and a flush of color rose to her cheeks. She looked across the table and saw in the darkness of Ali's eyes that he, too, remembered.

Now, in a voice that only she knew he had to strive to control, he asked, "Did you enjoy the museum, Elzakir?"

"Yes, my lord."

"When the wives of our foreign visitors come," he said, addressing the other women, "you'll be accompanying them to the museum and the university."

"We are going out?" Zaida asked.

Genevieve nodded. "You'll be participating in the conference. That's why we're all together at dinner tonight, to discuss our plans. From now until the conference, you'll be having dinner with your husbands several times a week." She inclined her head toward Sheik Turhan. "With your permission, sir."

"Of course." He leaned over and pinched Zuarina's cheek. "I like having Zuarina with me. But she's too thin, yes? I must fatten her up before the wedding day comes." He took a date from his plate and held it to her lips. "Eat, my sweet pigeon," he crooned. "I like my women with more meat on their bones."

Obediently Zuarina opened her mouth and took the date. But her eyes were cast down, and her face grew pale.

Across the table from her, Genevieve saw Rupert's face tighten. How could he bear to have Turhan touch the woman he loved like that? She looked at Ali. He, too, was watching Rupert, and there was a strange, almost angry expression on his face.

You're his friend, Genevieve wanted to say. Can't you help him? But she knew in her heart that no one could help Rupert. He was in a precarious situation, out of his element in a foreign country with a way of life so different from his own. She didn't know what the penalty was for kidnapping in Kashkiri, but she knew that it would be harsh. Kashkiri, as with many other Arab countries, believed in capital punishment for offenses much less serious than kidnapping.

A chill of fear went through her, for Rupert and for Zuarina, who was her friend.

All through dinner Turhan insisted on feeding Zuarina tidbits from his plate: a slice of orange, a fig, a cream-stuffed date. And each time he lifted something to her mouth, his fingers lingered against her lips.

He touched her constantly, with pats and little pinches. He stroked her hand and crooned, "Eat, little dove. Eat for Turhan."

First he fattens her up, Genevieve thought with distaste, then he tests to see if she's plump enough for the coming meal.

She looked at Rupert again. His face was tortured, his eyes downcast, his mouth set in a hard line. Genevieve wanted to weep for him and for Zuarina, who, for as long as Turhan desired her, would have to submit.

Making love could be so beautiful with the one you loved, Genevieve thought sadly, but how terrible it must be if you weren't in love. And she resolved that when she and Ali were alone, she would plead for Rupert and Zuarina and ask him to intercede with his father.

She would do it tonight, if he came to her.

He came, but it was late.

"You knew I would come?" he asked with a smile.

"I hoped you would." Genevieve got up from the chaise to greet him. She wore a sheer ivory satin nightgown, and her pale hair hung softly about her shoulders. She touched his face. "You look tired," she said.

"I had a long session with my father after dinner." He cocked one eyebrow. "Congratulations, Genny. I didn't think you'd pull it off, but you did."

She grinned at him. "It wasn't the success I had hoped for, but it was a beginning. Elzakir at least made an attempt to talk, and so did Zaida. I'd hoped Zuarina would, but . . ." She shrugged.

"But my father didn't give her a chance. Is that what you're trying to say?"

Genevieve nodded. "She doesn't love him, Ali. She loves Rupert. Can't you do something? Can you talk to your father?"

"I speak to him about affairs of state. I'd never discuss his personal life."

"But Rupert is your friend." She shook her head and frowned. "I wish he'd run away with her. I wish he'd sling Zuarina over his shoulder and run like hell. I wish—"

Ali grasped her upper arms. His fingers bit into her flesh. "You don't know what you're saying," he said. "If Rupert and Zuarina ran away together, and if my father caught them, as he most certainly would, they'd be sentenced to death."

"You . . . you can't be serious."

"I'm deadly serious. Stay out of this, Genny. As soon as the conference is over, I'm going to send Rupert back to England."

He wished things weren't like they were. He had tried to bring about changes, but changes took time. His father was a strong man, an even stronger ruler. He could be reasoned with, but he couldn't be pushed. He'd dug his heels in when Ali had suggested the conference, but he had finally given in. At first he'd said that he wanted only other Arab countries to participate. It had taken all of Ali's powers to convince his father that Japan and some of the Western countries should be invited, too.

There had been another battle when Ali had wanted a New York public relations company to assist in setting up the conference, and yet another when Turhan discovered that the Jordan of Cunningham, Tabler, Randall and Jordan was a woman.

One hell of a woman. Ali drew Genevieve into his arms. He felt the tension in her body and knew that she was still upset about Rupert and Zuarina, and though he knew he shouldn't interfere, he said, "I'll talk to my father, but he wants Zuarina. He won't give her up."

"But you'll talk to him."

"Yes." He tilted her face for his kiss. "Now can we go to bed?" he asked.

"I thought you'd never ask," she answered in a throaty whisper.

His eyes went smoke dark. He took her hand and led her into the circle of light from the bedside lamp. "Lift your arms," he said, and when she did, he pulled the gown over her head and tossed it aside. Then he looked at her slowly, drinking in every sweet line of her body. His gaze lingered on the rise of her breasts, the rosy nipples, the flare of her hips and the long and shapely legs.

He lifted the long blond mane off the back of her neck and, encircling that slender white column with his hand, he brought her closer.

Her lips parted. The pink tip of her tongue came out to touch the corner of her mouth. "Now you," she whispered. "Take off your robe, Ali."

He pulled it over his head. She looked at the low-riding briefs.

"You take them off," he said.

She put her hands on the bare skin of his waist, and he shuddered. She ran her fingers under the elastic and pushed the briefs down to his thighs, then reached around and began to caress his round, firm buttocks before she slipped the briefs down to his ankles.

He kicked them aside and reached for her.

"Wait," Genevieve said gently, and began to caress him.

His body began to shake, and he reached for her. He ran his hands over her breasts and rubbed his palms across the tender peaks.

Genevieve put her hands on his hips and, when she sat on the edge of the bed, she drew him to her. She rested her face against his stomach and kissed him there. When she felt his muscles contract under her lips, she put her arms around his hips and drew him closer and began again to caress him. When his body shuddered, she bent her head and feathered kisses where her hands had caressed.

Ali gripped her shoulders. His fingers dug into her skin. He threw his head back. The cords in his neck stood out, and he moaned aloud into the silence of the room until, no longer able to bear the sweet torture, he broke away.

Quickly he eased her back onto the bed and, covering her body with his, he surged into her, once, twice. Deep and hard.

Genevieve whimpered in pleasure, and gripping his shoulders, she lifted her body to his. It was too fast, too strong, too good.

She began to spin out of control.

"Yes!" His breath came hard and fast. "Oh, yes," he whispered, and with a force that shook them both, it was finished.

Ali tightened his arms around her and held her so close he could feel the frantic beat of her heart against his. He soothed her with his hands and rested his face against the tangle of her hair.

"Genny," he whispered when he got his breath. He kissed her again and again. "My Genny," he said, and held her until her breathing evened and she slept.

He knew that he should leave. Last night he had awakened just as dawn streaked the sky. He'd barely managed to slip back into his own garden before the gardeners came to clean her pool and refill it with fresh gardenias.

There must be no hint of scandal. Talk would not affect him, but it would hurt Genny. His father would be amused, but the harem women would gossip, the ministers would know and whatever confidence in her ability they'd had would be lost.

But oh, he wanted to sleep here with her. He wanted to curl his body against hers and feel that sweet round bottom against him. He wanted...

With a smothered groan Ali made himself move away from her. She murmured in her sleep, but she didn't awaken.

He slipped from the bed and stood for a moment looking down at her. Her face was relaxed in sleep, her lips still swollen from his kisses. He pulled the sheet up over her bare shoulders, then bent and kissed her brow.

"Until tomorrow," he whispered.

But Ali didn't see her the next day. News came while he was having breakfast that the forces of Omar Haj Fatah had gathered in Rus al D'hran, a village one hundred and fifty miles from Kashkiri City.

"I've called out the army," Turhan informed Ali and the ministers at a hurriedly called meeting that morning. "They'll reach Rus al D'hran in a few hours and wait on the outskirts of the city until I give the command for an attack." He turned to Ali. "The air force is on the alert. We may not need them, but I want you to contact Colonel Ridaya. If Haj Fatah advances, I'll want them called out. You'll act as liaison."

Ali nodded. "The conference is less than a month away. Haj Fatah has to be stopped soon, or we'll have to cancel it."

"No!" Turhan said furiously. "That's why he's doing this. That's what he wants." He began to pace up and down the meeting room. "The conference is our opportunity to take our place not only in the Arab community, but in the Western world, as well." He slammed a fist against his open

palm. "By Allah, I won't let him get away with it. I won't
let anything interfere with the conference. I want that bastard and I want him now." He looked around the room.
"Understood?"

The ministers, their faces grave and filled with worry,
nodded.

"There'll be no talk of canceling the conference," he said
to Ali. "It won't take me a month to wipe him out. The
minute he makes a move, I'll go in and hit him with everything we've got." He looked around the room at his ministers. "I don't want any of you to leave the palace without
bodyguards, especially you, Ali. You're not to leave the
palace unless you're well protected. Haj Fatah would like
nothing better than to get his hands on you, on any of you.
And if he does . . ." Turhan shook his head. "I will not bargain with a man like Haj Fatah."

The room grew silent.

"You men are more than my ministers," Turhan went on.
"You are my friends. And you, Ali, are the son I hold dear
to my heart. But I won't deal, not even for you."

Turhan studied the map spread out in front of him. "Ali,
I want you to contact Colonel Ridaya. Tell him I want every
available plane fueled and ready. You're to coordinate
things."

"Yes, Father."

"Tell the American woman to stay in the harem. Under
no circumstances is she to go outside. Omar Haj Fatah
would like nothing better than to get his hands on her. And
tell Rupert Matthews I want to see him. He may be able to
help in keeping this out of the press."

With a brief nod Ali left the meeting room. He'd call
Rupert first, he decided, then he'd phone Genny.

He hurried down through the corridors to his quarters.
Passing one of the servants, he said, "I'll be leaving the

palace. I want a car and two armed guards at the front gate in twenty minutes.''

"I will see to it, *sidi*.''

Once in his rooms Ali went directly to a wall closet, slid back the doors and took down a shoulder holster. The gun was in a drawer at the back of the closet. He checked it and, when he came out into the room, he took his robe off, put a shirt and trousers on and strapped the holster and the gun over the shirt before he picked up a loose-fitting jacket. That done, he dialed Rupert's quarters. He drummed his fingers impatiently on the telephone until a voice said, "Mr. Matthews's rooms. May I help you?"

"This is Ali Ben Hari. Let me speak to him."

"I'm sorry, sir, but Mr. Matthews is not here."

"Where is he?"

"I'm not sure, sir, but I believe he went out with the American lady."

"What?" A chill of fear like the cold dagger of death stabbed into Ali's midsection. "What time did they leave?" he asked in a tight voice.

"Over two hours ago, sir."

"Where were they going?"

"To the hotel, I believe. The lady needed to check on something there."

Ali pressed his fingers against his forehead.

"Call me the minute they return." He hung up, then quickly placed a call to the hotel. He asked for the manager. When he came on the line, Ali said, "This is Ali Ben Hari. Miss Jordan had an appointment with you this morning."

"Yes, Mr. Ben Hari. Her appointment was at nine."

"Is she still there?" Ali glanced at his watch. It was a few minutes after twelve. "I'd like to speak to her."

"I'm sorry, sir, but Miss Jordan isn't here."

"What time did she leave?"

"Miss Jordan never arrived, Mr. Ben Hari. Perhaps she forgot or—"

Ali put the phone down and leaned against the wall, his hands covering his eyes. When he straightened, he picked up the phone and asked for Haifa.

"Have you heard from Miss Jordan since she left the palace?" he asked.

"No, sir. Is anything the matter, sir?"

"Perhaps. Did she mention going anywhere besides the hotel?"

"No, Mr. Ben Hari. She said she had to check on a room there."

It doesn't mean that something has happened to her, he tried to tell himself. She and Rupert may have decided to go the museum instead of to the hotel. Perhaps they lost track of time. Perhaps...

He dialed the captain of the police and, when the captain came on the line, Ali told him that both Genevieve and Rupert might be in trouble. "I want every one of your available men out looking for them," he said. "She's an American, fair skinned, light golden hair..." He put a fist against his mouth, unable for a moment to go on. "There'll be a handsome reward for the man who finds her."

He had to tell his father. He... Ali sucked his breath in. His father's words, "I will not deal with a man like Haj Fatah," came back to him.

If Turhan wouldn't deal, even for him, he would not raise a finger to help Genevieve or Rupert.

If Haj Fatah had her... Ali's hands tightened into fists. "If you touch her, I'll kill you," he said aloud.

He glanced at his watch. He had to talk to Colonel Ridaya. He picked up the phone again. "Colonel Ridaya," he snapped. "This is Ali Ben Hari."

Ridaya came on the line. "I know of the situation with Haj Fatah," he said immediately.

"I want your planes fueled and ready."

"They will be ready, sir."

"Very well. You'll be contacted."

Ali left his quarters and hurried through the corridors. If Omar Haj Fatah had Genny and Rupert, it would be Turhan he would be in touch with. His father had to know.

All of the ministers had left the meeting room except for Madih. Turhan looked up from the map spread in front of him when Ali entered. "Did you contact Colonel Ridaya?" he asked.

Ali nodded. "The planes will be ready for takeoff."

"Good. Haj Fatah hasn't left Rus al D'hran. He—" Turhan paused. "What is it?" he asked. "What has happened?"

"I think Rupert and Miss Jordan have been taken."

"What in the hell are you talking about?"

"They left the palace this morning for a nine o'clock appointment at the hotel. They never arrived."

"Zfft!" Turhan spit out. "Why couldn't she have stayed in the harem with the other women? That's where she belongs." He took a breath. "Have you alerted the police?"

Ali nodded. "I'm leaving for there now."

"They're capable of handling things."

"I want to be there."

Turhan started to object, then he shook his head and said, "Go then." But as Ali started out the door, Turhan said, "Ali!"

He turned, waiting.

"If he has them..." Turhan's mouth tightened into a straight line. "I will not bargain with the bastard."

Ali stared at his father. "I know," he said.

The police could find no trace of either Genevieve or Rupert.

Ali had never been afraid of anything before, but he was afraid now. If anything happened to Genny... No, he couldn't think about that now. He had to think clearly; he had to think the way Omar Haj Fatah did.

He thought of what he would do to Haj Fatah when he got his hands on him, and every barbaric thing he'd ever heard or read about came back to him, things his ancestors had done to their enemies, things he would do slowly and with an unholy joy if Haj Fatah so much as put a hand on Genny.

He spent the rest of the day with the police, but kept in constant communication with the palace. Haj Fatah's forces had not moved from their position in Rus al D'hran. He spoke to Colonel Ridaya. The planes were fueled and ready.

At seven o'clock he went back to the palace. A servant said, "Your father is at dinner, *sidi*. He asked that you see him the minute you arrived."

With a nod Ali hurried to his father's apartments. Two of his ministers were with him. Zuarina sat by his side.

"Any word?" Turhan asked.

"None."

Turhan waved him toward a place at the table. "You must eat," he said.

"I can't."

"My lord, Turhan, has told me that Miss Jordan and Mr. Matthews have disappeared." Zuarina's face was very pale. "Has there been any word of them, Mr. Ben Hari?"

"I'm afraid not."

She lowered her eyes, but not before he saw the fear there.

"Everything is being done," he said gently. "We'll find them, Zuarina. We—"

A servant burst into the room. "Sheik Ben Hari..." He put a hand to his chest as though to catch his breath.

"Yes? What is it? Speak up, man."

"It's the Englishman? He—"

Ali started toward him. "You've heard? What is it? Did he call? Did he—"

"He's here, sir."

"Here?"

"A car drove into the patio only a few moments ago. They threw him out. He's badly hurt. He—"

Zuarina jumped up. Her eyes were wide with fear.

"I've sent for the doctors, Sheik Turhan. The servants are bringing the Englishman now." He turned back to the corridor. *"Alla, alla!"* he called out. "Hurry!"

They carried Rupert in on a litter. Ali rushed to his side, and gasped when he saw Rupert's torn clothes and bloodied face. He knelt beside his friend, but before he could speak, Zuarina ran forward and flung herself down beside Rupert.

"Rupert!" she cried. "Open your eyes, my love." She kissed his bleeding lips. "Oh, love, please!"

There was a shocked silence. Ali swung around. His father's face had gone a mottled purple; his eyes were dark and threatening.

Ali put a hand on Zuarina's shoulder. "I must speak to him," he said gently.

She raised her tear-filled eyes. "He mustn't die," she whispered. "Oh, please, Ali Ben Hari, don't let him die."

Rupert's eyelids flickered. "They have her," he said in a voice so low Ali could barely hear him.

Zuarina grasped his hand and covered it with kisses. "Rupert," she wept. "Oh, Rupert."

He raised his hand and touched her cheek.

Ali turned to one of the servants. "Take her back to the harem," he said. "Quickly. Get her out of here."

She looked at Rupert.

"Best you go," he whispered.

Zuarina pressed her delicate hands to her mouth. "Take care of him, Ali Ben Hari," she begged.

"I will," he promised. "Go now."

He watched her turn away. She looked at his father, then, openly weeping, ran out of the room.

Ali knelt down beside Rupert again. "Can you tell me what happened?" he asked.

"We were on our way to the hotel." Rupert closed his eyes. "Car pulled alongside. Forced us to stop. Four men."

"What kind of a car?"

"Mercedes. Gray." He opened his eyes. "Shot the driver. Pulled us out of our car into theirs."

"Where did they take you?"

Rupert shook his head, winced and said, "Blindfolded. Somewhere in city. We..."

His voice trailed off.

"Water!" Ali yelled, and a servant handed him a glass. When he turned to take it, he saw his father and stiffened because he'd never before seen such rage on his father's face.

He held the water to Rupert's lips.

"They kept us there." Rupert drank. "Tied us, put us in a dark room. Hot. No food, no water." He tried to sit up, gasped and fell back on the litter.

"Take it easy."

No food or water. Bile rose in Ali's throat, and he clamped his teeth together to keep from being sick.

"Came for me. I fought, I didn't want to leave Gen." He grasped Ali's hand. "Sorry, Ali. Too many of them. Hurt me pretty bad."

"The doctors are on their way."

Rupert grasped Ali's hand. "Omar Haj Fatah's men . . . They said . . . tell you . . ." He fought to get the words out. His eyelids fluttered. "Call off the conference or she . . . Gen . . . They'll kill Genny."

Ali bent over his friend. "Can you tell me anything?" he pleaded. "Think, Rupert! What part of town did they take you to? Do you have any idea?"

"Remember tracks, railroad." He put a hand to his head as though trying to collect his thoughts. "Maybe . . . maybe ten minutes later they turned off highway."

Two doctors hurried into the room. Ali squeezed Rupert's shoulder. "The doctors are here," he said. "They'll take care of you."

"Want to help, Ali. Sorry . . ." He winced. "She's an American. They won't hurt her." He brought Ali closer. "Zuarina," he whispered. "Your father knows. Protect her."

"I will." Ali nodded to the doctors and, when they began to examine Rupert, he went over to his father.

"Your friend is a dead man," Turhan said. He looked at Ali through eyes narrowed with anger. "You knew about this?"

"Genny told me."

"If he has touched her, I will have him castrated before I kill him."

Ali gripped his father's arm. "I know Rupert and I trust him with my life. Believe me, their love has been innocent."

"I'll have her banished, put out on the street with the other common prostitutes."

"Father, please . . ." Ali ran a hand over his face. I don't have time for this now, he thought. I've got to find Genny. Find her before . . . But Rupert was his friend, and he said,

"Sometimes love happens. Whether you seek it or not it comes, and there isn't anything you can do about it."

Some of Turhan's anger faded. "I said I would not bargain with Omar Haj Fatah and I won't. Not even for you, Ali. But I'll release you from your duties here and pray to Allah you find her in time."

It was something. He touched his forehead and his chest, then bowed.

"Take your guards when you go."

"I will." Ali hesitated. "There is something else I would like to ask of you, Father."

"If it's about your English friend—"

"It is. I ask you, for me, to do nothing in haste. Wait until this emergency with Haj Fatah has been resolved. Speak to Rupert then, and to Zuarina. I'll stake my life that they're innocent, but if they aren't—"

"They have betrayed me," Turhan said. He turned, and with his hands clenched behind his back he strode up and down the room. "But I'll wait until I have crushed Haj Fatah before I deal with them."

"Thank you, Father."

"About the American..." Turhan looked at Ali. "I had planned to have the air force attack Haj Fatah's stronghold tomorrow, but I'll wait for two days. If I haven't heard from you by then, I'll order an attack."

Two days. Ali let out the breath he had been holding. It wasn't much, but it was something.

"Two days," he said, then turned and ran out of the room.

Chapter 12

Everything had happened so suddenly. She and Rupert had been talking about the conference. She'd looked up when the limousine turned off the highway onto the road that led to the hotel, and that's when she'd noticed the gray Mercedes.

"The car that turned when we did is following awfully close," she'd said. "Why don't they pass instead of crowding us?"

Rupert had swung around, then he'd turned back, a look of alarm on his face, and tapped the window that separated them from the driver. *"Yala!"* he'd yelled.

The driver hit the gas. The limo shot forward, throwing Genevieve—who had leaned forward to see what was happening—back against the seat.

"What is it?" she'd cried.

"I'm not sure, but I think we'd better get the bloody hell out of here."

She looked back at the gray Mercedes. It, too, had sped up.

"Don't let them get around us," Rupert shouted to the driver. "Don't—"

A shot rang out. The limo swerved and veered to the side of the road.

Rupert put a hand against her back, "Get down!" he ordered.

Genevieve hadn't been sure what was happening. Why would anyone want to stop them? My God, why were they being shot at?

Another tire exploded. The limo tilted, scraped rock and skidded to a stop. Bullets slammed against metal. Genevieve heard car doors slam and steps running toward them.

The door opened. A man with a rifle reached in and grabbed her. She screamed, and when she tried to fight him, he cuffed her hard against the side of the head. She shrank back, but he grabbed her wrist and dragged her out.

Two men pulled Rupert out the other side. He swung at one of them, and the other man hit him across the face with the butt of his rifle.

Genevieve saw their driver jump out of the car, shooting as he came. A man fell. Another screamed in pain and grabbed his shoulder.

A third man fired. The driver's mouth opened, and a bright red stain appeared on the front of his white robe. He fell backward onto the hard ground.

Genevieve screamed and tried to struggle free from the man who held her. He slapped her across the face. She cried, "Bastard!" and struck him with her fist. Blood spurted out of his nose.

"American bitch," another man said, and shoved her into the gray Mercedes.

Rupert lay on the floor of the car. She knelt beside him and, ripping at the scarf that covered her head, tried to staunch the blood that ran down his forehead.

"Who are they?" she whispered. "What do they want?"

"Omar Haj Fatah's men." He gripped her hand. "Be careful. They're dangerous."

"What are they going to do with us?"

"Probably hold us for ransom. They—"

The back door opened. Two men lifted the wounded man into the back seat, then got into the front. The man Genevieve had hit sat on the jump seat holding a bloodied handkerchief to his nose.

The car leaped forward. The man on the jump seat grasped Genevieve's hands and thrust them behind her back, then took a dirty rag and bound it over her eyes. She heard Rupert groan and knew the same thing was being done to him.

She tried to listen for sounds that might tell her in which direction they were going. There were many sections of the city she wasn't familiar with, but still she tried. They passed over railroad tracks. What seemed like twenty or thirty minutes went by before the car stopped. Someone reached in and yanked her out. A man said, "Move, English," and she heard them pulling Rupert after her.

They were taken into a building, down a flight of stairs. A door opened. They pulled off her blindfold and pushed her forward onto a cement floor. She stumbled and fell, then struggled to a sitting position and looked up to see them shoving Rupert into the room.

The door slammed and locked behind him.

"Are you all right?" he gasped.

"Yes. Are you?" Blood had run down his face where they'd struck him with the rifle butt.

"What...what do you think they're going to do with us?" she asked.

"Hold us until Sheik Turhan accedes to their demands, probably."

"Will he?"

Rupert looked at her, then away.

"Tell me the truth. Do you think he'll give in to their demands?"

"I don't know, Genny, but I know that Ali will demand that Turhan do something. He—"

"But he's not the sheik," she said.

The room was unbearably hot and dark, except for the light that came in through a narrow opening of glass at the top of the door. There were jagged cracks in the four bare walls. The cement floor was damp and dirty and littered with trash.

"Ali will find us," she said.

"He'd jolly well better." Rupert tried to smile. "You're an American—they wouldn't dare hurt you, Genny." Rupert leaned back against the wall.

Her knees hurt from when she had fallen, and the rope that bound her wrists burned into her skin. The heat, the lack of ventilation and the smell of the trash made her feel ill.

Hours went by. They were thirsty, but when they called out for water, no one answered. Finally, toward dark, the door opened, and two of the men who had brought them here came in.

"On your feet, English," the taller of them said. His face was dirty and unshaven. A scar ran from his nose to his right ear. He yanked Rupert up and shoved him toward the door.

"Where are you taking him?" Genevieve cried.

"He's going to deliver a message for us." The two men laughed. "A message to Sheik Turhan Ben Hari."

"For God's sake let the woman go," Rupert begged.

"Let her go? Why should we do that, English?" the other one said. He was shorter than his companion, and his skin was sallow, his face pockmarked. "She's going to help us overthrow Sheik Turhan. But if he proves to be stubborn, we'll have other uses for her." He bent down and grasped Genevieve's chin, then snaked a hand across her breasts.

When she cried out and tried to move away, Rupert brought his bound fists up and clubbed her attacker across the back of his head. The man slumped against the wall. The tall man knocked Rupert down and struck him again and again on his already battered face. The other man pushed himself away from the wall and kicked Rupert in the side.

Genevieve struggled to her feet and, though her hands were tied, she tried to put herself between Rupert and the man who had kicked him.

"You're going to kill him!" she screamed, and finally the one who had Rupert on the floor said, "Enough. We want him alive when we deliver him to Turhan Ben Hari."

They grasped Rupert under his arms, lifted him and dragged him toward the door. Genevieve, weeping, frantic over how badly he'd been hurt, tried again to go to him.

"S'awright," he managed to whisper through his cut and bleeding lips. "Hang on, Gen. Ali'll—"

"Shut up, English!" The shorter man hit Rupert on the side of the head, and he slumped. Then they dragged him away.

Genevieve was alone with her fear. They had said they were using Rupert to deliver a message. Did that mean they were going to hold her for ransom? That they were going to keep her here in this dank, dark room until Ali's father paid or did whatever they asked?

With her back to the wall, her knees drawn up to her chest, Genevieve waited. At last a man she had not seen before came in. He untied her wrists, then he went out. When he came back, he brought a pitcher of water and a dish of what looked like lamb stew.

"How long are you going to keep me here?" she asked, but he went out without answering and locked the door behind him.

She drank thirstily and, although she wasn't hungry, she made herself eat.

At last, exhausted by all that had happened, she leaned her back against the wall and closed her eyes.

"Ali," she whispered. "Oh, Ali." And with his name on her lips, she drifted into a fitful sleep.

Ali tried every connection he knew: police informants, men in prison who might have had a connection with Omar Haj Fatah, prostitutes who might have serviced Haj Fatah's men. He offered money, he pleaded, he threatened. No one had any information.

Then a break came. A young prostitute, whose name was Melea, came to the police station and asked for him. He had her brought into one of the private offices.

"I have heard you will pay a lot of money for information about Omar Haj Fatah," she said.

"I will pay."

"How much?"

"More than you will earn in five years on the streets." Ali leaned forward, hands clasped between his knees. "What do you know of the kidnapping? Do you know where the American woman has been taken?"

"No, *sidi*."

"Then why...?" He felt sick with disappointment. "Then why are you here?" he asked angrily.

"I have heard that Omar Haj Fatah sells women."

"Sells them? What in the hell are you talking about? What has this to do with the American woman? What...?" Something cold clutched at Ali's insides. He leaned forward and grasped the girl's hands. "He sells them into slavery?"

The girl glanced around as though afraid someone might be listening before she lowered her voice and said, "There is a man here in the city. His name is Faouzij. It is said that he works with Haj Fatah. They steal women."

"Women like yourself?"

She shook her head. "No, *sidi*, they take young women from respectable homes. When I heard that the American lady had been kidnapped, I thought Omar Haj Fatah might have taken her to sell. It's said in the city that she is very beautiful."

"She is." Ali let go of the girl's hands. "But I don't think that's why she's been kidnapped, Melea." He got to his feet. "Where does Haj Fatah sell the women?"

"In Jadida."

Ali nodded. He had heard rumors of the slave trade in Jadida, but he hadn't believed them because it was hard to believe that such things still happened in the 1990s. The thought of it sickened him. As soon as this was over, as soon as he'd found Genny, he'd attend to the matter of Jadida. But for now he had to concentrate on finding her. His father had given him two days. His time was almost up.

He paid Melea. "Be careful," he said when she turned to leave. "Stay off the streets until Haj Fatah has been taken. Stay with friends or in a hotel. Don't go out until the rebels have been subdued."

"*Shukran, sidi.*" She touched her forehead, then turned and hurried out of the office.

He debated telling her story to the police, then decided he wouldn't. Melea had taken a great risk by telling him about the slave trade to Jadida. On the off chance there might be someone with the police who had a connection to the trade or to the country, he'd be better off keeping the information to himself. Meantime he had to concentrate on finding Genny.

Although the police had searched the area from the railroad tracks to the edge of the city, they hadn't found anything. There was a labyrinth of twisting streets and narrow alleys there, houses and apartments, small businesses and warehouses. They had searched them all, but they'd found no trace of Genny.

He talked to Rupert again. His friend had suffered broken ribs, a smashed cheekbone and injured kidneys, but he was going to make it.

Rupert was under house arrest. At the very least, he'd be sent back to England.

When this was over, when Genny had been found, he'd try to help Rupert. But first he had to find Genny.

"Is there anything you haven't told me?" he asked Rupert when he returned from the police station that day. "Anything at all?"

"No, Ali. I'm so sorry. I should have done something. I should have taken a guard that morning. I should have—"

"You didn't know there was trouble," Ali told him. "By the time word came that Haj Fatah had gathered his forces, you and Genny had already left for the hotel. It wasn't your fault, Rupert. You did what you could. We'll find her."

Pray Allah we'll find her.

Rupert's other concern was for Zuarina. "Protect her," he begged Ali. "Nothing happened between the two of us, Ali. I swear on my mother's grave, nothing happened."

"But you do love her?" Ali asked.

"Yes, oh, yes, I love her."

Ali squeezed his friend's shoulder. "I'll protect her," he promised. "Father won't do anything until this thing with Omar Haj Fatah has been settled."

Settled. A day and a half had gone by. He hadn't slept, nor had he eaten. He spent most of his time with the police. He went with them when they searched the streets, and returned with them to question anyone who might have a connection with Haj Fatah.

On the evening of the second day they brought in a man who had been known to do favors for Haj Fatah.

Nasir Moustafa, a small man with a scrawny neck and bad breath, would admit nothing. Yes, he knew who Haj Fatah was, he said, but he didn't know him.

A policeman hit him across the face with his revolver.

"Don't!" Ali said sharply.

The policeman spit out of the side of his mouth. "He knows something, *sidi*," he said. "I've seen him with Haj Fatah's men and I've heard that he sells information to them. If anyone knows about the American woman, it will be this one."

The policeman raised his gun again, but before he could strike out, Ali said, "Give him to me."

The prisoner's eyes went wide with fear.

"I'll take him to the palace," Ali told the policeman. "We have special ways of getting information from scum like this."

That hadn't been true since the days of his great-grandfather. But Ali wondered as he looked at the man before him if he could resort to torture. If it meant saving Genny's life, could he do what his people had done to their enemies so long ago?

"Give him to me," he said again.

"No!" The man pushed himself back as far as he could in the chair. "No, *sidi*. Please, *sidi*. I'm only a poor beggar who scrounges where he can for a few coins."

Ali bent over him. "Tell me what you know," he said in a cold and deadly voice. "Or I swear by Allah—"

"I saw you and the American woman together in the museum, *sidi*. I told Haj Fatah about her, that it seemed from the way you looked at her that she was important to you." He put his hands up over his face. "But I swear to you, Ali Ben Hari, I didn't think he would harm her. I didn't think—"

Ali knocked the man's hands away from his face. "Where is she now?" he cried.

"I do not know for sure, *sidi*. But…" The man's face was white with fear. "Haj Fatah will kill me, he—"

Ali tightened his fist around the front of the man's robe and shook him hard. "I'll kill you if you don't!" he roared.

The man's Adam's apple bounced up and down. "There is a building…" He struggled to break away, but Ali only tightened his grip. "It…it is in the Zagora section of the city. They have used it before. Perhaps she is there."

Ali yanked him up out of the chair. "Take us there," he said.

"You will protect me, Ali Ben Hari? You won't let him take me?"

"The police will protect you," the officer in charge said. He motioned to one of his men. "I want five extra cars," he snapped. "Everybody's to be armed." He brought out handcuffs and cuffed Nasir Moustafa. "If you're not telling the truth, I'll turn you over to Ali Ben Hari," he warned, and shoved Moustafa ahead of him out the door.

Ali sat in the lead car next to the police captain, every muscle in his body tense. He leaned forward as though to make the car go faster.

I'm coming, Genny, he said over and over again in his mind. I'm coming, my darling.

The door clicked open.

Genevieve blinked. The light from the other room hurt her eyes, but after a moment or two she recognized the sallow-faced man who'd kicked Rupert, the man who'd had his hands on her.

She shrank back against the wall. He laughed and, reaching out, he pulled her to her feet. "We're moving," he said. "I wish I could keep you here, but I've got my orders." He grabbed her wrists and tied them together. He grasped her chin and said, "We've got a little time before we leave, time enough for you to be nice to me."

He pulled her up against him. He smelled of raw garlic and sweat. Genevieve's stomach tightened. "Ali Ben Hari will kill you if you touch me," she said.

"He'll never find me, woman. Nor will he find you. You're going to a place where no one will find you." He slid his hand down over her hips and around to her backside. "Nice," he murmured, and his breath came fast. "Nice."

She brought her knee up, fast and hard. He whoofed in pain, clutched himself and backed away. "American bitch," he managed to say. "For that I'm going to—"

"You're going to do nothing," the man in the doorway said. "If Omar finds out that you've so much as laid a hand on the woman, he'll have your head. If there's a mark on her, I'll tell him you put it there. He's getting a king's ransom for her, you fool. She'll bring more than any of the others, and we'll both get a cut of it." He took a small revolver out of his pocket and waved the other man away. "Go get the car," he ordered. "We've got to be at the meeting place within the hour. That's where they're picking her up."

The sallow-faced man, bent over and holding himself, hurried out of the room.

"Listen to me . . ." Genevieve wet her lips. "Ali Ben Hari is a rich man. He'll pay you—"

"He'll pay us with a sword in our bellies."

"No . . . wait . . ." She fought for the words to make him understand. "He'll double whatever you're getting from Omar Haj Fatah. Take me back to the palace. I'll protect you. He'll pay you double . . . triple what Omar Haj Fatah will pay."

"Money would do me no good if Omar Haj Fatah found what I'd done." He shoved Genevieve toward the door. "It won't be so bad," he said. "Maybe you'll be lucky enough to find a master who'll be kind to you."

"A master?" Genevieve stared at him. "What . . . what are you talking about? Where are you taking me?"

"To a place where Ali Ben Hari will never find you," he said. "To Jadida."

"Jadida?" The name had no meaning for her. She knew almost all of the Arab countries. But Jadida? She'd never heard of it. She . . . Suddenly Genevieve's mouth went dry, and her heart began to pound so loudly she was sure he could hear it. Haifa had told her there were two countries where slaves were still sold. One was Oajdaa; the other was Jadida.

Trembling so badly she could barely speak, she managed to say, "Call Ali Ben Hari. Talk to him. He'll give you anything. I swear—"

"That's enough!"

"Please—"

"Enough!" He raised his hand as though to strike her, then, thinking better of it, he shook his head and said, "You need a strong master, American, a man who will tame you.

I'm sorry that I won't be the one to take you to Jadida. I'd like to see for myself the man who will buy you.''

He grasped her wrists. She pulled away from him and in the struggle felt her gold bracelet break. When he let her go, she started to stoop down to retrieve it, then hesitated and instead brushed it aside with the toe of her shoe.

"Come on," the man who held her said. He put his hand on her shoulder and shoved her out the door ahead of him.

The lead car screeched to a stop in front of the warehouse.

"There." The prisoner pointed a skinny finger at the dilapidated building.

"It looks empty," the police captain said. "If you've led us on a wild chase, I'll have your hide, old man."

"No, no, they've used the building before. I swear by Allah that I do not lie."

"You'd better not be lying." Ali got out of the car. He grabbed Nasir Moustafa and headed for the building.

"Surround the building," the captain told his men. "Don't let anyone get away. You, Samal, Rhama, Kouchaib and Youssef, come with me." He caught up with Ali. "You have a gun, Ali Ben Hari?"

Ali nodded grimly. "I have a gun," he said.

They ran toward the building. The windows had been broken, and trash covered the floor.

The man Samal kicked at the dirt. "No one has been in here in months," he said.

Ali shook Moustafa. "If you've been lying—"

"I haven't, my lord Ali Ben Hari. I swear by Allah that I'm telling the truth. There is a basement. Perhaps that is where—"

Ali shoved him toward one of the policemen and raced toward the stairs that led downward. His heart pounded hard in his chest. He said every prayer he'd ever known. Let her be there. Let Genny be safe. Let her be... His hand tightened around his gun.

The police captain caught up with him. "Let me go first, sir..."

But Ali rushed on ahead. There was a hall. Ahead of him he saw a small room with a table, folding chairs, a bottle half-filled with water, dishes of half-eaten food.

Allah, he prayed. Allah.

He saw the room that opened off it, and ran toward it. The door was open. The room was empty.

He slumped against the wall and put a hand over his eyes. She wasn't here. This wasn't the place. Thieves or vagabonds had used it. The man Moustafa had lied.

Ali pushed himself away from the wall and started out of the room. He kicked something and looked down. It was a gold bracelet. The gold chain bracelet he'd given her.

He cried out. The police captain ran in. "What is it, sir? What...?" He looked at the bracelet in Ali's hand. "Is it hers?" he asked.

"Yes." Ali tightened his hand around it. "Yes," he whispered. "It's hers."

Chapter 13

"I'm sorry." Turhan got up from behind his desk. "I gave the order for the attack an hour ago. My ground troops are in Rus al D'hran, and Colonel Ridaya's planes are in the air. Once and for all I'm going to finish with Omar Haj Fatah."

"Whatever the cost," Ali said bitterly.

"Whatever the cost. I'm sorry." He put his hand on Ali's shoulder. "I know you care about the woman."

"Yes."

"There will be other women."

"Dammit, Father! Don't you understand? I care about Genny. She's important to me." He tried to hold his anger in check as he swung away from his father and started toward the door.

"Where are you going?" Turhan demanded.

"To Rus al D'hran. That's where Haj Fatah will be. I'm going after him."

"No!" Turhan's voice cracked like thunder across the room. "I won't allow you to endanger yourself—"

But it was too late. Ali had slammed the door behind him.

He went to his own quarters. He'd had no sleep, except for a few hours at the police station, and nothing to eat for over a day. He asked his manservant to bring him coffee and something to eat, then stripped and got into the shower. He turned the water to cold and stood under it until he felt numb but more alert than he had before.

He phoned Colonel Ridaya. "I want a copter ready for takeoff in thirty minutes," he said. "I'm going to Rus al D'hran."

He made himself eat, then dressed in a clean black robe, strapped a bandolier around his chest and took an automatic rifle from the rack at the back of his closet.

The copter was waiting for him on the roof. He strapped himself in. "Let's go," he said to the young pilot.

It took over an hour to reach the site of the battle.

"Landing's going to be risky, sir." The pilot motioned toward the other helicopters in the area and the Pitts Special S-2As that were strafing the advancing rebel troops.

A voice came over the radio. He listened and said, "We're being advised not to attempt to land this close to the fighting. There's a landing area about ten miles out of town—"

"Put it down there." Ali indicated a clearing off to the right.

"But, sir—"

"Now, soldier."

The copter pilot's jaw tightened. He swooped down. Antiaircraft fire belched up from below. The pilot darted a glance at Ali. "The colonel will kill me if anything happens to you," he muttered.

"If it happens to me, it'll happen to you, too. You won't have to worry about the colonel."

Another blast came from below. The copter bounced.

"Steady," Ali said. "Steady, son."

They were over the clearing. Ali unstrapped his safety belt, ready to jump before it touched ground. Eight feet from touchdown, he turned back to the pilot. "That was damn good flying," he said. "I'll see that you get a promotion." Then, with a quick salute he dropped to the ground and watched to make sure the copter got out of the area before he turned and ran toward the fighting.

Minutes merged into hours. There was no sense of time, only of battle, of hand-to-hand-fighting, of dust and sweat and the cry when a comrade or an enemy fell. The last time he'd fought like this had been five years ago, in a battle with the tribes of the Taziris. He'd forgotten the terrible cacophony of noises: of rifle and cannon, of planes overhead and the whirr of rotors when the copters swooped low to lift wounded or drop supplies.

Ali fought alongside his father's men. When their commanding officer went down, he was the one who took charge. He drove the men on toward the front lines of Omar Haj Fatah's defenses, and passed the word from man to man that Omar Haj Fatah was not to be killed; he was to be taken alive.

Night came, and still the battle raged. Casualties mounted on both sides. Bright streaks of orange gunfire shot through the darkness of night. Ali and his men crept forward. When the fire became sporadic, they rested. He tried to put Genny out of his mind and concentrate on what he had to do. He had to defeat the rebel army of Omar Haj Fatah; he had to find Haj Fatah and force the truth out of him.

In those lonely and fearful hours he was tortured by thoughts of Genny. Where was she? What had they done to her? Had they harmed her? Was she alive?

He thought of what he would do to Haj Fatah if Genny had been harmed. Every barbaric thing that man had ever done to man burned through his brain with a kind of evil relish. Omar Haj Fatah would tell him where she was. He'd beg to tell him before he was through with him.

Just before dawn they inched forward and, when the first gray light streaked across the sky, they attacked with everything they had.

It lasted for two hours before the other side raised the white flag of truce and threw down their arms to surrender.

Ali and the other officers went forward to meet with the officers of Haj Fatah's army. The men had rounded them up, and they had been bound, arms behind their backs.

"Where is your leader?" Ali tightened his hand around his rifle. His face showed all the strain of battle. "Where is Omar Haj Fatah?"

"He's dead," a man down the line of prisoners said.

Ali swung around. "Who said that?"

"It was me, Excellency." A man in a torn and dirty robe stepped forward. "I saw him fall early this morning."

"Liar!" Ali shouted. "You're protecting him. You—"

"I, too, saw him fall," another man said. He pointed to a distant field where many men had fallen. "It was a little after dawn—the attack had already begun."

Ali's face went white. He grabbed the second man by his shoulder and thrust him ahead. "Show me!" he commanded.

One of the officers went with him. "If you're lying," he threatened, "I'll kill you."

The man's skinny face went taut with fear. "I swear by Allah, I saw him fall. That's why we lost. Our leader was gone—the fight went out of us."

The field was littered with the dead, and the air filled with the groans and cries of the dying. This was the cost of war and rebellion, and it sickened Ali. Please, Allah, he prayed, let this be the end of it. Let there be no more fighting, no more bloodshed here in Kashkiri.

"There he is!" The skinny man stopped beside a body that lay facedown in the dirt.

Ali's heart thundered against his ribs.

The officer rolled the body over. "He's alive," he said.

Ali bent over Omar Haj Fatah. He grabbed the front of the bloodstained shirt. "Where is she?" he cried. "What have you done with her?"

Haj Fatah tried to focus with eyes already fading into death. "Where you'll never find her," he whispered.

"Tell me or I'll—"

"You'll what? Kill me?" Omar tried to laugh, but he spit blood, and with a grotesque and deadly smile he mumbled, "You're too late, Ali Ben Hari. Too..."

His eyes snapped back. He gasped, and was silent.

"No!" Ali grasped his fallen enemy's shoulders and shook him. "No!" he shouted. "Don't die! Damn you, Haj Fatah, don't die! Don't—"

"Sir?" The officer cleared his throat. "He's dead, sir."

Ali let go of the lifeless body. He raised his face to the heavens, and a great cry that came from the depths of his soul welled up into his throat. He clenched his jaw so that he would not scream aloud.

"Pass..." He fought to keep his voice even. "Pass the word. I want my father notified immediately that the battle is over and that...that Omar Haj Fatah is dead." He turned and started back across the field.

"Where will you be, sir?"

Ali stopped. Without turning he said, "I wish I knew, soldier. I wish to hell I knew."

* * *

Genevieve had been locked inside a truck with two guards—a man and a woman, both armed, both dangerous—for two days. For the first part of the journey her hands were tied and her eyes were covered. When they started across the desert, they untied her and took the blindfold off her eyes.

Several times they stopped somewhere along the road, and while the woman guarded her, the man went in and brought back hot food.

Genevieve made herself eat because she had to be strong enough so that when the opportunity came, she would have the strength to take advantage of it.

"Where are we going?" she asked. "Where are you taking me?"

"You'll find out when we get there," the woman said.

She pretended to know only a few words of Arabic, hoping that she would learn something from them if they thought she couldn't understand. But they were careful. It was only on the second day that she caught the word "Jadida."

Dear God! The guard had been right. They were taking her to Jadida.

"We'll be there by tonight," the woman said. "As soon as we're paid, we can start back to Kashkiri." She looked out of the narrow window. "I hate this damn country. It's nothing but desert."

"Desert and oil and money," her companion said with a laugh.

"But what do they do for pleasure?"

"They make their own." He winked and nodded toward Genevieve. "This one will surely bring pleasure for anyone rich enough. She'll warm some wealthy man's bony backside when the desert nights grow cold. But it's a shame to waste one so lovely on the rich."

"Don't get any ideas, Faiz. You touch the girl, and you'll never return to Kashkiri with your manhood still attached. I'll—"

The truck began to slow down. She glanced out of the window, then knocked on the partition separating them from the driver. "What is it?" she called out. "Why are you stopping?"

"The radiator's heated up," he said. "Bring me some water." He got out of the cab and slammed the door behind him.

The woman picked up a half-gallon jug and handed it to the man.

"You take it," he said. "I'm tired."

Mumbling obscenities under her breath, she opened the back of the truck and jumped down.

"How much are you being paid to take me to Jadida?" Genevieve asked in her almost-perfect Arabic.

The man stared at her. "You understand!" he said.

"How much?" she asked again.

"Enough."

"Ali Ben Hari will give you twice what you're getting if you take me back to Kashkiri."

"Ali Ben Hari will castrate me if he ever gets his hands on me."

"He'll give you enough so that you'll be able to live like a rich man for the rest of your life," Genevieve went on as though she hadn't heard him. "And I—" she made herself smile "—I'll give you whatever you ask for, too." Her tongue darted out to wet the corners of her lips. "Anything," she whispered.

His nostrils flared. "Anything?" he asked hoarsely.

"And without a fight, Faiz." She touched his hand. "That's your name, isn't it? Faiz?"

He swallowed hard. "The woman would tell. She'd kill me."

"Get rid of her."

The hood was slammed back down. She heard the woman approaching.

"Money," Genevieve whispered. "All you'll ever need, and—"

The woman climbed back into the truck. She looked at Genevieve, then at Faiz. "What in the hell's going on here?" she asked.

Faiz cleared his throat. "Nothing," he croaked. He turned away from Genevieve. "Nothing," he said again.

She knew that she had lost.

The village was little more than a community of tents on the edge of the desert. Her tent, larger than most but not luxurious, was comfortable. There were two women servants: a tall woman in her sixties, and a younger woman whose face was tattooed with stars. There were two guards outside the tent.

The women tended her as though she were a prized race-horse, or a lamb to be fattened for slaughter. She was bathed in water-buffalo milk. Her skin was oiled, and her finger-nails were painted.

They tried to tempt her with special treats: a tender breast of chicken, a choice piece of lamb, the ripest pomegranate. They brought her *baklava* and *kumafah*, a sweet pastry made with strands of butter-coated dough filled with cheese and nuts.

When she tried to fight them, the women threatened to call the guards.

"Do you want *them* to hold you down while we bathe you?" the older woman asked. "Or stuff food in your mouth? That's what they'll do if you refuse to cooperate with us."

Genevieve had no choice but to obey them, at least for the present. She could only wait and hope that an opportunity would come when she could escape.

The dialect was different here than in Kashkiri, but by listening carefully and asking for a word or a phrase to be repeated, Genevieve began to understand much of what was being said.

Every day the slave trader, whose name was Abdula, came to inspect her. A short, bearded man with four chins and a belly that bounced when he walked, he carried a whip and was always accompanied by a male slave.

It was the slave who frightened Genevieve. The man was at least five inches over six feet, and wide as a barn door. His head was shaved, and the only hair on his face was a black mustache, whose ends had been oiled and waxed and hung in a curling wave five inches down from his mouth.

He always stood one pace behind the slave trader, muscled arms across his massive chest, while the two women servants paraded Genevieve in front of their master.

"She is too thin," Abdula complained one day. He pinched the skin of her upper arm, and when she slapped his hand away, his slave stepped forward.

"Let me have her for a day, master," he said. "I will teach her to behave."

"The last time you tamed one of the women, she was of no use to anyone ever again. You'll keep your hands off this one. She's going to make me a rich man."

The slave wet his lips. "Just one night, master, and I'll be your slave forever."

"You'll be my slave forever, anyway," Abdula said with a laugh. He prodded the slave with the butt of his whip and said, "Do you think I'd give such a woman to you, you great ox? If you do, you're even more of a fool than I thought.''

The slave's small pig-eyes smoldered with anger, but he didn't speak.

''I have already spread the word that I have a rare and exotic jewel in my possession,'' Abdula said. ''The sheiks are coming from every part of Jadida to see her.'' He rubbed his hand around and around over his belly. ''I'll exhibit her the first day, but I won't let the bidding for her start until the last day. By then their appetites will be whetted. They will bid higher and higher, and when it's over, I'll be as rich as any of them.''

Abdula laughed, and with a sly look he said, ''She's not for one such as you, Brahim.'' He flicked the whip against the big man's thigh. ''Come along. There are things I must attend to.''

Brahim didn't move. ''You have given me other women,'' he said. His hands, each the size of half a ham, clenched and unclenched.

The air inside the tent crackled with danger.

In a voice so low Genevieve could barely hear, Abdula pointed to the tent flap. ''Go,'' he said, and there was something so sinister and evil in his eyes that a chill ran down Genevieve's spine.

Brahim lowered his gaze, then, like a large dog who has been chastised, he turned and left the tent.

The women who attended her talked of nothing but the festival. There would be music and dancing, they said, acrobats and snake charmers, fortune-tellers and magicians. And the slave auction, of course. That was the highlight of the festival.

Each evening, when the sun had set behind the distant dunes, they took Genevieve out of the tent so that she might walk about. She wore a black robe, a black head scarf, and instead of the type of veil she had worn when she went out in Kashkiri, her entire face was covered from forehead to throat by a thin black veil. Genevieve had heard of countries where that kind of face covering was practiced. As she stumbled about in the semidarkness, barely able to see, she wondered how the women of those countries could bear to be imprisoned by the clothes they wore, almost unable to see in order that no man but their master might see them.

Would this be her fate? Would she...? No, she promised herself. She would never submit. If Ali did not come in time, if she were sold...

The thought came once, and once only, that she would find a way to kill herself before she submitted to the indignity of the auction block. But she knew, even as the thought came, that as terrible as her situation was, there had to be hope that somehow she could escape, hope that Ali would find her.

But sometimes in the night, when the two women were sleeping, she wept with despair. How could he find her? She was hundreds of miles from Kashkiri, in a different country, a dangerous country. He would look for her in Kashkiri, and after a while, when he could find no trace of her, he would think that she was dead. And eventually he would go on with his life. His life without her.

On the morning of the first day of the festival, the women bathed and perfumed her body. They dressed her in a filmy crepe de chine jeweled and sequined top that barely covered her breasts. Arabian trousers of cotton gauze were pulled below her waist to show the lines of her body. Full and flowing over her legs, tight at her ankles, they were also jeweled and sequined strategically, so that her long legs were clearly visible.

She wore a chiffon overgown in a pale shade of green over the top and the Arabian trousers. But rather than conceal, the gown seemed only to emphasize her near nakedness.

They brushed her hair so that it hung in loose ringlets over her shoulders. They put gold earrings in her ears, rings on her fingers, gold bracelets around her ankles. And finally they covered the lower half of her face with a veil as sheer as the overgown.

When she was ready, Abdula came to inspect her.

"Ahh." The sigh, long and drawn, out, whispered from his lips. "Yes, oh, yes. She's perfect. I'll send someone for her when it's time." Abdula smiled shyly. "I'll give them only a glimpse of her today. By Friday their mouths will be watering."

He snaked out a hand and patted Genevieve's cheek before she could back away. "You're going to make me a rich man, darling," he said with a chuckle.

"You bastard!" she said in Arabic.

"Ah." He pretended to recoil. "You have spirit. Men like that—it offers a challenge." He grasped her chin. "But when you are shown, don't do anything stupid, because if you do, I will give you to Brahim. By Friday you'll be happy to be sold to someone else, anyone else."

He let her go.

The two women looked at her when he left. "Be careful," the older woman whispered. "He is a devil. If you displease him, he will do what he says."

The other woman led her to a cushion. "Compose yourself," she said. "For soon it will be time."

Genevieve closed her eyes. From outside the tent she could hear the excitement of the crowd, the music, the bleating of lambs, the squealing of pigs, laughter and song. She smelled sweetmeats and incense, perfumes, spices and camel dung. And through it all she could hear the voice of the auctioneer shouting, "What am I bid?"

A man came to the opening in the tent. "It's time," he said.

"Come." Each woman took one of Genevieve's hands and brought her to her feet. "Remember," one of them said, "do not do anything. Do not say anything. Stand submissively. Do what you're told. It will be over in a minute or two, and you will return here."

They led her from the tent into the boisterous, carnival-like atmosphere of the festival. Through a haze of dizziness she saw the colored streamers, the dancers, the acrobats and the soothsayers.

The crowd surrounding the tent grew silent and parted to let her pass.

She took a deep breath and clamped her jaw hard against the wave of sickness that rose in her throat.

"This way," the man who had come for her said.

Ahead of her she saw a young woman being led away by a man old enough to be her grandfather. The woman was weeping. The man had a triumphant smile on his face.

The auction block loomed in front of her. She raised her eyes and saw the man who stood there, hands on his hips, waiting for her.

The breath clogged in her throat. She began to tremble.

Someone led her up the steps of the block.

There was a buzz of talk, then the crowd grew silent once again.

The auctioneer took her hand and led her to the center of the block. "Feast your eyes," he said to the men who crowded around. "This is a jewel of the rarest quality. She is an American, not a girl you will have to tutor in the ways of love, but a woman of experience who will set your body on fire with passion."

Genevieve looked down into the sea of black robes and lusting eyes.

The auctioneer turned her slowly around. "Look, gentlemen, for looking is all you can do today. Have you ever seen such a form? Have your eyes ever been bedazzled by hair of spun gold, by eyes as green as the sea?" He captured Genevieve's wrists and held her arms behind her back so that her breasts were thrust forward.

"Have you ever seen such breasts, my friends? What would you give to touch them, to fondle and suckle them?"

There were deep-throated murmurs from the men who pressed even closer.

"Sell her now," one of them cried. "By Allah, would you torture us? Begin the bidding. I offer ten thousand *diharas*."

"Twenty!" Shouted another man.

The auctioneer laughed. "Save your money until Friday, my friends." He nodded to the guards who waited below. "This is the last you will see of her, other than in your dreams, until then."

He pushed Genevieve toward the guards. They took her arms and began shouldering their way through the crowd amid cries of, "I will pay a fortune for you, my beautiful one.... You will be mine on Friday, oh queen of love.... I will cast out my other women when you are mine...."

She smelled their sweat; she felt their hot breaths.

She would have fallen if the guards had not held her, but she made it back to the tent before she fainted.

Chapter 14

On Thursday night the women who guarded Genevieve gave her a sleeping potion. In the throes of a dream she cried out for Ali, and coming awake she heard one of the women whisper, "I cannot help but feel sorry for her. Poor woman, never again will she see the man who walks in her dreams."

Genevieve turned her face into the pillow and, with her fist against her mouth, wept silent tears for the love she had lost, the love she would never have again.

The next morning they bathed her in perfumed water and applied emollients to her skin, then washed and curled her hair so that it fell in softly undulating waves over her shoulders.

They outlined her eyes with kohl, put mascara on her lashes and painted her lips. They hennaed the palms of her hands, the soles of her feet. And though she protested and tried to fight, they rouged the areolae of her breasts.

A storm raged inside her. She had decided, as in the lines of the poem, that she would not go gently into whatever it was that fate had in store for her. She would fight the guards when they came to get her, fight them when they put her up on the block and fight the man who bought her.

Most of all, she would fight against the sickness and the fear that even now rose like bile in her throat.

The noise outside the tent became louder, the voices more clamorous as the men who were going to bid for her discovered where she was being kept. The guards were doubled, but even then, they had trouble holding the prospective buyers away.

The women dressed her as before, but this time the outfit was even more revealing. A pale turquoise swatch of chiffon barely disguised the outline of her breasts. The chiffon trousers were cut to fit at the low line of her hips, but this time there were no jewels or sequins to hide her body.

"The overgown?" she asked. "The veil?"

"There will be no overgown or veil today," one of the women answered. "You must be displayed for all to see."

"I won't go out like this," Genevieve said defiantly.

"You will do as you are told." The older woman fastened emeralds to Genevieve's ears and an emerald the size of a thumbnail in her navel.

When Genevieve struggled, she said, "Stop this at once, or I'll call a guard to hold you. If it's necessary, you'll be taken to the block with your arms bound and a rope around your neck."

And when Genevieve stared at her in horror, the younger woman, the one with the stars tattooed on her face, said, "Don't be afraid. When a man pays a fortune for something, it's not likely that he will abuse it."

Something. The sickness threatened to come again. She had become a something.

"You'll live like a queen if you please your new master," the woman went on. "What does it matter that you will have to sleep with him? One man is the same as the next. He—"

"They're ready for her," one of the guards called out.

"Don't be a fool," the older said. "If you try anything, they'll make sport of you, and in the end it will be the same. You're only a woman—you can do nothing to defend yourself against them."

Though Genevieve wanted to fight, she knew they were right; it would do her no good to struggle. She could not allow herself to be trussed up like an animal and led, with a rope around her neck, to the block.

"Hurry it up!" A guard opened the tent flap. "They're getting impatient out here."

The two women took her upper arms. "Let me alone," Genevieve said, and there was something in her voice that made them loosen their grips.

I will *not* let them see my fear, she told herself. I will *not* be sick, or faint or cower. I will look these bastards in the eye and somehow I will survive until Ali finds me.

With his name a murmured prayer on her lips, she stepped out into the crowd.

There was a collective gasp, then silence. The guards started to take her arms as the women had done, but when they did, she said, "I don't need your assistance," and they, too, let her go.

She paid no attention to the men crowded around. With the guards surrounding but not touching her, she walked head high and shoulders back, toward the auction block and mounted the stairs unassisted. She did not look down, but kept her gaze straight ahead, away from the men that crowded in below.

"This is the one you've been waiting for," the auctioneer called out to the crowd. "Nothing is hidden from you today, all her charms are revealed. See how soft her curves, how smooth her skin. Think of owning such a creature, my lords. Think of the pleasure a woman like this will bring.''

He took Genevieve's hand. She didn't flinch, but stood as though he had not touched her.

''What am I bid?'' he asked.

''Twenty thousand *diharas*,'' a man called out.

The auctioneer sneered. ''You insult the lady, sir.''

''Fifty thousand,'' someone else shouted.

''Seventy-five.''

The bids went on, higher and higher. To two hundred thousand *diharas*, two hundred and fifty.

''One million,'' a man said.

The crowd gasped.

''One million, sir?'' The auctioneer smiled uncertainly. ''You're offering one million *diharas*?''

''You heard me.''

His voice. Ali's voice. Dear God, was her mind playing tricks on her?

For the first time she gazed down at the scores of men crowding around the auction block. Some of them had their faces partially covered, but otherwise they all looked the same.

The auctioneer scanned the crowd. ''Would anyone like to raise that offer?''

There was silence, a low rumble of disbelief and anger.

The man who had bid for her came forward. He was dressed in a black robe. A black *howli* covered most of his face. He stepped closer to the block and held up a chamois bag. ''It's in gold,'' he said. ''Count it.''

Genevieve looked down at him, and for a moment she grew faint. But she sucked air into her lungs and made herself look straight ahead.

The auctioneer took the bag.

"Give it to me!" Abdula, his fat belly jiggling with the effort, climbed up onto the block and snatched the bag out of the auctioneer's hands. He hefted, then he opened it. His eyes widened.

He looked from the gold to the black-robed man. "Give him the woman," he said.

Genevieve began to tremble.

"Come." For the fraction of a heartbeat their eyes met. Before she could speak, he grasped her hand. "You belong to me now," he said, and led her down the steps.

A man pushed his way to the front of the crowd. "You're mad to pay so much money for a woman," he said angrily. "It isn't fair that you do."

"What I do with my money is my business."

"I was prepared to pay half a million."

"And I was prepared to pay a million." Ali's hand tightened around hers.

The man swore. "I will give you a million and a half. I do not have it with me, but—"

"Step aside," Ali said.

The beefy face grew dark with rage. "Do you not know who I am, sir? I am Sheik Raja al-Kadiri."

"I don't care if you're the king of Persia. Get out of my way." Ali elbowed past the man. "Come, woman," he said, and pulling Genevieve after him, he led her to where two of his bodyguards—the two that had been in the desert with him—were waiting with horses.

Sheik Raja al-Kadiri and some of the crowd followed.

"We must get away quickly," Ali murmured to his men. "There is one who might make trouble." He took a robe from a saddle bag and handed it to Genevieve.

"How did you find me?" she whispered. "How did you—?"

"Be careful," he warned. "We're not out of danger yet."

She pulled the robe over her head, and he helped her to mount. "Let's go," he told his men. Behind him he could hear the angry murmur of the crowd.

The rode to the edge of the village, where the desert began. Other men were waiting for them there, camels saddled and ready to go.

Ali helped Genevieve off her horse and clasped her in his arms. "I thought I'd lost you," he cried. "I was so afraid, Genny, so afraid I'd never see you again."

She clung to him, weeping against his shoulder, unable to speak because the terror of the past days and nights was still with her. She couldn't believe that Ali was really here, that he'd come to take her away.

"We should go, *sidi*," one of the guards said. "I don't like this place."

Ali held her away from him. "Are you all right?" he asked. "Are you able to travel?"

"Yes." She managed a smile, but she didn't want to let him go. She wanted to keep holding onto him because if this was a dream, she didn't want it to end. She touched his face. "I knew you'd come," she said.

They rode straight out into the desert. Four of his bodyguards led the way, two followed behind. Genevieve had no idea where they were going, but she was with Ali—that's all that mattered.

An hour out of the village one of the guards called out, "We're being followed." Ali wheeled his camel around, but the guards said, "There are only three of them, *sidi*. You and the woman go on—we'll handle this."

"It will be Sheik al-Kadiri, the man from the auction. Be careful."

"Have no fear." The guard laughed, then with a whoop he raised his rifle over his head and, whacking his camel, started running back toward the men following them. The three others followed his lead, standing in their saddles, shouting their war cries as they raced toward the other riders.

The men who had been pursuing them stopped, and as Ali watched, they turned and began to gallop back the way they had come.

They rode on until dark. Then, guided by the stars, they went on. It had been a long and frightening day, but though Genevieve was tired, she didn't complain. She wanted to get as far away from the village where she'd been held as she could. And though she knew she was safe now with Ali, she kept looking back over her shoulder to make sure no one was following.

It was almost midnight before they reached the camp where more of Ali's men were waiting.

Ali helped Genevieve off the camel. "You must be exhausted," he said as he led her toward a tent.

She shook her head. "I still can't believe you're really here." She clung to his arm. "How did you find me? How did you know where to look?"

"I questioned a prostitute by the name of Melea. She told me about the slave trade here. She said that Omar Haj Fatah sometimes sold women at Jadida, but at the time I didn't connect it to your disappearance."

He put his arms around her. "I found the place where they'd been holding you and Rupert."

"Is Rupert all right?"

"He was pretty badly beaten up, but he's going to make it."

Ali hesitated, reluctant to tell her that Rupert was being held under house arrest until Turhan decided what to do with him. He had exacted a promise that Turhan would do nothing until he returned, but he feared for his friend's life and knew that if he had to, he would defend it with his own.

He brought Genevieve back into his embrace. "The police and I went to where you were being held, but by the time we got there, you'd been taken away. I found your bracelet."

He remembered again the terrible fear he'd felt when he picked it up, the fear that had stayed with him all the long days and nights since she had been gone.

"Why were we taken, Ali? Rupert thought it had something to do with Omar Haj Fatah. Is that true? What did Haj Fatah want with me?"

"He'd gathered his forces to march on the city. He thought if he had you, he could force my father to surrender."

"But your father wouldn't have surrendered," she said in a quiet voice. "If you hadn't found me..."

He put his arms around her. "But I did find you," he said against her hair.

She closed her eyes, and it was a moment before she could ask, "What happened? Did Haj Fatah stage another attack?"

Ali nodded. "There was a terrible battle. Haj Fatah is dead, Genny. The fighting's over."

"Then the conference can still take place." She stepped out of his embrace. "But there's still so much to do," she said. "We've got to get back to Kashkiri."

"Right now all you've got to do is rest." He took her hand and led her into the tent they would share. She settled back against a pile of soft pillows, and while they waited for their dinner to be prepared, he began to tell her of the battle and all that had happened afterward.

"I didn't know where to look for you until I remembered what the girl Melea had told me about the slave trade in Jadida," he said.

He told her then of the other villages he had gone to, of places like the one where she had been held.

He had been to other slave auctions before he had heard about the festival that was to be held in a place called Sefoua.

"I was here when they showed you five days ago," he said.

Genevieve looked at him, startled. "I didn't see you."

"I didn't want you to, not then." But he had seen her, up on the block, and for as long as he lived, he would never forget the rage and the sickness he had felt when the auctioneer had paraded her for all to see. He'd wanted to take her and run with her, but he'd known that he would never have got away with it.

He'd had five days to plan, to get the money it would take to buy her, to get the guards necessary to protect her.

She was safe now, and he knew as he gazed at her that he would never again let her go. But he wouldn't tell her, not yet.

A guard brought their dinner, but halfway through the meal Genevieve's eyes drifted closed and her head began to nod.

"Sorry," she mumbled. "I haven't been able to sleep, except for last night when they gave me a sleeping potion."

"It's all right, Genny." Ali took the tray and put it outside the tent. She lay back against the pillows. He covered her with a blanket, then came down beside her and took her in his arms.

As gently as though she were a child, he began to stroke her back. "Sleep, Genny," he murmured. "Sleep, my love."

And he said a prayer of thanksgiving to Allah that she had been restored to him.

* * *

She was on the block. The men were calling out their bids. They went higher and higher, calling out, "Fifty thousand... One hundred thousand... One hundred and fifty thousand..."

"Give her to me," Brahim said.

"Sold!" The auctioneer began to shove her off the block.

Sweat glistened on Brahim's bald head. He reached up for her with beefy arms and dragged her down off the block.

"No!" The scream tore from her throat. "Brahim, no!"

"Genny? Easy, sweetheart. Easy."

"No!" she cried. "Let me go!"

"Wake up, Genny. It's only a dream. Wake up."

She trembled in his arms. "No, it's—" she shuddered against him "—a dream?" she whispered.

"Yes, love." Ali tightened his arms around her. "Nothing's ever going to hurt you again," he said. "You're here with me now." He put a hand against the back of her head and pressed her face to his shoulder. "You're safe, Genny. Go back to sleep, my love."

He held her trembling body close to his, and though he wanted her with all the passion and the fear he'd held in check since the day she'd been taken, he only stroked her and held her until at last she was once again asleep in his arms.

It was late morning before she awoke again. Because there was no pool in this desert oasis, but only a watering hole, Ali had brought a basin of water for her to bathe in. She took off the turquoise chiffon, and with a shudder of distaste rolled it up into a ball and tossed it aside. She thought of all the men who had seen her yesterday, of Ali, who had looked upon her almost nakedness, and for a moment shame flooded through her.

When she realized she still wore the emerald earrings and that the large emerald was still in her navel, she removed them. They were an expensive souvenir of her trip to Jadida, and for a moment she was tempted to throw them as far as she could out into the desert. Then she curled her hand around them and smiled. Only a fool would throw away a fortune in emeralds; she wasn't a fool.

"I didn't realize how tired I was," she said when she came out of the tent dressed in the white cotton pants and shirt that Ali had put out for her.

"You've been through a lot, Genny. You needed to rest." He glanced down at the rolled-up material in her hands.

"Bury it." She held out the emeralds. "I was wearing these when you rescued me. What should I do with them?"

The jewels sparkled in her hand.

"Wear them in good health," Ali said with a chuckle, and closed her fingers around them.

"We'll leave here tomorrow," he told her while they ate. "I have a plane waiting half a day's ride from here." He reached for her hand. "I'll be happier once we're out of the country."

"Yes, so will I."

"Genny..." Ali hesitated, then because he had to know, he asked, "Who's Brahim?"

She stiffened.

"That's the name you called out in your sleep last night."

The hand that held her fork started to tremble. "He's Abdula's...Abdula's slave," she murmured.

"Abdula?"

"The slave trader. The one you gave the gold to. He's a terrible man, an evil man. But Brahim..." She shuddered. "Brahim is monstrous, monstrous in every way. He's huge, built like an overweight linebacker. Bald."

"I saw him watching you."

"Abdula threatened to . . . to turn me over to Brahim if I didn't behave. He said he'd . . . he'd given Brahim a woman once, a woman who needed to be taught a lesson, and that after that, she was of . . . of no use to anyone."

Ali swore under his breath. He wanted to ride back to the village and wipe it off the face of the earth. He wanted to kill Abdula. He wanted to get his hands on the man who had so terrified Genny.

"When I heard your voice, when you bid for me. . ." Her eyes widened. "You paid a fortune for me," she said. "You paid a million *diharas* in gold for me!"

"You're worth every penny." Ali grinned. "If I start taking it out in trade now, maybe by the time you're eighty you'll have paid me back."

She looked shocked, then she chuckled. The chuckle turned into laughter, and the laughter into tears. Suddenly all the horror and the fear and the humiliation of the last ten days caught up with her and she couldn't stop crying.

Ali put his arms around her, and unmindful of the guards who stood at a respectful distance, she sobbed against his shoulder.

"It's all right," he whispered against her hair as he carried her into the tent. "You're safe, Genny."

At last, when her sobs had subsided to shuddering sighs, he laid her down upon the cushions and cradled her to him. He stroked her back and told her how beautiful she was.

"I love you, Genny," he said. "I think I've loved you since that night in Rome beside the Trevi Fountain."

"Ali." She gazed at him, tears still glistening on her lashes, and her eyes were wide with wonder.

"I've wanted to tell you all these weeks, but I was afraid, Genny, because we're so different. I was afraid you could never love me."

"But I do. Oh, darling, I do."

He felt the sting of tears behind his eyelids and, because he didn't want her to see them, he kissed her gently, her cheeks, her nose, and nuzzled against her ear. He kissed the white column of her throat and her shoulders. And when at last he felt her grow warm and pliant, he began to kiss her breasts.

Though his body throbbed with desire, he held himself back because she was so infinitely dear to him. He knew what she had suffered and that if he hurried her now, she might never recover from the terror of her captivity.

Reverently he caressed her breasts, and when she sighed with pleasure, he took a rosy tip between his teeth and began to softly lap and circle with his tongue.

She arched her back. "Oh, darling," she whispered, and tightened her hands on his shoulders. "Come over me," she pleaded. "Cover my body with yours. Hold me, Ali. Oh, darling, hold me."

He eased himself over her. He took her whispered breath, then, grasping her hips, he joined his body to hers. And because he had wanted this so badly, he cried out when her warmth and her softness took him in.

"Genny," he gasped. He rocked her close and moved his body against hers. "You feel so good. So good, Genny."

But how could he put into words all that he was feeling? How could he tell her of the terrible fear that he'd lived with these past days, the terror he'd known when he'd thought he had lost her. How could he tell her the thoughts that had tortured him every minute of the day and night, wondering where she was and what she might be going through.

As long as he lived, he would never forget the rage and the sickness that had gripped him when they'd brought her up to the auction block that first time. He'd seen her terror, her revulsion, seen the expression of pain and humiliation in her eyes. He'd wanted to kill every one of the avaricious bastards who were putting her through this, but he'd had to stand silently, biding his time, planning how he would rescue her.

His arms tightened around her, and he held her with all his passion, all his love and his fear. They were one now; she was a part of him now. He covered her, moved with her, held her.

Did she understand the intensity of his desire, the constant need he had to merge his body with hers, to become a part of her, to touch her, to love her?

He heard her murmured sighs of pleasure, and with a cry he rolled so that she was on top of him. "I love you," he said in a voice as frantic as the body that moved under hers. "There'll never be anyone else for me, Genny. Only you."

He reached for her breasts. She moaned and strained against him.

"Not yet," he pleaded, though his body was dangerously close to exploding.

He tried to go more slowly. He looked up at her with love-filled eyes. Her head was thrown back. Her glorious hair streamed like spun gold over her shoulders and bare breasts. She looked at him with her wondrous green eyes. She whispered his name, "Ali, darling..."

He thought he would die with loving her.

Their cadence quickened. She closed her eyes. Her teeth clamped hard on her lower lip, and she began to tremble.

"Genny!" he cried. "Genny, girl!" He rose up against her, loving her as he'd never thought it was possible to love, shaking with a passion that left him weak and spent.

She collapsed over him, and he took her mouth. "Love you," he said again and again. "Love you, Genny."

For a long time they didn't speak. He stroked her back; he kissed the side of her face. He didn't know his eyes were wet until she raised her head and said, "Ali? Darling, what is it?"

He shook his head, unable for a moment to speak. But at last he said, "I thought I'd lost you." He tightened his arms around her. "I didn't think I'd find you again."

Genevieve touched the side of his face. "When I thought I'd never see you again, I wanted to die." She kissed his tears.

"I'll never let you go again."

"No, never."

"We belong together, Genny."

"Yes, Ali."

"Swear that you'll never leave me."

"I swear."

He held her close, and at last they slept.

When she awoke in the morning, she remembered that she had sworn she would never leave him.

Chapter 15

At noon the next day they reached the airstrip where Ali's private jet waited. Only then did Genevieve allow herself to relax.

When the plane taxied down the airstrip, she rested her head against Ali's arm and closed her eyes. She'd always been afraid to fly, but she wasn't afraid now. She desperately wanted to be in the air, to know that at last she was safe.

It's over, she told herself when the plane rose above the desert and turned east toward the coast. I'm safe; I'm with Ali.

Last night she had sworn that she would never leave him. She had meant it then, and she meant it now. She loved Ali with all her heart but . . . And it was the "but" that worried her. Ali was Turhan Ben Hari's son. One day the sheikdom would be his. That meant he would never leave Kashkiri. Could she, as much as she loved him, live the kind of life she would have to live in Kashkiri? Could she give up everything she had worked for, the kind of life she was used to, to stay in Kashkiri with him?

Sooner or later it was something they would have to talk about, but because she didn't want to talk about it now, she said, "Tell me about Rupert. Is he really all right?"

Ali hesitated. They'd be back in Kashkiri soon, and she'd find out then what had happened between Rupert and his father. He didn't want to upset her after all she'd been through, but he knew he had to tell her.

"What is it?" Genevieve asked. "Is something wrong with Rupert? Is he—"

"He's recovering, Genny, but he..." Ali shook his head. "My father has placed him under house arrest."

"Under arrest?" She stared at him. "But why? Does your father think the kidnapping was Rupert's fault?"

"No, it's not that." Ali reached for her hand. "When Haj Fatah's thugs threw Rupert out in front of the palace, the guards brought him to my father's apartments. I was there when they brought him in. So was Zuarina."

"Zuarina?" Genevieve looked at him anxiously. "Go on," she implored.

"Rupert was bleeding and only semiconscious. The guards put him down, and when they did, Zuarina ran over and knelt on the floor beside him. She called him her love. She kissed him. She..."

"Dear God. And your father saw? He heard?"

Ali nodded. "I think if I hadn't stepped in, he'd have killed Rupert on the spot. When I left to find you, I made him promise he wouldn't decide anything until I returned."

"What about Zuarina?"

"She's in seclusion. I'm not sure what's going to happen to her. Father has threatened to throw her out into the street, but I—" Ali raised his shoulders "—I just don't know. I'll talk to him as soon as we return, but I'm not sure how much good it will do. As for Rupert, he'll very likely be sent back to England."

Genevieve closed her eyes and leaned her head back against the seat. He knew that she was thinking about Rupert and Zuarina, and he was sorry he'd told her because she didn't need the added strain now. She'd lost weight since her capture. There were patches of fatigue under her eyes, a pucker of worry between her finely arched brows. He wished that instead of flying back to the city, to all of the problems that lay ahead of them, they could go to the house in the desert and return once more to the oasis where they had first made love.

But they couldn't. They had to go back because of the conference. And Rupert. But once Rupert was safe and the conference was over, he'd take Genny back to the desert.

But you can't stay there forever, a voice inside his head warned. Life isn't a desert oasis; it's reality. You have to face the reality of who you are and what your responsibilities are.

Some day he would rule as sheik of Kashkiri. That was his destiny; that was what he had been born to do. He was his father's son, and he knew what his responsibilities were.

Could he turn his back on them? Could he, for Genny's sake, turn and walk away from his country, his people?

Last night Genny had sworn that she would never leave him. He knew that she loved him. But she didn't love Kashkiri; she would never agree to living in the harem.

He would make many changes when he became sheik of Kashkiri, and though it went against all tradition, one of the changes would be that a wife could live with her husband. But until then... He groaned inwardly. Would Genny agree to live in the harem until then? Would she quietly wait for the night when he would send for her?

He didn't think she would.

He reached for her hand and brought it to his lips. What was he going to do? What in the name of reason was he going to do?

An air-conditioned limousine waited at the airport for them.

"Your father is most anxious to see you, Ali Ben Hari," the chauffeur said when he held the door for them. And to Genevieve he said, "We have all been concerned for your safety, madam. It's good to have you back."

"Thank you. It's good to be back." And while she was glad to be back in the safety of the sheikdom, she dreaded returning to the confines of the palace and to the harem. That would be the most difficult of all.

A servant greeted them when they stepped out of the car. "Your father is waiting for you in his chambers," the man told Ali. "He also would like to greet the lady, sir."

"I hope you're up to this," Ali said with a grin.

"I'm up to it." She glanced at her wrinkled clothes. "But shouldn't I change before I see him?"

He shook his head. "I don't think Father would like to be kept waiting."

So once again she was back in Turhan's domain, Genevieve thought as she and Ali followed the servant. And though she hated the restrictions of the palace, after the nightmare of her imprisonment, it was a blessing to walk once again in the flower-filled patios and down the clean mosaic-tile corridors.

Turhan rose to greet them when they entered his apartments. "*Marhaban*, welcome," he said. "*Mesa al khair*, it is an evening of goodness now that you have been restored to me." He kissed Genevieve's hand, then he embraced Ali. "Praise Allah that you have returned safely, my son." He smiled at Genevieve, then asked, "Where did you find her?"

"In Jadida," Ali said grimly. "On the block, being auctioned off to the highest bidder."

"Zfft!" A look of disbelief crossed Turhan's face. "How can that happen today? What did you do? Ah, don't tell me. You were the highest bidder."

Ali nodded. "We have to do something about the slave trade in Jadida, Father. I want the men who deal in the trade and I want the man who bought Genny from Haj Fatah. His name is Abdula. He's a slimy, avaricious bastard who buys and sells women. I want to see him get what he deserves."

"I'll speak to their ambassador tomorrow. Unless I'm assured that the slave trade is halted immediately, I'll report it to the United Nations and to the Association of Arab States. As for the slave trader Abdula, I'll make his arrest a condition of the agreement."

Turhan gathered his dark robe around him as he sat down on a plush red velvet cushion. "It must have been terrible for you, Miss Jordan," he said.

Genevieve nodded. "And for all those other poor women that Abdula bought and sold."

"If you don't feel like working on the conference, I'll call in someone else."

"I'm quite all right, Sheik Ben Hari. We have two weeks before the conference."

"Then perhaps you'll arrange another dinner meeting with the wives. Please instruct Tamraz that she will sit at my side."

Genevieve moistened her lips. "Sir, about Zuarina—"

"I don't care to discuss Zuarina."

"Ali told me what happened, Sheik Turhan. I'm so sorry. I know how distressed you must be, but believe me, nothing happened between Rupert and Zuarina. She holds you in the highest esteem." She stopped and drew in a breath. "May I see her?" she asked.

"No."

"Surely it will do no harm for me to speak to her."

Turhan glared at her, but Genevieve refused to be intimidated. "I want to see her," she insisted.

"There is an old Arab saying that a good woman is a silent woman." Turhan frowned. "It would do you well to pay attention to that."

"Perhaps I will...when hell freezes over," Genevieve replied with a frown that matched his. "But right now I'd like to see Zuarina."

"All right!" Turhan threw his arms up as though to ask why Allah had seen fit to inflict him with this aggressive woman. "But don't ask me to be lenient with her. She's a wanton, a betrayer, an adulteress—"

"She's a woman in love. I know how upset you are, sir, but—"

"Upset!" Turhan's face grew red with anger, and he glared at Genevieve. "At first I was going to throw her out into the street, where she would either have starved or gone to work as a prostitute. But I have decided to be lenient. Madih has asked for her, and because he is a friend, I have decided to give her to him."

"Madih?" Of all Turhan's ministers, he was the one Genevieve liked the least. In his late sixties, he was a portly and unpleasant man with a perpetual scowl and the unpleasant habit of sucking his teeth. The very idea of Zuarina's being forced to become one of his wives sickened her. "You can't do that," she said.

"Can't? Can't?" Turhan's face turned even redder. "Get her out of my sight!" he roared. And to Ali he said, "I told you this woman would be hard to tame. But, by Allah, if you intend to keep her, you'd better tame her."

Ali reached for her hand. "I intend to keep her," he said.

The women crowded around her, and Haifa, who had never shown any emotion around Genevieve, clutched her to her bosom and kissed both her cheeks.

"What happened to you?" Zaida asked. "We heard that you had been kidnapped. Is that true?"

"It's true."

"Where were you taken?" Tamraz put her arm around Genevieve. "Did they harm you?"

"Weren't you frightened?" Fatima wanted to know. "What did they do to you? How was it that Ali Ben Hari found you? How—"

"Don't ask so many questions," Haifa snapped. "Can't you see that my mistress is tired? She must rest now. Later you can talk to her."

But the women were reluctant to let Genevieve go.

"Did you hear about Zuarina?" Elzakir pressed closer. "She betrayed Sheik Turhan with the Englishman."

"She has been taken out of the harem and is imprisoned somewhere in the palace," Fatima said.

"She will be banished," Kamilaba put in. "Thrown out onto the street without a penny. She—"

"Enough of your gossip!" Haifa took Genevieve's hand. "Come," she said, "you will bathe and then you will rest." Turning away from the other women, she led Genevieve away.

"Don't mind them," she said when they were alone. "They like nothing better than gossip, and though it might not seem so, they're concerned about Zuarina." Her face wrinkled in a questioning frown. "Is it true? Was the Englishman her lover?"

Genevieve shook her head. "No, it isn't true."

"It is said that when they carried him in, wounded and bleeding, Zuarina threw herself upon him and declared her love."

"But she and Mr. Matthews weren't lovers, Haifa." Wanting to put an end to the conversation, Genevieve said, "You can run my bath now, please, and then perhaps I'll rest for a while."

But Genevieve didn't rest. As soon as she had bathed and dressed, she phoned Turhan's secretary. "Sheik Turhan said that I could see Zuarina," she said. "I'd like to visit her to-night."

"I will arrange it, madam. I shall send someone for you."

She smiled when she put the phone down. She had won a round; she only hoped that she would be able to win the battle.

When the servant came for Genevieve, he led her through an older section of the palace she'd never seen before. The tile was worn, and the corridors were dark. There were no lovely Moorish arches here; no trees or flowering plants graced the patios.

At last they came to a room that opened off one of the corridors. The servant spoke to the guard there, and to Genevieve he said, "I'll return in one hour."

The guard unlocked the door, and Genevieve stepped into a dim entryway.

"Zuarina?" She hesitated. "Zuarina, it's Genny."

"Genny?" The young woman had been standing near a narrow window looking out into the barren patio, but when she heard Genevieve's voice, she whirled around. "Oh, Genny, is it really you?" she cried, and ran across the room to throw herself into Genevieve's arms.

For a long time Genevieve held the other woman without speaking. But at last she said, "Come sit down, dear."

Zuarina wiped her tears away with her fingertips and allowed Genevieve to lead her to a chair. "I was so afraid for you." She clung to Genevieve's hand. "That night when they brought Rupert in..." She began to weep again. "I'm such a fool," she said. "I did such a terrible thing. But when I saw him, I couldn't help it, Genny. He was bleeding, and his face was so bruised, so battered." She tried to control herself. "Is he all right? Have you seen him?"

"No, Zuarina, but Ali told me that he's recovering. He's going to be all right."

"What will Sheik Turhan do to him?"

"I'm afraid he's going to send him back to England."

Zuarina closed her eyes. "At least he'll be safe." She hesitated, and in a barely audible voice asked, "Has Sheik Turhan decided what is to become of me?"

Genevieve wanted to lie. She wanted to tell Zuarina that she didn't know what would happen to her. But the other woman looked at her so imploringly, so fearfully...

"Please, Genny?" Zuarina said. "If you know something, tell me. How am I to be punished? Will I be whipped? Thrown out into the street? What?"

Genevieve shook her head. "No..." She hesitated. "Turhan isn't going to punish you, Zuarina. But he—" she covered the other woman's hand with her own "—he has decided to give you to Madih in marriage."

Zuarina's eyes went wide with shock. "He...he can't do that. I won't marry Madih! I can't marry him!" Zuarina grasped Genevieve's hands. "Can't you talk to him, Genny? Can't you do something?"

"I've already talked to Ali," she said. "He's agreed to speak to his father." She smoothed Zuarina's hair back from her forehead. "Do you have a family? Someone who would take you in?"

"I have no one, Genny. My mother and father died a few years after I married Baraket." Zuarina shook her head. "I have no one," she said again.

"You have me," Genevieve put her arms around the other woman. "You have me," she said.

"My father is adamant," Ali said when he came to her that night after dinner. "He's determined that Rupert be banished from Kashkiri and that Zuarina marry Madih."

"Madih's old enough to be her grandfather!"

"I know, Genny, and I'm sorry. But it's better than I'd hoped for Zuarina. At least here in the palace she'll be well taken care of. She won't be harmed."

Turhan is taking her away from the man she loves, Genevieve thought. He's forcing her to marry, to *sleep* with a man she has no feeling for. Is that better than being thrown into the streets? She didn't think so. "When will Rupert leave?" she asked.

"In a few days. He's stronger now. He'll be able to make the trip." Ali went to her. "I don't want to talk about Rupert and Zuarina," he said.

"I want to help them," she said.

"I know, Genny. And so do I." Ali put his arms around her. "I haven't given up," he said. "I'm going to talk to my father again."

Genevieve nodded. Taking his hand, she led him to the chaise in front of the French doors. "We have to talk," she said.

"Talk?" And because he was afraid of what she might say, he said, "I'd rather make love."

She smiled. "So would I, but first..." She tried to think of the words to tell him how she felt. "I saw Zuarina tonight," she said at last.

He waited.

"I told her about Madih, that your father has promised her to Madih."

"You shouldn't have done that."

"Why not? When would you have her find out, on her wedding night?"

She got up and began to pace the room. "I wonder if your father would have been so upset if he'd discovered that Zuarina had fallen in love with a Kashkiran."

Ali stiffened. "What are you talking about?"

"Is it because he feels betrayed, or is it because he's been betrayed by an Englishman, a foreigner?"

Genevieve came over and stood looking down at Ali. "I'm a foreigner," she said gently.

"Genny—?"

"We love each other, Ali. I know that there will never be another man for me, that forever and always I'll love only you. Last night—" she fought to hold back the tears "—last night I swore that I would never leave you." She sank to her knees beside him and took his hands. "But I don't know how we can live together, darling. I don't see how we can ever make it work."

"What are you saying?"

"That I can't spend the rest of my life here in the harem waiting for the night when you will come to me."

"That will change when I become sheik."

Genevieve shook her head. "That could be twenty or thirty years from now, Ali. Your father's a strong and vital man. He's going to live a very long time."

"I'll insist that we live together when we're married."

Married. It was the first time he'd said the word. She leaned her head against his knee, and when she raised her face to look at him, there were tears in her eyes. "But don't you see?" she whispered. "Even if we were able to live together, I'd still be a virtual prisoner here within the palace walls. I couldn't live like that, Ali. I couldn't raise our children that way.''

Children. His and Genny's children. Something deep within him stirred.

"Perhaps it wouldn't be as difficult if we had a son," she went on. "But if we had a daughter, daughters..." She touched his face. "I couldn't raise them in a harem, Ali. You can't ask me to do that."

"But I love you." He clasped her head between his hands. "Doesn't that mean anything to you, Genny? Doesn't my love mean anything?"

"It means everything to me, darling. But I'm afraid that if I stay here in Kashkiri, if I live as a Kashkiri woman, that something inside me would die." She bowed her head. "I'm afraid our love would die."

She closed her eyes and let the tears fall.

The room grew silent. From somewhere in her garden a nightingale called to its mate.

"You're asking me to give it all up," Ali said. "Everything. My right to the sheikdom. My country. I've been born and raised to be the next sheik of Kashkiri. It's what I have to do."

"I know," she whispered.

He stood up and lifted Genevieve to her feet. "I love you," he said when he let go of her hands. "We belong together. If you love me..." The words hung, suspended in the stillness of the night.

He drew her into his arms. He leaned his face against the soft spill of her hair and felt the tension in her body.

"Genny...?" But there were no words, nothing left to say. He let her go. He ran a finger down the side of her face. "I love you," he said again.

And before she could respond, he turned and left the room.

Chapter 16

Ali almost didn't see the figure step out of the shadows into the corridor ahead of him. This particular wing of the palace was rarely used. As far as Ali knew, Rupert was the only one being housed in this section, and only because he was under house arrest.

He flattened himself against the wall. Why in the hell was the man sneaking around? Could it be one of Haj Fatah's men? A diehard out to revenge his leader?

Ali waited. The man stepped from the shadows and began moving toward the older part of the palace where the woman, Zuarina, was being held. He reached a patio and, when he began to cross it, he stopped and looked around.

A gasp escaped Ali's lips. Rupert? Good God, it was Rupert. How had he...?

Ali ran toward him. Rupert whirled. The moon glittered on the revolver in his hand.

"Rupert! It's me, Ali."

"Ali?" The hand holding the gun fell to his side.

"What in the name of all that's holy do you think you're doing?" Ali demanded.

"I'm going to see Zuarina."

"Zuarina? Don't you realize if any of my father's guards spot you, you're dead? How did you get away?"

"I told the guard I was ill. When he opened the door, I hit him and took his gun." He faced Ali. "I'm going to see her," he said. "You can't stop me."

"That's impossible. And even if you did manage to get in, you'd never get out. The guards would be alerted, and my father would have you shot."

"I'm willing to risk it." There was a determined expression on Rupert's face. "I damn well don't want to live without her, Ali. If it means giving my life to see her again, to spend one minute or one hour with her, then I'd gladly give it." He shook his head, and with a sad smile he said, "Do you know I've never even kissed her? I've never held her in my arms and told her that I loved her?"

"Rupert—"

"You can't talk me out of it, Ali. In another day or two your father's going to send me away. I've got to see Zuarina before I go, and as soon as I get to England, I'm going to do everything I can to get her out of Kashkiri."

"She's going to marry Madih."

Rupert's face went cold and still. "Get out of my way," he said.

"No." Ali took a deep breath. "Go to my quarters. I'll bring her to you."

"But—"

"The guards won't stop me. If they do, I'll say that my father sent for her." He grasped Rupert's shoulder. "Go back the way you came. When you get to the jade salon, you'll find a door at the far end. Follow the passageway. It leads directly to my apartment." He gave Rupert a gentle shove. "Go on," he said.

Ali waited until Rupert had disappeared into the shadows before he turned in the direction of the old building. He walked boldly through the corridors to the place where Zuarina was held. When he reached it, the guard shouted, "Stop! You can't come this way."

"It's Ali Ben Hari," he said curtly. "I've come for the woman. My father wants to see her. Bring her out at once."

"But I—"

"At once!"

The guard opened her door and called out, "Woman! Come immediately!"

She came, dressed in a black robe, her eyes wide with apprehension, her arms crossed over her chest as though to protect herself.

"Ali Ben Hari—"

Ali silenced her with an uplifted hand.

"Go and put a veil on, woman," he ordered. "It isn't fitting that anyone should look upon your shameful face."

She looked stunned, then she bowed her head and ran back into the room.

"What will my lord, Turhan, do with her, sir?" the guard asked.

"I don't know." Ali shrugged. "She's no concern of mine. When we leave, go into her rooms and stay there until she returns. Admit no one. Speak to no one. Do you understand?"

"Yes, *sidi*."

Zuarina appeared behind the guard. Ali grasped her arm. "Come," he said, and pulled her after him into the corridor.

She didn't speak for several moments. Then she said, "Where are you taking me?"

Ali stopped and looked behind him. "To Rupert," he whispered.

"Rupert . . . ?" She swayed and would have fallen if Ali hadn't been holding her.

"Be quiet, Zuarina. If anybody see us, we'll both be in more trouble than I want to think about."

But nobody did see them. When they reached the door of Ali's apartment, he led her inside.

"Rupert?" he called out softly.

"Thank God." Rupert got up from the sofa. "I was afraid . . ." He saw Zuarina. "My dear," he said. "Oh, my dear."

And with a cry she ran into his arms.

For the briefest of moments Ali looked at them, then he turned away and went into the other room. He stood for a moment in front of the French doors, gazing out into the garden. Then with a sigh he went to the phone. "Give me Colonel Ridaya," he said. "This is Ali Ben Hari."

The colonel came on the phone.

"I want a jet gassed and ready to leave within the hour," Ali said.

"Very well, sir. What is the destination?"

Ali smiled. "London, Colonel. Nonstop to London."

Ali had known that all hell would break loose, and it did. He had seen his father upset before, but never like this. So angry that he couldn't sit still, Turhan stormed up and down the room, his face tight with barely controlled rage.

Colonel Ridaya stood at attention, eyes straight ahead, shoulders back.

"I'll have you stripped of your command," Turhan shouted. "Who gave the order for the plane? By Allah, if you don't tell me, I'll have you flogged."

"I gave the order," Ali said.

Hassan Madih pushed himself up from the red leather hassock where he had been sitting. "You, Ali Ben Hari? It was you who sent my bride away?" He turned to Turhan. "You promised her to me. You said—"

"I know what I said." Turhan waved his hand as though shooing a fly. "Leave us. You, too, Ridaya. I'll deal with you later."

He waited until the two men were out of the room before he turned to Ali. "You call yourself my son," he said. "Would a son do this to his father? Would he betray the man from whose loins he had sprung?"

"I'm your son," Ali said quietly. "That will never change, but I make my own decisions. If there are times when we disagree, then I must do what I think is best. Only yesterday you were appalled at the selling of women in Jadida, yet you were going to give Zuarina to Madih."

"That's different."

"Is it? Did you give her any choice? Did you ask her what she wanted?" Ali shook his head. "She might as well have been your slave, Father, a woman to be sold to the highest bidder."

"How dare you say that to me? Damn you! And damn your English friend to hell." Turhan turned back to his desk and snatched up the telephone. "I'm going to call the department of immigration in London," he told Ali. "I'll have Zuarina back on the next plane."

"No." Ali took the phone out of his father's hand. "That's beneath you," he said.

Turhan froze.

"We've had our differences, Father," Ali said quietly. "There have been times when I've disagreed with you, but I've always respected you. I don't want that to change." He put the receiver back on its cradle. "Let them alone," he said. "Let them get on with their lives."

Turhan clenched his jaw. "It's the American woman, isn't it? She's the one who has made you do this. She's the one who's changed you."

"Genny didn't have anything to do with it. She doesn't know they're gone."

"But you did it for her—because she became friendly with Zuarina, because she didn't approve of my methods." Some of Turhan's anger faded, but the hardness in his voice did not. "I asked you once if you would take her for your mistress, and you told me that she would never agree to such an arrangement. I'm telling you now that you can never marry her. When you marry, it will be to a Kashkiran woman who will give you Kashkiran children."

Turhan put his hands down flat on his desk and faced Ali. "You're my first-born son," he said. "The sheikdom will be yours one day. It's your heritage—it's what you were born for. There's bedouin blood in your veins, just as there is in mine. Our ancestors fought and died for this land. Would you turn your back on it for a woman? Would you throw it all away, your country, your tradition, your birthright?"

There was sadness as well as a fierce strength in Turhan's voice. "If you marry the American, you give it up," he said slowly. "For your sake I wish it were not so, but it is. Marry the American, and you lose it all, your country and your birthright."

Ali's gaze didn't waver. "Have you finished?"

Turhan ran a weary hand across his face. "Yes," he said, "you may go now."

Ali took a deep breath. "You won't interfere with Rupert and Zuarina? You won't try to bring her back?"

Turhan shook his head. "The Englishman is your friend. I suppose I must respect that. He's welcome to Zuarina if he wants her."

"Thank you, Father."

"I will yield on that, Ali, but I will not yield on the issue of the American. It's her or the sheikdom. The choice is yours."

Ali nodded. "Yes," he said. "The choice is mine."

The harem women talked of nothing else that day.

"The Englishman has kidnapped Zuarina," Fatima announced when Genevieve came into the courtyard that morning.

"Sheik Turhan had promised her to Madih." Elzakir's eyes had held a glint of malicious glee. "I wasn't enough for the old rooster—he wanted a third wife." She chuckled. "But Zuarina didn't want him, and now she's flown the coop. It serves the old man right."

"If my lord, Turhan, finds them, they'll be severely punished," Seferina said.

And Tamraz, with a twin girl clinging to each of her hands, frowned at Genevieve and said, "You and Zuarina are friends. If you know where she is, it's your duty to tell Sheik Turhan."

"I don't know where she is." As puzzled over the couple's disappearance as the other women were, Genevieve went back to her own quarters and tried to phone Ali. His manservant answered and said that he wasn't available. She paced up and down. What had happened? How had Rupert and Zuarina managed to escape from the palace? Where were they?

She tried to phone Ali several more times that day, but the answer was always the same—he wasn't available.

The next morning her phone rang, and when she picked it up, Ali said, "I want to go to the desert. Can you be ready this afternoon?"

"Yes, of course. But why—"

"We'll talk about it later. Don't take Haifa— I want to be alone with you."

"Ali..." She lowered her voice. "I know Rupert and Zuarina have disappeared. That's all the women have talked about. What happened? Do you know where they are?"

"Later, Genny," he said.

At three o'clock Haifa came to tell her that Ali was waiting for her in the front patio and that his servant would escort her there. She picked up the small bag she had packed and followed the servant.

He had little to say on the way to the airport. It was only when they were on the plane that Ali told her that he had helped Rupert and Zuarina escape from the palace and that he'd put them on a plane for London.

"They're together," he said. "They're safe. As soon as legal papers have been arranged, they'll be married."

Genevieve squeezed his hand. "I know how difficult it must have been for you to go against your father's wishes, but I'm so grateful that you did. I'm so glad they're safe."

"Yes, so am I. God knows it's rare enough to find happiness in this world."

There was something in the tone of his voice, something in his face, that frightened her.

He remained silent and thoughtful for the rest of the trip. It was only when the plane began to circle low over the desert and she clutched the armrest that he turned and took her hand.

"Close your eyes," he said gently. "I'll tell you when we're down."

Genevieve kept them tightly closed until the plane bumped down, raced across the runway, then slowed and skidded to a stop.

"You can open your eyes now," Ali said with a smile. And when she did, she saw the car waiting at the side of the tarmac.

The chauffeur took her bag, and Ali helped her into the air-conditioned car. He knew by her expression that she didn't understand why he had brought her here; he wasn't sure himself why he'd wanted to come. He'd only known that he had to get away from the palace for a little while.

He leaned back against the leather seat and closed his eyes, and as he breathed in the soft desert air, a feeling of peace flooded through him, for this was the place he loved most in the world. He was a man of the desert, like his ancestors before him. He'd been born of bedouins, and forever and always this love of the desert would run through his veins. It was a part of his heritage; it was in the marrow of his bones. Each time he returned, it was like a renewing of his spirit. And when he left, he left a part of himself in the desert.

He looked at Genny and thought how dear she was to him, how much he loved her. He thought of what he had to do.

When they reached the villa, he said, "You look tired. Why don't you rest before dinner?"

She nodded. Worrying her bottom lip, she said, "How long will we stay? The conference is in less than two weeks. I still have a lot to do."

"I know. We'll fly back tomorrow."

"Tomorrow?" He saw the uncertainty in her eyes. "Why have we come?" she asked.

"I felt the need to sleep in the desert tonight."

Genevieve stared at him. "I don't understand," she said. "Why—"

But Ali shook his head. "Tonight," he said. "We'll talk about it tonight."

She went to her room, but instead of resting, she sat by the open window and watched the dunes turn from amber to gold in the setting sun. And though the night was warm, there was a chill inside her body that wouldn't go away because she knew that Ali had brought her here to end it between them. They'd had all they were ever going to have. This was the end; this was the final goodbye.

When the hour for dinner grew near, she bathed and, when she had done her makeup, she pulled her hair back into the chignon she had always worn in New York. The chignon had suited her there. It was only here in the desert, because that was the way Ali liked it, that she'd worn it loose over her shoulders. But she was leaving the desert. Soon she would be back in New York.

She took a deep breath and straightened her shoulders. Ali mustn't see how deeply this hurt, how wounded she was. She opened the closet door, took out a flamingo-bright kaftan from the closet and slipped it on. The color would give her courage.

Ali was waiting for her when she went into the dining room. "Would you like an aperitif before dinner?" he asked. "I've had the servants stock the liquor cabinet for the visit the conferees' wives will make. Would you like a sherry, or do you prefer vodka?"

"Vodka," Genevieve said. "On the rocks."

He raised one eyebrow, but made no comment.

The glass was cool in her hands, the liquid soothing on her tongue.

"Only ten more days," he said.

"Ten more days?"

"Until the conference."

"Yes." She took another sip of the vodka. The taste turned bitter in her mouth.

"I've ordered some special dishes for dinner tonight, typical regional dishes. I hope you'll like them."

"I'm sure I will."

Genevieve tightened her fingers around the cool glass. They were being as formal as though they'd just met. Would you care for an aperitif? Yes, thank you. Would you care for another? Yes, thank you. Shall we say goodbye forever?

Dear God, how could she bear it?

She tried to force a smile to her lips. When the dinner was served, she said how delicious it was and made herself taste a little of everything.

They lingered over the rich Arabian coffee, and when they had finished, Ali said, "Let's walk for a bit."

As they stepped out into the night that was fragrant with the scent of desert roses, they heard the faint and plaintive voice of the muezzin from the village calling the faithful to prayer. As his voice faded, there came the soft, sad sound of a lone flute, and when they passed one of the tents, they saw a robed man sitting cross-legged on the ground, playing while his wife and his children gathered around him.

Ali put his arm around Genevieve, and they stood in the shadow of the palms until the last notes faded and the night grew silent.

"Come." He led her in the direction of his tent. When they were inside, he said, "You've been very quiet all evening."

"You've been quiet since we left Kashkiri City." She clasped her hands together. "You've brought me here to tell me something, haven't you, Ali?" She drew in a steadying breath. "I . . . I think we've come to say goodbye. That's it, isn't it?"

"Yes, Genny."

She closed her eyes, and when she opened them, she said, "We both knew it had to end, that—"

"I came to say goodbye to my land, to my desert."

"To..." Genevieve stared at him. Slowly she shook her head. "I don't understand," she whispered.

Ali took her hand and led her to where the Persian carpets and the satin pillows covered the floor. "I love you," he said. He dropped to his knees and brought her down beside him. "I'm a rich man, Genny. I have oil interests all over the world. We'll live in New York or anywhere you like."

"Ali..." So stunned she could hardly believe what was happening, Genevieve clung to his shoulders. She had prepared herself for the knowledge that she must leave him, but she hadn't expected this.

"I know how you feel about Kashkiri," he said. "And it's all right—we won't have to live here. As soon as the conference is over, we'll fly to New York and be married there."

Married. This was happening too fast. "Ali..." She tried to gather her thoughts, to bring everything into focus. "This is your country," she said. "You belong here. Some day you'll become the sheik of Kashkiri. You can't... you can't give that up because of me."

"It's you I can't give up." Ali tried to smile. "By the time my father steps down, little Ismail will be old enough to take over the reins." He put his arms around her and brought her close. "I've made up my mind, Genny," he whispered. "I won't let you go."

He began to unfasten her hair. When she tried to speak, he stopped her words with a kiss. And though at first she resisted, soon her lips parted and softened.

"Ali," she said. "Oh, darling." Her arms crept up around his neck, and her body pressed closer to his.

He let her go long enough to take off his white robe, toss it aside and slip the kaftan over her head. Then he laid her down on the thick Persian carpets and took off her bra and her panties and gazed at her there in the lantern light. He ran his hand across her belly and thought how it would be when she began to swell with their child, their son or their daughter.

"I'm going to fill you with my seed tonight," he said. "I'm going to give you our child."

"Ali . . . ?" His name trembled on her lips.

"I'm going to watch it grow." He stroked her belly. "And though you're beautiful now, you'll be more beautiful then."

He rested his head against her stomach. "My Genny," he whispered. "My love."

Tears stung her eyes. "I love you," she said. "I love you so much."

He came up beside her and, when he had drawn her into his arms, he kissed her mouth. The kiss deepened and grew. Her tongue met his, and he sighed with pleasure.

He kissed her throat. He nibbled and savored each tender earlobe and the delicate skin behind each ear. Her skin was satin soft and lightly scented. He remembered the gardenia pool and how, after she swam, her skin smelled of the white flowers.

He flicked his tongue against her breasts, and she held him there with her fingers threaded through his hair, and pressed her body closer.

"Come over me," she whispered.

"In a moment, my love."

"Please, Ali. Now, Ali."

How he loved it when he knew she wanted him as much as he wanted her, when every moment delayed increased the promise of the ecstasy to come.

He patterned kisses across her stomach and her thighs. He nipped then stroked her inner thighs with his tongue, and though she said, "No, oh, no," her body began to quiver like a captured bird beneath his hands and mouth. And when he found the warm and fragrant core and touched her there, a moan escaped her lips and she said, "Oh, please, yes, please."

He held her there. He loved her there. Loved her until her body shook like a leaf caught by the wind and she clung to him, whispering his name again and again into the silence of the night. Then he came up over her and filled her with his throbbing love.

In that final moment, when together they found that peak of rapture, he cried, "I love you! I love you, Genny!"

Genevieve held him close. She soothed his hair and kissed his brow. She kissed his shoulder and licked his skin because she loved the taste of him, the scent of him. She whispered, "Ali? Darling?" but he didn't answer. His body relaxed over hers, and his breathing evened.

She knew they had to talk, but it was late and he was tired. Tomorrow, she thought, we'll talk tomorrow, then she, too, slept, warm in the comfort of his arms.

She awoke to the sound of the muezzin and lay with her eyes closed, listening, for it was like no other sound in the world: mystic and musical, eerie and solemn.

Beneath her head she felt the steady beat of Ali's heart, and when she opened her eyes, she saw that he was awake and that he, too, was listening to the call of the muezzin. She started to speak, then stopped because there was an expression on his face of love and longing, and of a belief that lay deep within him. Time could not change it, and distance would not weaken it, for this was a part of his heritage, a part of the land he loved.

She closed her eyes and knew what she must do.

When the call of the muezzin faded, she kissed Ali's chest and said, "Good morning, darling."

It took a moment for the shadows in his eyes to disappear. "Good morning, Genny." He brushed the hair back from her face. "Did you sleep well?"

"I always do when I'm with you." She sat up. "What time do we have to leave?"

"After breakfast."

"Then we'd better get ourselves together."

"There's time." He smiled, but when he made as though to pull her down beside him, Genevieve shook her head and said, "We have to talk, Ali."

"We talked last night."

"You talked."

"But—"

She pressed a finger against his lips. "It's my turn now." She reached for the kaftan and slipped it over her head because what she had to say was important; she couldn't do it without the protection of her clothes.

"You told me last night that you would leave Kashkiri, that we would live in America." A slight smile curved her lips, and she shook her head. "Somehow I can't see you spending the rest of your life in New York."

"Then we'll live in Europe." He raised himself onto one elbow. "What's this all about, Genny? What are you trying to say?"

"That I can't let you do it."

Ali stared at her. She saw the shock in his eyes.

"This is where you belong," she said. "Your home is here. You can't turn your back on Kashkiri, Ali."

"I've made my decision."

"But it has to be *our* decision, something that both of us think is right." She shook her head. "And I know that what you've decided isn't right. You'd be as unhappy spending the rest of your life in America as I'd be, spending mine in Kashkiri." She searched for the words to make him understand. "I couldn't bear watching you be unhappy, Ali. I couldn't stand knowing that after a while you'd resent me for taking you away from the life you know and love."

Before he could speak, Genevieve covered his mouth with hers. "It isn't going to work," she whispered against his lips, and knew that if a heart could break, hers was surely breaking.

They lay in each other's arms without speaking, and though he argued, she would not waver from her decision. When the conference was over, she would leave. They had had all they were ever going to have.

Chapter 17

The banquet room of the palace glittered with the light of sparkling chandeliers and glowing candles. Men, some of them in business suits, some in white robes, and women in colorful kaftans, sat together on overstuffed cushions on the floor while they watched the rhythmic undulations of a belly dancer.

This was the last night of the conference, and the guests were in a festive mood. The conference had been everything Ali had hoped for. Men from different countries, not just Arab states, but from the West and the Far East, had met together and accomplished the one important thing that he had envisioned; they had come to know one another. The business side of it would profit all of them, but more importantly the men gathered here had developed a mutual respect for one another. They would leave with a better understanding of each other and of their respective countries.

And while the men had had their meetings, Genny and the women of the harem had entertained the foreign ladies. So that the guests might take back a special remembrance of their time in Kashkiri, Genny had purchased silk kaftans in a warm variety of colors for them to wear tonight. They looked, Ali thought, like a flutter of butterflies.

And Genny was the most beautiful butterfly of them all.

It was a minor miracle that the women of the harem had taken to the role she had trained them for. At first they had been shy with the foreign guests, but little by little, with gentle prodding from Genny, they had accepted their roles as hostesses. Tonight they seemed relaxed and happy as they chatted with the wives of the visiting delegates.

This, all of it, had been Genny's doing. She was a remarkable woman, a special woman. He remembered that the first time he'd seen her in New York, he had been taken aback by her professional demeanor and he'd resented her taking over the meeting. He'd been arrogantly male those first few days they had spent together, for though he'd been attracted to her, he hadn't had the slightest idea of how to deal with her. He'd never known a woman like Genny before. She intrigued him, puzzled, angered and excited him as no woman ever had.

Without her expertise, her innate sense of how things should be done, tonight couldn't have happened. He was proud of her, and he loved her so much his bones ached with wanting her.

"The conference has been a great success, hasn't it?" his father said, breaking in on Ali's thoughts. "This morning the Texan told me that he and his associates have agreed to build the refinery here." Turhan bit into a fig. "I've been working on the deal for months, but we couldn't come to terms."

Ali raised an eyebrow.

"I have you to thank for it. After you talked to him, after you explained the benefits on both sides, he seemed almost eager to sign the contract." Turhan took another fig. "You're responsible for the conference, Ali. It was your idea. You talked me into it, and I'm grateful." He looked in Genevieve's direction. "You talked me into hiring her, too, and now I have to admit that much of the success of the conference belongs to her."

Ali followed his father's gaze. She turned and saw him watching her, and her hand went to her throat as though to still the rapid beat of pulse there. For a moment her green eyes softened, then she looked away.

She was glad that this was almost over. She had done her job; the conference had been a success. The day after tomorrow she would return to New York.

She knew that Ali was still watching her, but she would not allow herself to look at him again. They had seen little of each other since their return from the desert. He had tried to talk to her the day they left, tried to make her change her mind. "I love you," he'd said over and over again.

"And you love Kashkiri."

"I don't want it to end this way."

But Genevieve had remained adamant. She had convinced herself that if Ali left Kashkiri, a part of him would always be sorry that he had, for he belonged to his world just as she belonged to hers.

This past week she had taken a group of the foreign wives to his villa. That had been painful for her because every time she'd looked out toward the desert, she'd seen Ali's black tent. She had remembered the love they had shared there, the love that could not be.

The belly dance ended. The guests applauded, and when the applause died down, Turhan rose to his feet.

"Ladies and gentlemen," he said in English. "It has been my pleasure and my honor to have you here in Kashkiri. In this time we have come to know and to understand one another, and from now on we will deal with each other as friends rather than as strangers. Next year we'll meet in Japan. The following year in America. It pleases me that this conference has been a beginning. We will go on from here toward a better understanding, and hopefully better business for all of us.

"The conference was the idea of my son, Ali Ben Hari, and I thank him for convincing me that it was indeed a good idea."

"Right on!" the man from Texas called out.

Applause and laughter followed his remark, and when the applause died, Turhan said, "I'd like to take this opportunity to make two announcements. First, the Kashkiran ambassador to Italy retired this week, and my son Ali has accepted the ambassadorship." He smiled at Ali. "I hope you'll like Rome. I hear it is a most romantic place."

Ali smiled back. "That's what I hear," he said.

"Now to my other news," Turhan said. "I'd like to announce the engagement of my son Ali..."

Genevieve clenched her hands together in her lap. Dear God, it had already been arranged. Couldn't he have waited until she left. Couldn't he have...

"To the woman who has been your hostess here in Kashkiri, Miss Genevieve Jordan."

There was a stunned silence before the guests began to applaud. Mrs. Sumoto, the wife of the Japanese delegate, said in her careful English, "Happy news. Very happy news." And the man on the other side of Genevieve kissed both her cheeks.

Genevieve sat frozen, unbelieving, unable to move as Ali came toward her. He took her hands and brought her up beside him. "Did you really think I'd let you go?" he whispered so that those close to them couldn't hear his words.

Genevieve clung to him. "Rome?" she said. "I don't understand," she said. "Your father…your life here… You can't give it up."

"I'm only giving up a small part of it, Genny. And just look what I'm getting in return." Then, unmindful of the people all around them, he kissed her.

Later, when he and Genevieve were alone, he said, "Father would like the wedding to take place here in Kashkiri. But if you'd like to, we can have a Christian ceremony when we get to Rome."

"Yes." She took a deep breath and tried to steady herself. "Yes, I'd like that."

Everything had happened so fast. She felt as though she'd been having a bad dream and that suddenly she had awakened to find things had turned out right.

"What about your father?" she asked. "How did he come to accept our marriage? You're leaving Kashkiri…you're giving up your claim as the next sheik."

"I never wanted to be the sheik, Genny. Besides, I'm not my father's only son. I think he finally realized that. Ismail will be eighteen in ten years. He'll be the next sheik of Kashkiri." He took her hand and brought it to his lips. "Kashkiri will always be a part of me, Genny. We'll live in Italy, but we'll visit New York and Kashkiri whenever we can."

He drew her into his arms. "You're not going to give me an argument, are you?" And when she didn't answer, he kissed her. "You belong to me," he murmured against her lips. "Say it, Genny. Tell me you're mine."

She smoothed the black hair back from his brow, and with the slightest of smiles said, "Of course I'm yours, darling. You paid a million gold *diharas* for me, didn't you?" She brushed his lips with hers. "I love you, Ali," she said. "Always and forever. Only you."

* * *

The women of the harem prepared her for the wedding. After she had bathed in perfumed oils and her hair had been arranged in silken curls, they hennaed her hands and her feet. They dressed her in an ivory-and-gold satin kaftan, put gold satin slippers on her feet and a veil over her face.

Three weeks had passed since she had seen Ali.

"It's the Kashkiran custom," he'd said the day after the banquet. "The groom may not look upon the face of his bride until after the ceremony, when, in a part of the ceremony, he lifts her veil. That's the beginning of their life together."

He'd kissed her and let her go. "It's going to be a long three weeks," he'd said.

It had been. But now the waiting was over. Within the hour she would be his. Forever and ever his.

From outside the harem walls she could hear the music of the musicians who would follow her to where the wedding would take place.

"Are you ready?" Haifa asked.

Genevieve took a deep breath. "I'm ready," she said.

They led her to where Ali waited. He wore a green robe that was heavily encrusted in gold thread and a head cloth that was held in place with a circlet of gold.

He was unlike any other man she had known, a man of the desert. But she felt no fear, no hesitation when she placed her hand in his.

She didn't understand all of the words of the ceremony. When it was her turn to speak, she looked at Ali. His face, through the gossamer veil that covered her face, was indistinct, as shadowed as a half-remembered dream.

He lifted the veil. He said, "I love you, Genny," and the dream became reality.

Afterward there was a dinner and entertainment. Belly dancers swayed to the strangely exotic music, whirling dervishes whirled, and jugglers juggled.

When it was over, amid jokes and jibes and laughter, they finally escaped to Ali's apartments. The following day they flew to his home in the desert.

Each night they slept in his tent at the edge of the rolling dunes, and when it came time to leave, there was no sadness because they knew that they would return.

It was almost midnight. There was no one else about. The only sound was the splash of water over the sea horses that pranced next to the figures of Neptune in the Trevi Fountain.

Genevieve leaned her back against Ali and listened to the music of the mandolins from the restaurant above. "I'm so happy," she said.

Ali put his arms around her waist, and when he did, she took his hands and guided them to her stomach. "Feel," she said. "Feel our child."

His hands moved, then stilled. He held her there, unable to speak. Afraid to speak. Then slowly, carefully, he turned her around so that she faced him.

"You're pregnant," he whispered.

She saw the shine of tears in his eyes, and she smiled and said, "You told me that night in the desert you would give me a child, Ali." She stepped closer into his embrace. "Our baby will be born in the spring," she whispered.

Our baby. He thought his heart would burst with loving her. He didn't speak, but only held her against his heart, his wife, his love.

And in a little while, with the faint soft music of the mandolins drifting in the night air, they turned away from the Trevi Fountain and went arm in arm through the quiet streets of Rome to the place that was their home.

* * * * *

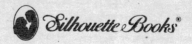